*The Ascension*
*Book Three*

# Out of the Dark

I0638467

Cover Illustration by Henning Ludvigsen.
Interior Illustrations by Henning Ludvigsen.

Brick Cave Media
brickcavemedia.com
2015

In loving memory of
Frank L. Parks Sr.
Nov 5, 1950 to Nov 2, 2010

By J.A. Giunta

THE ASCENSION
Book One: *The Last Incarnation*
Book Two: *The Mists of Faeron*
Book Three: *Out of the Dark*

  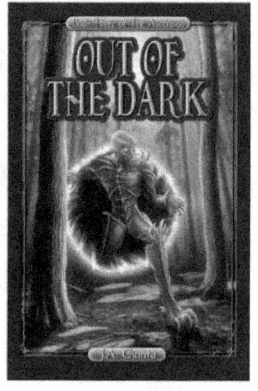

THE GUARDIANS
Book One: *Knights of Virtue*

# Out of the Dark

J.A. Giunta

# Acknowledgements

I'd like to thank Bob Nelson and Jenn Labuz for all of their hard work and dedication in bringing my work to print and help putting it in your hands. Social interaction isn't my strong suit, so I'm lucky to have found people who are not only good at promotion but willing to do it for me.

Thanks to Julie Ann Elefante for her help in editing this time around. Searching for mistakes is a never-ending battle, one far easier fought with a second set of eyes.

Thanks to Sharon Skinner for her insight as another writer. The book would've ended very differently if not for her.

And thanks once more to Henning Ludvigsen for all his effort in putting a face to my work. He's gotten very busy over the years, as one of the most talented character artists out there, and I was fortunate enough to have him finish out the trilogy.

# – 1 –

 he air shimmered and shook like ripples across water, carried outward by the force of an unseen stone. Another struck with a dull echo, breaking loose frozen leaves, threatening winter bark with the promise of destruction. Once more and snow melted, crying out in wisps of steam to the trembling of earth and trees. Birds took flight, and the forest grew quiet. The last tore it open, like the splitting of fine silk, a raw wound of empty black suspended in air. Violet fire ran its length as the tear became a hole. Chitin claws gripped either side, pushed and strained against the protest of a breach that longed to close. A taloned leg stepped forth, the runes engraved across its carapace reflecting silver moonlight. Beryl eyes broke through the Dark as the shiardin came into view.

1

*More insect than man, the hairless creature was encased in ebon shell from head to toe. Runes covered its body, across the length of each limb, circled torso and shoulders, crossed the top of its head and edged a prominent brow. Beneath the glowing emerald of its eyes, a ridged nose pressed flat over the gash that was its mouth. Blunted teeth and knifelike ears, spines jutting from every angle, it was a child of the Dark, the new scion of a once god.*

Shia, *born of hatred, as spoken in the first tongue, the language of the gods, and* urdin, *a swift messenger; its name was as dark a portent as its presence in the Light.*

Fluora tightened an empty grip, skin flushed to the elbow, and focused on the premonition with eyes wide and jaw clenched. She fought against the flood of emotion washing over and through her body, stood firm against the tide threatening to pull her under. He was there in the impenetrable black, she knew, could feel him in every torrent that raked her spirit. Imprisoned or not, he was there staring back.

Revyn was still alive.

*The shiardin took in long whiffs of air, snuffling the bitter wind, before fully stepping from the rift. Its head cocked to one side, it sniffed again and was off.*

*The scent was a palpable tendril of silver light, much brighter than the moon, more alive in its flicker and wending path and filled with the warmth of a living soul. It made the pain of dying bearable, masked the stench of burning carapace.*

*The forest sped past, a blur of trees and snow, ice and a trail of black. The ground hissed at every step, each footprint an ember blown to life then left to fade to ashen scars. Claws tore at the trees in an effort to bound ahead, leaving gashes and cracked chitin in their wake.*

*Powerful legs pressed down, talons ripping through stone and soil, and propelled the shiardin over obstacles three men high.*

*Scent and sense commingled to the shape of a man, a mass of coursing* furie *thumped in time to an inner drum. The argent strands grew thicker, drew her on without relent, even as her body burned away. Long hair, tapered ears, the dirtied skin of a hunter, he was all that would quench the holy fire within.*

*He looked up at the last, and she knew without ever having seen him that he was Unther, the once Archer God of Stars and Sky. His godhood stripped, he knelt in mortal flesh over the carcass of lifeless prey.*

*The shiardin leapt, its fading body burst apart into shadow and black mist. The darkness engulfed Unther like a blanket of starless night, a constraining second skin that swept over every inch. Smoke rose from the struggling body, muted flames against the chill. It fell inward and shook, trembled and collapsed across the cold of unforgiving dirt. The dark mist bellowed out in its final silent throe, sank into frozen soil and a ley line far below.*

*Fluora tried to break free the seer sight, fought the current of golden* furie *that swept her headlong toward darkness. The acrid scent of burning flesh reached her nostrils, a minor eddy in the maelstrom compared to muscles taut and near to tearing. Screams followed in the torrent, bounced off earthen walls and crashed back down upon her, buffeting her eyes, snapping at her hair. Empty black loomed ahead, where the river of* furie *splashed its spent runes and disappeared into a void. She saw nothing in its depths and feared it might claim her.*

*Again the screams rang out.*

Her eyes opened as the shockwave flashed out in a

ring of visible sound. The chair splintered beneath her. The bed rose and flipped, striking the wall behind, while the dresser in front upended and crashed into shards. Smoke swept the length of her pale skin as she fell to her back. Fiery hair splayed out beneath her, singed at the tips.

The premonition had ended, but the screams would not abate. They haunted with their echoes, taunted from the river heading straight into the black. It took long moments to settle in, to shake loose the grip of mindless fear, the irrational anxiety of being swallowed by a vision.

To realize the screams had been her own.

*   *   *

Barr sat in the grass before a rift he'd just opened. He leaned back on both hands and stared up at the night sky, at the twinkle of stars slowly crawling overhead. It didn't matter they weren't real, that the sky was far removed from the underground city. It felt good on cool nights to look up at the enchantment and become lost in its wonder.

Light snoring broke his reverie. Aren slept close by, his chest rising and falling with the steady rhythm of deep slumber. The massive war hound, of late, was always close at hand. His wounds had all been healed, as were everyone else's, and yet, since their battle with Revyn...

Barr blinked away the dark thoughts. No amount of brooding would bring back all those lost in the struggle nor undo the damage Revyn and his shapelings had wrought across Taellus.

*Are you alright?* Idelle asked, her voice a soothing presence in his mind. Even taller than Aren, the giant hawk perched atop the fountain outside his home. Barr could hear the trickling water in her thoughts. Near sleep herself, she rested on one foot and ruffled her feathers. *You should try to rest.*

*I will.* He turned his attention back to the rift. *Soon.*

As she closed her eyes and drifted off, Barr shifted his vision to the runic spectrum. Countless, empty runes floated in air, no bigger than a fingertip and stacked one upon another. Like a transparent swarm of bees, it was difficult to see them individually, especially when the light of nearby life structures outshone them. The grass beneath him, the trees, bushes and earthen paths, even his own body, all glowed with a brilliant golden light, as if each were a vessel filled with the *furie* of a ley line. The complex patterns swirled and moved in time to a steady motion, oblivious to the surrounding chaos.

They were all divine runes, the language of creation. He recognized some of them, as he had that first time when his spirit swam the depths of a ley line beneath Karon-Rai and again when trapping Revyn in the Dark. There were still far too many for him to fully understand. At least his head didn't hurt as much while focused on them anymore.

It was the rift that troubled him, how easily he could weave one in a runic language he barely knew. His past life as Alanara, an accomplished traveler, afforded him the vast knowledge of arachon portal making. These rifts, however, were not woven in arachon, and the speed with which he wove them felt more a second nature than any product of learning. That's what had been nagging him at the back of his mind. The rifts were stable, safe, but he didn't know why.

Without that knowledge, how could he be so sure?

Was there risk of opening a portal to the Dark, as with traversing the mists? He didn't think so, since he was using his own *furie*. What if it was some sort of trick, a subconscious thought planted in his mind by Revyn? Did the god plan to somehow break free, using Barr as an unwitting accomplice?

Perhaps he was over-thinking the situation. He let out a sigh and studied the glyph more closely, before the pain behind his eyes became too much to bear.

The structure seemed fairly simple. Sigils moved in steady motion within each ward, which in turn revolved through five separate spheres. It was night time on the other side of the rift, but the field of grass outside his mother's estate on Faeron glowed bright with *furie* and life. It lit the bottom edges of the rift in a backdrop of yellow-gold, like staring through a sheet of ice at the midday sun.

It was then that he saw sigils disappearing from view for a brief moment and reappearing on the opposite side of its ward. He trained his eyes on a single rune, followed its course and was surprised to see the entire glyph fade to the background as his vision shifted of its own accord. He still looked at the same glyph, but most of its parts were dimmed. Everything took on a bluish cast, as if the world had been encased in sapphire. Even the runes had lost their fiery glow and were replaced with an azure sheen. His vision switched again, to a vibrant panorama of silver and pale light, as if the moon embraced all with its touch. Runes shimmered like quicksilver, reflecting every motion like polished mirrors cast adrift. It was easier then to see each ward spin from one color to the next, to realize what was happening before his eyes.

The glyph existed on three different planes.

Barr was looking at the structure in its entirety, in

its form on the physical, ethereal and astral. It took some practice to intentionally switch between them and even longer for the nauseating vertigo to pass. He noticed not all runes passed from one plane to another. Most stayed in the physical, with specific runes moving back and forth within the spheres, but what surprised him most were the ones that never left the other planes.

How he was able to conjure these rifts, with runes in the ether and astral, suddenly became more troubling and an even greater mystery.

He spent hours poring over every sigil and what its place was within its ward, what its primary function had achieved and how it affected surrounding runes. Despite the intricacy of traversing three planes in a single glyph, the structure itself was fairly simple. From what Barr could discern, through trial and error, none of the wards altered when a sigil was removed – where a more complex ward might divert its purpose if tampered with. Neither did any of the wards or the glyph itself work once a rune was removed. The rift simply closed until the rune was put back.

After manipulating the glyph for so long a time, Barr began to recognize and understand individual runes and how they were used. He had no names for them, as he did with every other runic language, and the symbols were too different to draw comparison. He persisted until he knew which runes could form various wards. The harder he worked at it, the easier he understood. It felt as if he'd known them all along and was only just then recalling how each one could be used.

He began to wonder if the rift on Faeronthalsos was a natural occurrence or something similar to his own. He made a mental note of it and moved on.

His rifts were so unlike the arachon portals that

even the mindsets behind them were dissimilar. An arachon portal brought two places in the physical plane together, like folding a piece of parchment. His rifts, on the other hand, traveled into the ether, drew stability from the astral and returned to the physical at another location.

While scholars in the past had been adamant the other two planes existed in far removed places, much as Taellus was far from Faeron or Danarriden, Barr could see with his own eyes the truth. All three realms existed within the same space, like three pieces of parchment pressed impossibly tight against one another. By shifting his vision, he could scrawl runes in both the ether and astral, while his body remained constant in the physical. It was the runes that existed in more than one plane at a time.

It was well into morning when Barr rubbed weary eyes. His head pounded from the mental exertion. He had improvised for the past hour, reworked runes in all three planes, until what remained was an elegant piece of Art: a self-sustaining glyph, drawing *furie* from the nearest ley line and warded against tampering. Not only could he weave permanent rifts, the glyph had burned itself into his mind – like storing it in a precious gem. He couldn't think a glyph into existence, as crushing a storage gem would, but it did make it easier to weave the runes much faster.

He considered heading to bed for some much needed rest. The others would be up soon, and he'd rather skip the lectures that were sure to follow. Then again, he could grab a quick breakfast and travel to the rift on Faeron. Even if it was a natural occurrence, its runes could reveal much. The more exciting and likely prospect was that it had been woven by –

Fluora's scream pierced the quiet; Barr was up and

running before he could finish the thought.

\*   \*   \*

Barr had heard the release of *furie* that accompanied her scream, felt it grip him by the spine and tingle up to the nape of his neck. The hair on his arms still stood on end as their house came into view. All thought of sleep and weariness had left him, replaced by fear for Fluora's safety. His mind raced as fast as his body. They should have been safe in the underground city, where the only way in were through portals conjured by travelers; where thousands of Protectors had sworn to safeguard any life within the city. Not that the Oath had done anything to save his uncle Therol.

He forced that thought aside.

*Aren, Idelle!* Barr shouted in his mind to wake his friends. *There's trouble at the house.*

By the time he arrived in their bedroom, Hanar was already there and cradling Fluora's head in her lap. She was kneeling on the remains of a splintered chair. The entire room looked as if a storm had raged through and dashed everything to bits. Whatever magic had been unleashed, it didn't appear to have caused Fluora any bodily harm. Her freckled skin was pale, but he saw no sign of burns or scorch marks on her fingertips. He rushed over and knelt beside them both.

*What happened?* Idelle asked.

"Is she alright?" Barr asked. *I'm not sure.*

He saw Fluora wasn't wearing her blindfold. Her eyes were wide open, the dark blue orbs ringed in black still haunted by premonition. He caught sight of the silken cloth, shook out the debris and covered her eyes.

*I'm here.* Aren rushed in and looked around. He shook out his coat and lay down at Fluora's bare feet, covering them with his warmth. *Did she do this?*

Hanar said, "Her breathing has steadied."

*Maybe*, Barr replied. *She can weave but why do this? More likely it had something to do with whatever vision she saw.*

The two fingers Hanar held at Fluora's neck were covered end to tip in runes filled with silver. Despite her new role as an arbiter, the obsidian golem was now truly an arachon. Barr was glad she'd chosen to remain their Protector. He could hear and feel the thrum of healing Hanar channeled into Fluora, like a warm buzzing in the pit of his stomach.

"You think she was injured by a vision?" He took up a pale hand and squeezed it between his own. He said more than asked, "How is that even possible."

"Just a precaution," Hanar said and ended the flow of *furie*. She brushed Fluora's hair with gentle fingers. The fiery curls looked like daybreak on the horizon of Faeron, like coppery amaranth kissed by both suns. "In case her mind was affected."

*Her mind*, Barr wondered. *The only time I can recall her seer sight causing her harm –*

*Was the day you met*, Idelle finished for him.

Aren licked a foot. *She'll be alright. Won't she?*

"Let's take her to the other bedroom."

Barr lifted her in both arms and carried her down the hallway. He knew she was strong, in body and mind, but in that moment she felt so very frail. Her cheek rested against his shoulder, where every breath touched his neck.

"Bring her to my room," Hanar said. "I will stay with her until she wakes. You look like you have not slept at all."

He set Fluora down on the bed and took the woolen blanket Hanar offered.

"Thanks," he said and covered Fluora. There were no chairs in Hanar's room, so he brought one in and took a seat near the bed. "I know," he told the golem in a weary voice, waving off any criticism she had in mind. He settled in for a nap and added, "Just wake me when she stirs. Please. And thank you, Hanar."

"Sleep well, Master."

Aren padded over and rested his bulk at Barr's feet. Without a word, he was soon dozing.

*I envy him that.* Barr blinked heavy lids, his body longing for sleep. He took Fluora's hand in his own and closed his eyes.

*Yes,* Idelle agreed, *being able to nap at a moment's notice can be quite useful.* Despite the mirth in her tone, Barr sensed her unease. She took wing and added, *I'll be close if you need me.*

Barr nodded with a sigh and drifted off.

\*     \*     \*

Dhar stepped from the portal into an immense hall beneath Dwendorim. He strained his neck to look up and ventured he could shift back to his true form, fly half a dozen beats and still have room to maneuver before reaching the vaulted ceiling. A mosaic of runic tiles lit the darkness at that height, blue steel sigils that shone like winter dawn across the ocean. A row of alcoves ran the length of all four walls, with pillars at either side that stretched up into the icy glow. The likeness of arachons long since passed had been carved into the pillars, interspersed with more runic patterns shedding light across the chamber. A decorative weave of precious metal and stone swelled the gaps with impressive whorls and spheres filled to varying degree. The walls bore the sheen of polished marble in ashen white, while the floor was wholly crafted for heavy travel. Rough stonework encompassed the entire area, with a bevy of wide tracks carved a finger-length deep. Small as a thumbnail, more blue steel runes lit the inside of each track.

He glanced back at the portal, a pane of churning silver liquid that hummed in the quiet. It looked the top of a long oval, halved and stretched thin. He had the urge to reach his hand in, to wave back at the traveler who had fashioned it, but thought best not to risk losing an arm should it close.

Another traveler stood waiting a good distance away, this one shaped of red granite and reflecting light off its silver runes.

There were no exits in the grand chamber.

"Welcome, friend Dhar'paogi," the golem said with a tilt of its head. He began conjuring another portal as the first disappeared. "It is a pleasure to see you again. I trust all is well at Naerat Sanae?"

"As well as can be expected," Dhar replied, a hint of sadness in his voice. He bowed his head in return, his features no longer hidden behind the dark of a cowl. Since regaining his memories at the Mirror Pool, his eyes and skin appeared normal. He walked with strength and confidence. He had cast aside his old garb and now wore what humans referred to as battle robes – heavy linen reinforced with leather and steel braces. "Thank you for asking."

Truth be told, his kin had suffered a great loss at the battle of Geilon-Rai, maybe even more so than the elves. Dragons were never intended for propagation. A mated couple would be lucky to bear a clutch of two or three in as many centuries. Immortal by design, as had been all of the first children races, too many offspring would have meant outgrowing their mountain home and filling the skies of Taellus until the world was shrouded in shadow. In short time there would have been little left by way of food to sustain them. Starvation would not have killed them but merely forced them into slumber, an eternal hibernation without the promise of coming spring.

The portal opened before him to the thrum of *furie* in his ears, rising up as if an unseen veil had been lifted.

He stepped through to a circular courtyard, to fresh air and the scent of birch. Two full commands were there to greet him. Once golem Protectors, sworn to uphold the Oath, they had chosen to leave the protectorate and had been remade as arachon – in honor of the ancient people they once called Masters. Animated stone, statues given life, the golems had evolved into a species as complex as any born of flesh.

The white glow of *furie* from their eyes followed him as he headed for the main road. Zheren saluted, ebon fist to chest, and bowed his head. The others followed suit as the portal closed.

Dhar returned the gesture, forcing a steady pace despite his eagerness to be away. They had fought at the elven tree city. All of them had, every arachon, every last one of them. So why was anger so bent on rising within him that he could feel it burning the back of his throat with bile. Because they had suffered fewer losses? Or was it the death of a single dragon far outweighed any other's sacrifice?

He sucked in a deep breath and let it out, willing his anger to be carried away with it. All blame fell squarely on Revyn's shoulders, on the god who had inflicted the shapeling curse upon Taellus.

Lycanthropy. What life would not turn, he had sought to crush underfoot.

Dhar shook his head and closed tight his eyes from the images that assailed him. Dragons falling like stones, spiraling downward on wings torn, burned or ripped away; the cries of his own blood as they were shredded in a chaos of *furie* and fire; his children roaring in pain, claws rending, scales failing to protect as they crashed against rocks and cold earth.

"Mind your steps."

*Enough!* he stopped and shouted in his thoughts. He cast off the painful images. They only served to remind him of Kaolanni. The young silver had good intentions, maybe even genuine feelings for him, but he was still too mired in the past to truly care for the future. Khrona had even gone so far as to call it an "obligation" to their kind.

Dhar was the last Patron, last of the first dragons Curoch had given life. With each generation since then, dragons had grown smaller, weaker and less fertile. Their mountain city, Naerakeilan, had been carved so high that modern dragons could no longer breathe the thin air. A new city had been crafted much further down the mountain, one too small and plain, one Dhar felt had no place for him. It had become a common hope he would take a new mate – or three – and reinvigorate their species, that his seed would make for stronger offspring.

"You lost?" The same female voice, reluctant, curt. He opened his eyes and saw a human sitting on the edge of a fountain, washing dirt and dried blood from her arms and hands. "You sure seem lost."

Her skin was covered shaved head to bare feet in blue runes, across corded muscles and a wiry frame. A young woman, she was half-naked but for the barest of

14

leather strips. No ink, those runes glowed with the power of *furie*, but their silvery cast paled in comparison to the second set. Formed of transparent black fire, they ringed her body an inch above the skin, ran the length of each limb, swirled her chest and shoulders then finished in a mask across the sapphire of her eyes.

He immediately knew what and who she was.

"You must be Sera." He was puzzled by the blood. "Were you hunting?"

Sera gave up cleaning her hands as a lost cause. She stood and flicked excess water in another direction.

"And you're the dragon," she said, sizing him up. "One of the golems took me out of the city."

"All done resting then?"

She shrugged, hands on her hips. "It's nice once in a while, but I don't belong here. I'm not safe to be around."

He knew she meant Master Therol, his once friend and mentor – and Barr's uncle. The old scribe had been like a father to Dhar, all those years spent trapped in an ill-formed body with no memory of who he was. If anyone had a right to take issue with her actions, it was he.

"You were not yourself," he said at last and offered his hand. "No one blames you for his death, least of all me. I too was made to betray friends at Revyn's bidding."

She nodded but did not meet his gaze. She gripped his forearm, surprised him with her strength. He was careful not to hurt her and briefly wondered if she were able to harm him. Their eyes met, and it seemed a corner of her mouth had moved up in the semblance of a smile.

"Have you killed many?" Sera let go her hold, but her eyes still held him fast. "Thousands?"

"If not more." He looked down at her feet, how runes colored each toe and rose up to form rings around her ankles. "Much more. I spent years on Danarriden for my atonement."

She had caught the last but must have sensed his reluctance to speak of it.

He did not care to think back on those days, when the death of his mate and then his daughter weighed so heavily upon him he had no recourse but to seek his own demise at the hands of an enemy. When the demons had stopped fighting back, when they fled rather than face him, he was left with no choice but to leave.

"Any Arch Demons?" she asked instead.

Her curiosity struck him as a bit odd. From what he knew of demon hunters, their short lives were filled with unending fighting and physical pain, loneliness with little to no rest and a bitter anger at the geas that ruled their existence. Not only were they compelled to hunt and slay, the curse drew demons to them like a lodestone. Why would she want to spend any amount of time talking of them?

"All five, though not at once." He looked up and saw something in her expression. Sadness or guilt, he could not be sure. "I am surprised at your interest. I would think by now you had had your fill of demons."

"Sorry. I just don't... I mean I haven't –"

She looked as if she struggled between a desire to say more and a sudden need to be elsewhere. The latter won out. She shook her head and turned away, heading for the eastern path.

"Wait," he said, uncertain if he had insulted her. "I meant no disrespect."

Sera stopped to regard him. "That was the longest conversation I've had in a long while. Thanks."

His brow crinkled in confusion. "My pleasure? Next time I shall try not to bore you so quickly."

"Next time then," she agreed and continued down the dirt path, past a pair of topiary columns.

Dhar watched until she disappeared into the garden.

\*   \*   \*

Barr woke to the scent of hot jasmine tea, freshly baked honeycakes with strawberry syrup, red potatoes in melted butter, spiced apple slices and cut melon. There were others he couldn't quite place. Cinnamon loaf covered in raisins and dates? His stomach rumbled, and he realized he hadn't eaten since late afternoon the previous day.

He was alone in the bedroom but could hear them all at the dining table. Whatever Aren was eating, it made Barr's middle twist even more with hunger pangs. When he stepped out from the hallway, he was surprised to find Dhar had come to join them for breakfast. Or was it lunch?

*It's lunch,* Idelle confirmed. *Sleep well?*

*Well enough,* Barr said and stretched his arms with a yawn. Aren kept eating, his attention focused on a stack of honeycakes. *At least he's using a plate.*

Fluora smiled at that and pulled a chair out beside her for Barr to come sit. He was glad to see her wearing a blindfold.

"You were supposed to wake me," he accused Hanar and took his seat. To Dhar he said, "Good morning."

Dhar bowed his head and chuckled, enjoying sliced ham and a hearty helping of potatoes.

Hanar put a plate of food down in front of Barr. "You needed rest," she said and joined them at the table. The chair squeaked in protest beneath her, but she paid it no mind. "You know better than to stay up all night."

"It wasn't *all* night. Just most of it." Barr took hold of Fluora's hand, leaned over and kissed her. Her color had returned, and she tasted of berries. "How are you feeling? Was it something you saw?"

"I am fine now," she assured him and gave his hand a squeeze. "Let us finish this fine meal before any talk of visions."

The food was wonderful and of such an abundance Barr wondered if Renahd had saved any for the others staying in Dwendorim. All five demon hunters, a small group of faeron and a handful of sylvannis had chosen to stay. Hanar was quick to reassure that Renahd and the other growers were stockpiling food in anticipation of commerce with all the major cities. The arachon did not require sleep, worked tirelessly at their crafts and only took time to rest for two hours a day.

They planned to reopen the portalis, a central hub of portals originating in Dwendorim and leading to any city who wished to partake. There were plenty of materials the arachon were in short supply of: precious stones and metals, wood from various regions but most of all they sought knowledge. With coin gained from selling produce or any number of crafts they had to offer, they could purchase books on a wide variety of subjects and hire master craftsmen to come teach and refine skills.

A small fee for use of the portalis, with a guarantee of safety from the Aegis, and soon Dwendorim's coffers would be overflowing. Such a vast sum could then be used to undo the damage caused by war and Revyn's shapeling disease. Nothing would bring back those who had died, but homes could be rebuilt, food and clothing given to the needy, hope restored to those lost in despair. Survivors could leave the past behind them and look forward to brighter days.

There was still much for Hanar and the other arbiters to decide, but their future as a people was filled with promise and joy – a happiness they planned to share with all of Taellus. Barr was proud to have seen them come so far, watched them assume the mantle of their makers and embrace their evolution from Protectors to a society of caring individuals.

"We still plan to invite other races," Hanar told them when the meal was finished. "Faeron, the sylvannis, the vardikor, all will be welcomed to come live here."

Dhar said, "That is very generous. I hope you will save me a small place to sleep when I visit."

"All of the homes in this corner are reserved for the Master's family and friends."

"Hanar, please," Barr said, "You don't have to call me that anymore."

"Yes, Master."

Fluora giggled at Hanar's smile.

Barr rolled his eyes and poked Fluora in the side. They sat on the edge of the fountain outside their home, while Dhar and Hanar rested in sturdy chairs.

"Not that I want to dampen the mood any," he said, his own smile fading, "but I'd like to hear what it was you saw last night."

*Wait,* Aren said. *I'm still eating.*

Idelle ruffled her feathers atop the fountain. *You know you don't have to stop eating for us to hear you.*

*Hmm, you're right. Go ahead then.*

Fluora took Barr's hand into hers, slipped her fingers between his and looked down for a long moment.

"What I saw," she began, "was Revyn."

Dhar sat forward. "How is that possible? It has only been three days."

Barr said, "I guess it was too much to hope that the Dark would destroy him. He's still trapped though? Tell us everything you saw."

"I could not see into the Dark, see him. I could only sense his presence." The hairs of her arms stood on end, and she shivered. "He has been drastically changed. At the tree city, when we fought, he was frightening; evil, scheming, all too willing to destroy everything around him, but he was only a god. What I saw last night." She put her other hand to the blindfold covering her eyes, as if she could push back whatever images she saw. "It was as if the Dark had railed against him with all that it had, and not only did he survive, he stood a conqueror in its midst."

"What do you mean?" Barr asked and lifted her head gently by the chin. "What did you see?"

"He has created new life, akin to an umbral but far more dangerous." Fluora looked him in the eyes from behind her blindfold. "He calls them shiardin, and he can send them through rifts from the Dark."

Dhar got to his feet. "Why did you not say something sooner?" he demanded. "How many of these creatures are running loose?"

Barr held out a hand, asking his friend for calm. He trusted Fluora. If she'd chosen not to tell them sooner, it's because there was nothing they could do about it. She probably needed time just to sort it out in her mind.

"Yes," she whispered to Barr. "Thank you." To the others she said, "I had to be sure what I saw had already happened and was not a premonition. It took a great deal of effort for him to open that rift, and even then he was only able to send a single shiardin through."

"Where?" Hanar asked. "Where did he send it?"

"A forest, I am not sure exactly where. All I can be sure of is that it had a purpose. It sought out Unther."

"Unther," Dhar repeated, "the Archer God?"

Fluora nodded. "Except he was no longer a god; he was mortal. I could see it in his aura."

Aren licked his chops before moving on to another plate. *How does a god become mortal?*

*I'm sure he had help*, Idelle offered.

*A punishment maybe*, Barr said, *from the others.*

"He was dressing a fresh kill," Fluora continued, "a stag, when the shiardin became like a black cloth. It covered him completely and pulled him down to a ley line, taking me with it." She swallowed, her voice caught in her throat. "It dragged us both through this river of blinding golden light. I tried everything to end the vision. Only when I saw where it was taking us, when I truly panicked, was I able to break free."

Barr put an arm around her and held her close. "It's alright. We need to find out how often he can do this, or why he's even able to open a rift in the first place."

"What about Unther?" Dhar pressed. "Where did the creature take him?" Fluora only shook her head, as if unable to speak. "Barr?"

"It took him to the Dark."

21

## – 2 –

ren didn't like these new rifts. It felt wrong, two paws in Dwendorim, the other two in Greywood. His hind end was still warm from the bright of midday, while ahead the winter sun was shrouded in icy gloom. The forest was a mass of thick colorless trees, with a blanket of dead leaves and snow at its feet. The skies rumbled in discontent, distant drums and a loud crack like the breaking of stone.

Flakes of snow touched his nose, caught him in the eye. Aren shook out his coat, and a flurry reached his tail. No, he most definitely did not like these rifts.

*You could've stayed*, Idelle teased.

He felt her in the freezing winds overhead, gliding through treetops and blinding mist. She slipped into a dive, upending his stomach with a wave of vertigo. The next rumble was his own. He looked back at the house, trying to recall if he'd finished all the honeycakes. Food always settled his stomach.

Idelle laughed.

*What's so funny?* He could see Barr and Fluora in a clearing up ahead. They'd been examining the spot where Unther had been taken for what seemed like hours. Hanar was off making important decisions, or so she'd said, and Dhar had gone looking for the scary demon hunter. Even if it was Revyn who had made her kill Barr's uncle, Aren didn't like her. She smelt like magic, and not in a good way. Idelle didn't answer him, only giggled some more and swooped by his head. *Stop that.* He thought a moment. *I don't suppose you see anything to eat.*

*Besides the stag?*

*I'm not eating that*, he said and shivered. Its scent was horrific, drowned out all else with the cloying rancor of spoiled meat. *Smells like it's been dead for days. Even bugs won't touch it.*

That caught Barr's attention. He and Fluora began looking closer at the stag, poking at it with a stick to see inside.

*You're right*, Barr said. *The meat's nearly black with decay, but nothing's touched it, not a single maggot or beetle. No bite marks on the bones.* Barr lifted a hind leg with the stick. *Nothing underneath either.*

"The ground," he heard Fluora say. A gust of wind picked up, so he wasn't sure if she'd said more.

*What about it?* Aren asked, inching forward into the cold. He wanted to go see but feared the rift might close behind him.

*It's black.* Barr grabbed another stick and dug at the frozen ground. *At least a finger-length deep.* "Careful," he said to Fluora. "Don't get any on you."

*What does it mean?* Idelle asked. She'd landed on a sturdy branch and watched them from above. *Is the earth dead like the stag?*

*I think so,* Barr replied. *Its pattern's been corrupted. Whatever the shiardin did, its touch must've caused this.* He left off the stag and began poking at the blackened shape that was Unther. He dug until the stick was half into the ground. *I think the soil's been damaged all the way to the ley line.*

He dropped the sticks, and the two of them headed back toward the rift. Fluora held onto his arm, though Aren knew she could see regardless of the blindfold.

"What did you mean by its pattern?" she asked.

*Finally,* Aren said and stepped back into the city. *I could use a nap.*

"It's a bit complicated."

Barr's tone and hesitance meant he just didn't want to talk about it. Aren would've shrugged if he could but instead found a warm spot to rest beneath his favorite tree.

Fluora was more persistent. "Too complicated for me to understand?"

She almost sounded upset, though Aren knew she wasn't. Head resting on his front paws, he opened an eye to watch. Idelle was already perched atop the fountain when they stepped back through the rift. He narrowed his eye at the strange doorway. Before they'd left for the forest, he'd circled it. When he'd stood in a certain spot, it'd vanished from sight, as if the rift was too thin to see from its side. He wondered if walking forward would've put him in Greywood or cut him in half.

"That's not what I meant," Barr said, "and you know it." Even Aren could see the playful twist at one end of her mouth, the poor attempt to fight back a smile at Barr's expense. "I don't fully understand it myself."

Aren shut his eye. Sleep was more interesting than the teasing and kissing. He heard the rift close, like a piece of cloth ripped in two – only backwards. The hair on his neck settled into calm. He didn't know why magic always caused his hackles to rise. In truth, it annoyed him, made him anxious for no reason he could see.

*Are you coming?* Idelle asked, though in the haze of drifting off, it sounded more like *Are you hungry?*

*What? Yes!* He blinked to clear his eyes and shook the sleep from his head. Another rift stood where the last one had, though this went to... *Geilon-Rai?*

*Hurry up!* He felt Idelle already swooping through the tops of the tree city. *Before the rift closes!*

His nails scraped against the cobbles, so fast did he run. He leapt through the rift and into Darleman without a second thought. How long had it been since they were here in the forest, outside the elven city – when no one was trying to kill them?

It seemed like a lifetime ago.

Barr chuckled in his thoughts. *Go have fun with the others. Fluora and I are meeting with the council.*

*Alright, give dad a lick for me!*

*Yeah, I'm not doing that,* Barr said and laughed along with Fluora. *I'll tell him you said hello. You can lick him yourself later.*

Aren wasn't really listening. He was running with all speed for the pens, focused on the trees and snowy forest floor. As glad as he was to be back home, everything had changed for the worse. His pace slowed as the sadness crept in.

Battle had rained down upon the forest, blackening trees and earth, splintering limbs and rock, uprooting entire boles until the landscape was unfamiliar. Bodies of the fallen no longer littered the floor, but their lifeblood stained the soil in dark swathes of sticky leaves and debris.

The pens had been destroyed, where a dragon had fallen and taken its final breaths impaled upon the wood. Sylvannis worked to remake it, shaping trees beneath their hands. The tingle of magic coursed through him as he stepped through the devastation and his memory of how it should be.

*Over here,* Idelle called. Her cry pierced the winter cold, from a field where hounds were training. *They'll fix it, Aren. Leave it be for now.*

Less than two dozen. That's how many war hounds remained. He stopped in the snow to watch them from a distance. Grief took hold of his heart and wrenched. It stole the warmth from his joy at being back home and soured it to a bitterness that threatened to choke the life from him. His friends were all gone. He'd never again hear them laugh. No more hunts, no more playing, they were gone forever. Aren turned back the other way.

*This isn't my home anymore.*

Idelle landed in front of him. *No, it isn't. But that doesn't mean we stop caring.* She stepped closer and nuzzled her neck against his. *Don't turn away from them now. They need you more than ever.*

He looked back at the field. Two Ballar and every hound stood watching, waiting for him to join them.

*They're still pups. I don't know a single one.*

*True,* Idelle said and took wing, *but they're also good friends you've yet to meet.*

Aren padded over to the clearing and was met by a female Ballar. She smiled and offered her hand for him to sniff. He did so only out of respect. He could scent any one of them, elf or hound, from where he stood.

She was dressed much like the other, heavy leathers with extra padding at the thighs and forearms, bones jangling from her shoulders – a mix of wolf and boar teeth. An ironwood long knife was sheathed at both hips and secured at the knee. Her hair was brown, tied in a weave of two braids down her back that joined at the waist. Grey eyes flecked with silver, she wore face paint across the bridge of her nose and again at either side of her neck.

"You must be Aren," she said in elven. Even though he understood her, his thoughts were in alixhiran, like Barr's. He gave a brief snort in acknowledgement. "I am Ellaena, Ballar Animwa, of House Talehn."

*She isn't blooded?* Aren followed beside her to the other hounds. *How is she supposed to train them?*

Idelle landed on a narrow boulder jutting up from the ground. *You don't need to kill to know how.*

The largest male stepped up to Aren with his head held high, ears straight up, hackles raised.

*I lead here,* he said and gave a low growl.

Aren looked down at the pup. He couldn't have been more than two years old. Aren eyed the other hounds, even the two Ballar, all waiting to see how he'd react. Without warning, Aren struck, biting down on the other's scruff and driving his face into the snow. He bit hard enough to elicit yelps of fear and pain. The male tried to pull away, frantically scrabbling its paws against the ground for any footing. Aren let out such a low, guttural growl that it shook the pup's body and caused others to back away. Only when the struggling ceased, when the male lay quiet and still, did Aren let loose his hold.

*You're not here to lead,* he told them all. *You're here to learn.*

The male got up and slipped back into the ranks behind him. Twenty war hounds sat at attention, their eyes trained upon Aren.

"All is well?" Ellaena asked him. Another brief snort. "Very good then. Let us begin."

They trained until sunset, when the tree line glowed like pale honey and gray skies gave way to stars. Every hound had already been bonded, but most Ballar were rebuilding the pens. The day's lesson had been all about discipline. A companion not only answered to their Ballar but answered to one another. They worked together to achieve a common goal, relied on each other to stay alive and bring down an enemy without mishap or injury.

It wasn't until Aren shared what he knew of combat and all he had learned since his own first day of training that he realized how experienced he truly was. He may have taken it for granted, that Barr and Idelle would be there for him every bit as much as he would be there for them. Seeing firsthand just how much had been lost, how many had died despite years of training, made him appreciate what he had all the more.

*Aww, you're going to make me cry*, Idelle said. Aren sighed and circled camp for a comfortable spot beside the fire. *I mean it. There could be real tears.*

The others were out playing in the snow, leaping one upon the other, chasing and being chased. The Ballar had finished work for the day and settled into camp for a hot meal and warm drink. They ate and laughed as their hounds romped in the cold.

"What say you, Aren?" Ellaena asked and took a seat by his side. "Any interest in one?"

"Or two," another said, and everyone laughed.

Aren studied the elf's face. She wasn't poking fun, as far as he could tell. She seemed genuinely interested. In what, he had no idea.

*She wants to know*, Idelle said, *if any prickled your skin.*

*Any what?*

"None?" Ellaena asked with surprise. "It may be too soon still, but we were hoping you would choose a mate today."

More drinking, more laughter.

*They're not teasing you, Aren. They want you to pick a female.* He gave her a questioning look. *You know.* For the first time, his sister seemed at a loss for words. *To be with!*

*Sometimes you make no sense at all.*

A few Ballar whistled a call to their hounds. Four females loped over to Aren and giggled, turning so he could see them from all sides. He looked to Ellaena in askance.

"Do any of these smell pleasing to you?"

*They're alright, I suppose.* He sighed again and eyed the camp for more salted venison. *Seriously, though, do you know what she's –*

A clump of snow hit him square in the face.

Idelle laughed so hard she fell from her perch. Aren shook the snow from his eyes and saw Kaela staring back. Smallest of them all, she was also the fastest. She laughed and bounded off.

"Kaela may be small," Ellaena warned, "but she is very agile. Think twice before accepting her challenge to catch her."

Climbing back to her perch, Idelle still laughed.

Aren was up and after with such speed that he drew startled gasps from the gathered elves. The runes along his ironwood collar began to glow. Fair or not, he was going to catch her.

Kaela jumped at a full run, touched all paws to a wide tree and pushed off in another direction. Aren slid and took the tree in his side, knocking the air from his lungs. He could no longer hear the cheering or laughter, the cries of encouragement. It all faded to distant quiet, replaced by determination and the steady rhythm of his heart.

He was almost on her tail when she leapt again, this time jumping from one branch to another. Aren stopped at its base, watched in astonishment as she climbed the tree to a dizzying height. She jumped out into nothing but cold air and landed on a snow bank, slid down to its bottom a fair distance away and kept running for all she was worth.

*She's crazy!*

*That was impressive,* Idelle said.

With longer strides and much more powerful legs, it didn't take long for Aren to catch up. He was almost on her once again when she purposely bit into a low branch, swung her body around and let it go right back into Aren's face. To his credit he kept running but smashed into a tree.

Her laughter was playful, as if she relished the chase far more than he did. Kaela pounced on him when he was down, nipped his ear and ran off.

Despite the humiliation and ever slow realization that he would never catch her, Aren left off and walked back to camp. He dropped beside the fire, winded and a little bruised. Kaela padded up and nestled in beside him.

*You really are crazy,* he told her.

She turned her head toward him. *I like you, too.*

"It seems Kaela has chosen for you," Ellaena said and shared a drink with the others. "May her litters be many and often!"

Aren snorted and closed his eyes.

\* \* \*

Barr and Fluora stepped off the southern lift, the only one of four still intact, and into Geilon-Rai. Their ascent was not as smooth as he remembered, but with so much damage across every facet of the city, he was glad they were spared the climb. He couldn't help but smile at the thought of his first time here. Only eight years old, he had to be carried up the leather rope ladder most sylvannis used. The lifts were primarily for anything too heavy for one person to carry, such as animals the Maurdon had trapped or hunted.

Two Gharak stood guard at either end of the passage leading into the chamber. Skilled warriors charged with the protection of Geilon-Rai from within, they also served as personal guard for the Speaker of the Sun. When Barr had lived here that was Roedric. So many of them were now gone, either slaughtered outright or lost in battle three days ago.

Tuvrin, the new Speaker, strode into the room with two more Gharak in tow. He smiled and embraced Barr as if they hadn't seen each other in ages. He hugged Fluora as well and kissed her cheek. One day soon, he would be as a father to her. Just how soon was in no way up to Barr.

"Thank you for coming so soon," Tuvrin said.

He wore the *feydra* of mourning, black feathers tied into his long braids. No longer First of the Maurdon, his dark hair was now woven in the more formal mien of a Speaker. Despite the years and hardship, he still looked every bit the man who had taken Barr in as his son.

Barr said, "I only wish it could've been sooner."

"And under better circumstances," Fluora added. "I am afraid we bring ill tidings."

His father's expression grew somber, all trace of their joyous reunion giving way to the heavy burdens of a new leader.

"Let us not keep them waiting then." Tuvrin led the way to the council chamber. "We will need to go around," he said and stepped under a broken tree limb hanging down from the ceiling. "All fires have long since been put out, but I fear our home is falling apart around us."

Barr had mixed feelings about his return to Geilon-Rai. His exile had been lifted. He was again a sage of the Illumin Valar, if he chose, but his old friend and mentor Seltruin was gone. He had no desire to live among the sylvannis in the tree city anymore, but without him they had no Valar. He was the last. What once might've been a happy occasion had become a burden of responsibility he neither wanted nor felt able to assume.

They continued past a corridor where limbs jutted up from the once smoothed earthen floor, and the exterior had collapsed inward from a great impact. A room on the right had been completely exposed, half torn away and hanging out in the elements. More than the destruction of the sylvannis' homes, the Great Tree had suffered injuries only a sage could mend.

Geilon-Rai rested atop and within a single enormous tree in the center of Darleman. Its roots reached deep into ley lines far below the city and wove through every tree in the forest. Chambers were shaped into hollow sections of the bole, while corridors ran through limbs and out into covered areas of interwoven branch and packed earth. The Great Tree, or Niyaen as the elves called it, was both sentient and alive. It provided warmth to the sylvannis, nutrients for their gardens, protection from harsh elements and prying eyes, carried moisture up from the soil to drink and molded to the careful will of elven hands.

Without Barr's help the Niyaen would wither and die – and the forest soon after. It wouldn't matter humans from Alixhir had discovered the truth, that elves existed after centuries of feigned extinction. Threat of war was a moot point if the Great Tree failed.

"Have there been more attacks?" Barr asked.

Without aid from the Shamarrin, their elven kin from Undersea, Geilon-Rai would have fallen long before the battle with Revyn. There were simply too few sylvannis, and now they numbered less than a thousand. When shapelings infiltrated the council and began turning the entire city, every elder and child had been fed upon. He dreaded the thought, but it was possible the sylvannis might not see another generation.

"No, thank Celene." Barr could hear the strain in his father's voice, the worry that went unsaid. "The Narohk have been doing an excellent job dissuading humans from venturing too close. Whatever orcs were in the forest Adrean and Teldein have forever silenced." Tuvrin allowed himself a smile then. "The Speaker of the Stars expressed his undying gratitude to the sylvannis for use of our sage. What you did for the wyndorrin will not soon be forgotten."

"I was glad to help them."

Fluora squeezed his hand and leaned in closer as they walked.

Two Gharak came into view, holding ironwood great swords crossed before the woven leaves of the council chamber. They withdrew their weapons and moved the leaves aside.

Tuvrin motioned for Barr and Fluora to enter and take a seat at the U-shaped table. Four others were already in attendance, two female and two male – one Barr recognized as Galdein. He and the sturdy Maurdon shook forearms with an unspoken promise to talk when they were able. He was glad to see Galdein had replaced his father as First.

Barr shared a smile in greeting with Lorelei, who had taken her father's seat as First of the Ballar. He knew the other two, as he had known all the sylvannis, but not well enough to call either a friend. Korein was an able Narohk, with a strong bow arm and the presence to lead. Taerra had the broad shoulders and unwavering stance of a Gharak. Though position did not always pass to the firstborn, Barr thought her a fine replacement for her father. He nodded to each in turn.

There were no Eneir to replace Landrin, Roedric's only son, nor Valar to take up the white robes of a sage. Barr felt keenly aware of the eight remaining seats. That none had survived of sufficient age to don the mantle of advisor spoke more of the plight facing the sylvannis than any visible damage to the city.

Shimmer globes lit the otherwise plain room. One's colored glass had been cracked, and its flickering glow was not as bright as the others.

As Speaker, Tuvrin sat at the head of the table.

"Please," he said and motioned for them to join him, "let us begin. I would first ask if any oppose lifting Barr's exile?" When none spoke up, he added, "I would also see him restored to house and rank, his name again on the Eondin Scrolls –"

"Father," Barr interrupted. He looked to the others. "Friends. I'm grateful to be allowed back into the city, to see my family again." He hesitated, unsure what to say. Fluora rested a hand on his arm, supporting his decision no matter the consequences. "But I've made a new home elsewhere. I'm not here asking to rejoin the sylvannis." He could see by the crestfallen and worried looks that they had expected or at least hoped to hear different. "I do still feel a duty to my oath as a sage. I came here to offer my help. I can train new sages, heal the Great Tree, but you'll still face threat of war from Alixhir."

Taerra said, "We would not be here if not for your aid against Revyn. It gladdens me to hear the Valar will live on." Her eyes were the earthen fire of leaves in early autumn, touched by the sadness of spring's passing. "Seltruin was a dear friend to my family. I trust your judgment as I did his. What would you have us do?"

"You could make a home in Dwendorim." Barr tried to gauge their reactions as each considered leaving the forest, abandoning the only home they'd ever known. Moreover, the Niyaen was a part of the sylvannis. To leave it behind would not be easy. "I've spoken with the arbiters. The arachon would be honored to have you."

Fluora leaned forward and said, "You would also be welcome on Faeronthalsos."

"To leave," Korein said, his painted brow furrowed, "would be akin to surrender." He looked to Barr. "Is there no other way?"

"There is," Barr replied. It was a drastic measure, one he'd hoped to avoid. He wasn't even sure it could be done. More to his father than the others, he asked, "If you could truly isolate Geilon-Rai from the rest of the world, wall the city off from all outsiders, would you?"

"If that were possible," Tuvrin answered and gave the question serious thought. "Yes." The others agreed. "Is it possible?"

Barr let out a breath he'd been holding. "I suppose we'll find out."

"The rifts," Fluora said, working through an idea. "You could leave one here to Dwendorim. The elves could come and go as needed, for food or rest, trade wares with the arachon," she turned her blindfold toward Tuvrin, "visit with family. Your new sages could train at the university."

Galdein looked surprised. "So we would not truly be isolated then? Some could live in the underground city while we repair."

Taerra cleared her throat. "Who else would have access to this rift? Not to offend the arachon, but I think many would be unnerved at strangers in Geilon-Rai."

"Let alone living statues," Korein added.

"Place guards," Fluora offered, "at both sides of the rift. Allow through only those who have permission."

Tuvrin asked, "This would not offend the arachon? I fear our arrangement would be a bit one-sided."

"No," Barr replied. "I think they'd be happy for the opportunity to speak with others and share knowledge."

"Very well." Tuvrin gave the other elves time to be heard if they chose. When none spoke up, he said to Barr, "You may create this rift in a place of Taerra's choosing. The Gharak will be responsible for its use. You have the freedom to call on whom and however many new sages you wish. Which leaves but one more issue to discuss.

"What are these ill tidings you spoke of?"

*   *   *

Dhar found her at a shaping pit on one of the lower levels, between two quarries and the tunnel entrance to an iron mine. Wooden scaffolding surrounded the upper half of a destroyer. From the waist down, it was still a solid square of white and blue granite molded together by *furie*. Shapers worked at the colossal golem's middle a good fifty feet up from the pit floor. He could see and hear the pale light beneath their hands. With practiced care, they smoothed away fine layers of stone until every detail of the soon-to-be arachon was perfect.

Rune crafters worked along the uppermost platform, gouging out its instructions with the same painstaking attention. Some no bigger than a palm, others larger than a man, the runes were woven about its body in an artistic pattern of symmetry. More arachon worked off in the distance, smelting blue steel in preparation to fill each shaped sigil. Dhar knew all that remained then was for enchanters to link the enormous body to a ley line, and the destroyer would open its eyes for the first time. It was strangely exhilarating to see the Art used with such finesse, to behold the living works of crafted artistry give life to yet another.

From the first arachon who had dwelled here, to the golems they conceived and gave life, on down to those few who remade themselves and then fashioned such a monumental image, both arachon of flesh and stone had forged immortality from imagination. The golems were no longer children doomed to fade in time and tide.

They had found a way to sire offspring.

"It's beautiful," Sera said in a hushed tone, as if she too were aware of the godlike implications. "Don't you think?"

A hundred paces away, seated knee to chest, she not only sensed his arrival but knew his dragon ears would hear her every word. Dhar walked forward with a smile of mild amusement. For reasons he did not yet fully grasp, he found this demon hunter far more interesting than the other four.

"I do. I have seen many things in my lifetime," he said and stopped a respectful distance behind her, "but few of this magnitude and import. May I join you?"

Sera patted the ground beside her and ignored the plume of dust. He sat, crossed his legs and leaned back to regard her. She kept her eyes forward, lost in the shaping. Her skin was alight beneath the ebon fire of her own runes. He wondered if she felt a kinship with the unfinished destroyer. She turned her head back toward him, resting a cheek on one knee.

"I can't be with you." Her tone was plain, a matter of fact. "Nor should you be considering it."

Did she know of Kaolanni? Regardless of how Dhar felt about the silver, he had made no promises – not to her or the conclave. More likely, Sera had spoken of her own affliction. He could change his appearance, become something other than a dragon, while she was bound by hers. He saw it in her eyes then. Every thought, every action, was tempered by the geas. She was a demon hunter, fated to be a weapon and a danger to those around her.

For Sera there was no escaping her flesh.

"I am not here to bed you," Dhar said and chuckled at her raised brow. "I thought you might like to go for a ride. I need to get back to Naerat Sanae before morning, but that leaves us plenty of time to go on a hunt."

She sat up, attention piqued. "Hunt demons?"

"I did not think you would go for the mere fun of it, so why not both?" He stood and offered his hand. "We could ask a traveler to take us anywhere you like."

"Alright." She got up in a single fluid motion, with no help from Dhar and body taut like a bowstring. "Not that it matters, but what of getting back?"

The thought had not occurred to him. He flew fast enough to reach home, or what had once been his home, from anywhere on Taellus in a short time. He might need to stop for a cow or two, but end to end a trek around the world took only a day.

"The arachon keep a traveler at World's Edge," Dhar said. "Since I need to return tomorrow, I can just bring you along."

"To North Haven?" she asked. Dhar hated the name humans used for Naerat Sanae, but he smiled and gave a nod. "A city full of dragons. I suppose that might be worth seeing."

Dhar started back up the ramp. "Not to worry," he called back. "If I see you having fun at any time, I shall find you a demon to make amends."

He glanced back and caught her smile, then saw it quickly replaced with a mask of stony silence.

It took less than an hour to reach the upper levels and find a traveler. Orelar, a white marble female, was happy to assist. Dhar enjoyed watching the arachon weave, no matter how simple the enchantment. As in everything they did, there was a beauty to their motion, an elegance to every act. Moreover, as a people, they shared a deep appreciation for life. They were welcoming, considerate and far more accommodating than his own kind. Perhaps that was why he felt more at ease in Dwendorim than he did in his own home – their home.

His mate and daughter had long passed; it was the memories that lingered. No matter how hard he tried to focus on the love, the laughter and warmth they had shared, guilt and shame overpowered any joy gleaned from the past. Perhaps that was why he took human form so often. He had grown uncomfortable in his own skin. Even the sight of other dragons weighed upon him, a constant reminder of what he had lost – and why.

"What now?" Sera asked quietly.

The portal closed behind her. She looked at him as if she recognized or at least understood the thoughts he struggled with. As if she took his somber quiet for what it was: mourning a loss that could never be replaced. He forced a smile and blinked the memories from his mind. They stood upon a cliff in the Ghaoylens, a mountain range overlooking the tall trees of Darleman.

"Now? We fly." He leapt from the ledge and shifted back to his natural form. One powerful beat sent wind rushing downward and raised him to equal footing with the cliff. He leaned his head in and offered his neck. "Hop on!"

Sera glanced over the edge and gave him a wry look. With a shrug, she grabbed hold of a scale and pulled herself high enough to get a leg up and over. She got to her knees, climbed further down his neck to just above the shoulders and secured her legs behind two ridges. She gripped the next set with both hands. Dhar looked back, and she nodded. A few beats to test her hold, and he felt assured she would stay firm. He swung left and glided down on a warm current.

Sunlight glinted off his scales the golden hue of pure *furie*. Its warmth tingled across the membranes of his wings, swept over his body and filled him with the joy of flight. It was moments like those, when he let the wind and warmth carry him, that he understood why Eoraini had been so enamored by flying. He kicked at the air and drove his wings in powerful thrusts. They breached the clouds and kept going, soaring up through a sea of white mist and roiling wind. They broke through the top in a burst of haze, to the clear blue of endless sky.

He leveled off and heard her laugh, an unbridled cry of delight that caused him to join her. Wings wide and held taut, he skimmed the tops in long strides. They rode the edge of each in turn, sliding down until the next and rising up with just a tilt. It was a game they played for a time, skirting from cloud to cloud and finding currents to glide upon.

Dhar dipped low and swung back, dropped below the downy vapor and headed for the forest. He tested Sera's limits at a gradual rate. He could have gone much faster, stole the breath from her lungs, sent her reeling from his back, but wanted to know what she could endure before exhilaration grew to panic. It was not his intent to scare her but to gauge the speed and mobility with which they could hunt.

His shadow stretched out across the treetops. Not the largest gold to have ever lived, Dhar was still the last Patron. Easily four times the size of other dragons, his body from snout to tail spike was the length of fifty men. His wingspan was half again as wide.

"Faster!" Sera yelled with a growing smile, struggling to see ahead through the wind.

A chuckle of molten flame, and Dhar summoned the *furie* to fly well beyond his natural ability. Trees the size of titans swayed in their passing. Wind howled around them, as if parted by a golden blade, and leaves rose up in a tumult that trailed in swirling streamers. He reared his head ever so slightly and careened them up into the blue, then spiraled in a backward fall that sent them racing toward destruction. He evened off at the last, felt trees scrape the plates of his underbelly and relaxed the flow of *furie*. They slowed to a thunderous pace, enough that Sera could again speak.

"That was incredible!" she shouted.

"I am glad you liked it," Dhar called back. "It is not every day I get to –"

Sera erupted in holy flame, a blue fire hot enough Dhar could feel it against his scales. Her legs tightened with noticeable strength, directing him to go right as if he were a mount. He leaned to the east. She gripped and pulled a neck ridge all the harder and only eased off once they were headed for the black plume.

He wondered how he could have missed it. The oily smoke clung to a treetop and dissipated in a haze. Dhar heard before he saw the flashes of violet light run up along its edge. Sera dug in her heels and pushed with both hands.

"Hold on!"

*Furie* shot them forward like a bolt. Sera's flames grew hotter the closer they drew. Once they were over the plume, Dhar dipped his head and let out a roar, raced down at the forest floor in the wake of streaming breath. He scorched trees and earth, opened his wings at the last moment and landed on all fours. Blackened earth rippled out, tossing rocks still on fire and splintering tree trunks in a town-sized radius.

Sera was already in air, landed in a roll and ran headlong for the demon. How or why it had gotten here was of far less significance than what the creature was doing. On two plated legs, bristling with barbs, and four arms the width of small trees, the horned elder held the bodies of two charred remains. It tossed the human corpses onto a black ritual pyre. The rising smoke flashed again with a jolt of violet. A portal opened as Sera reached the demon and attacked.

Dozens of lessers began pouring through, demons of leathery red flesh covered in plating and black spines. Others were mottled yellow, oozing noxious fumes from their bulbous bodies. Dhar wasted no time but moved to attack, when their eyes turned as one at the frenzied battle cries of a demon hunter.

He bathed them in a scalding blast that could have melted rock, a white-hot liquid that clung to all it touched and burned through without relent. Sera tore spines from the elder's back as she climbed. Her new weapons came alive with blue runes, enchanted by the geas. She drove them deep into demon flesh as she pulled herself inexorably toward its head.

Dhar smashed demons with his claws, driving bodies feet into blackened ground or careening off through a dozen trees. His tail crushed them by the handful, swept them into a mass and unleashed a surge of fire over dying and broken bodies. He reared his head, summoned *furie* to his throat and let loose a deluge of fire straight into the portal. Its edges burned and wavered. Demons ignited and burst apart in the same instant they stepped through. The portal collapsed, cutting a demon in two at the waist.

The elder reached for Sera and lost a hand for its trouble. Over and over, she drove the enchanted spines into its head. Fire erupted with each strike, the holy flames across her body eating away at the thick plates and demon flesh. The elder flipped its head forward and flung Sera upside down through the air. She collided with a tree, snapped wood and bone alike, then dropped to the forest floor on her front. Dhar was swiping and smashing a bloodied path to reach her. The elder picked up one of the spines and drove it through Sera's middle as she got to her feet. She looked down at it in disbelief, when the second punched through her chest.

Dhar roared with enough force to floor every demon but the elder. He leapt and grabbed hold, pulled it away from Sera and drove its body into the ground again and again. The lessers thought to flee and were consumed by *furie*-driven fire. Dhar hefted the broken remains of the elder, gave a wrenching twist with both claws and tore the demon apart. He let fall the bloodied remains and turned back toward Sera. For one of his size, he moved with great speed, closing the distance between them in a heartbeat. He shifted as he ran and reached her as she pulled the first spine from her stomach. She wretched dark blood across her front. The second spine would not give. It was lodged through her breastbone and a rib on the other side.

She collapsed into his arms.

"Sera!" Dhar wiped black ichor from her stomach to see the severity of her wound. He breathed easier when he saw it begin to close. "It is healing," he said and wiped blood from her face. "I have to pull the other one now." He took a deep breath and said quietly, "Forgive me."

She screamed as he pulled the spine free and tossed it aside. Her breath grew watery, and she coughed up thick spouts of blood and crimson bubbles. Dhar held her upright, trying to sound calmer than he felt.

"Alright," he soothed, wiping heavy clots from her chin. "Just try to breathe. You are already healing. The geas will not let you die."

She sobbed at that. Fresh tears ran down her cheeks in rivulets through blood – both hers and the demon's. A final cough and air flowed, sucked in with a ragged gasp. She gripped him by the robe and continued to sob, burying her face in the cloth. A soundless cry shook her between mouthfuls of air. He held her until she settled, until a sigh loosened her grip. She swallowed and leaned back, looked him in the eye.

"Thank you." Though he could feel her strength had returned, she allowed him to help her up. She wiped a cheek with the back of her hand. "I must look a sight." She gave a single laugh and sniffled. "Beautiful as the day I almost married."

Dhar's hands slipped down to hers. "Beauty is not always about appearance but emotion. How someone or something makes us feel when we look upon it." He glanced around at the carnage and back to her. "Right now I feel glad to be alive. You make me feel glad we are both alive."

Sera looked up at him as if he had caught her off guard. Puzzled, she stepped in closer, until their noses nearly touched. When he remained still, looking back just as puzzled, she grabbed him by the robes with both hands and kissed him. Passionate, hungry, she pulled at him as if the taste only filled her with more longing. He returned her kiss with an equal fervor, pushed her back against the broken tree. She smiled and bit his lower lip, put a leg behind his and brought them both to the ground.

They laughed and kissed again, rolled back and forth in an effort to pin the other's arms. Sera was on top and grinned down when he couldn't move. The sound of tearing robes then echoed through the forest. Dhar's open-mouthed shock only amused her even more.

The gray of winter day was soon fading into night, where blue skies far above gave way to starry black.

Not that either of them seemed to notice.

\*  \*  \*

Barr headed for the viewing chamber at the center of Geilon-Rai, where Valar for generations had performed the Restoration. It was as good a place as any to commune with the Great Tree. With so many elves hard at work, few would have idle time to spend with the Niyaen – the Pillar of Life. It truly was that, Barr mused, supporting both the forest and all life that made a home there. What would become of the sylvannis if they were forced to live without it?

He pushed the thought aside. There was too much to be done to even contemplate failure.

The others were busy as well. Aren and Idelle trained with the Ballar. Fluora and Lorelei had left together, and his father begged off to pen letters to the other Speakers. Barr wished he and Fluora had brought happier news. That Revyn was still alive and able to attack did little to lift spirits. If anything, it called into question the loss of life that had already been sacrificed to wondering what the inevitable coming battle would cost them.

No one would be safe until Revyn was destroyed.

Barr passed many in the corridors and was surprised to see them smile or bow a head in respect. There were so few left, it was possible they all knew he'd returned to aid them as a sage, however he could. He had expected toleration, not open appreciation. Even before his exile, he had never been so well received.

*They know the truth now*, Idelle said.

*Maybe so.*

He stepped out into the viewing chamber. Though he had seen it many times before, it still struck him with a sense of beauty and awe. The entire room was a dome, its walls formed of shaped branches reaching up from below and smoothed to a warm glow by the tree itself. Its ceiling was opened wide at the center, though vibrant boughs blocked much of the sky. The enormous trunk, a hundred arm lengths wide, was encircled by a walkway so elves could touch the Great Tree without hampering its growth. It filled the chamber with warmth, with a soft glow as if sunlight shone through all around. Birdsong accompanied the flutter of wings far above, where spring remained eternal.

Corridors branched off in two more directions, but one had been damaged in the attack. The north wall had collapsed inward, and scorch marks ringed the opening in a swirl of charred branch reaching inside. A body length west would have breached the chamber. Had the Niyaen been exposed, the battle might have been Geilon-Rai's last.

Barr approached the tree with solemnity, mindful of the burden he'd placed upon himself, of how much life relied on the tree to sustain them and what his actions might mean for the future of all sylvannis. He'd pledged his life to protect them, the elves and subsequently the tree. No amount of self-doubt would sway him now.

He touched both palms to the Great Tree.

A wave of agonizing pain and desperation washed over, drove him to his knees and sapped *furie* from his body in great tugs at his spirit. He may have cried out. He couldn't hear anything above the tumult of distress in his ears, the piercing wail of a thousand dirges begging for release. It burned his flesh as it scoured his spirit. Shedding light on any darkness, laying bare any secret, across every ripple of silver liquid in the vast ocean of his soul, the Great Tree merged its essence with his.

A single root was immersed in the golden flow of a ley line. The others had burned away in an attempt to heal the forest. Now he faced annihilation as well; an endless winter filled with darkness, a withering lamentation of hushed quiet and bitter solitude, the whispered promise of eternal rest weighed upon him like a mountain, a starless blanket of despair and uncertainty.

*No.* Soft, assured, it was his own voice in the wind. *No*, it called again, *I will not succumb to fear.* He flexed both hands, reaching his fingers deep through earth and stone. *I will never lose hope.* His skin tingled with the touch of a ley line. *I am loved*, two more, *and will never be alone.* The last three bubbled past, and the shiver of renewed life grew to a triumphant thrum throughout his body.

*I am everlasting*, the voice went on, his or the tree's he couldn't be certain. His fingers curled, and roots turned back through the soil. *I am the Light.* The city glowed as a single entity, spread its warmth to every tree in the forest and as one healed its wounds; knit every splintered branch, soothed every burn, smoothed each earthen surface and again made whole its home. *I am the Dark.* Its ironwood roots shot through the ground like bolts of lightning, arcing in thousands of directions. He gritted his teeth, and heavy thorns burst forth from the shaping limbs. His body tensed with the effort, beaded with sweat, and snow melted in a nimbus about the city half the width of the forest. *I am everything.* He cried out against the strain, eyes shut tight, hands tensed and alive with *furie*. Roots widened and twisted, raced toward the surface and breached the forest floor. *And nothing.* One upon another, roots joined together or intertwined, formed layered walls of impenetrable ironwood. Barbed, hard as steel, they stretched up into the night, like petals of a flower half as tall as any tree.

The barrier fully encompassed the affected area of Darleman, where all trace of winter had been erased by the weaving. It surrounded Geilon-Rai, cut the sylvannis off from all contact but the rift to Dwendorim.

*I am free.*

Barr opened his eyes to see runes spiral down both arms and out his hands, unraveling from his own, and back into the Great Tree. He saw all three planes at once; the physical, ether and astral. Empty runes spun their course. It was difficult to tell where he ended and the tree began. Even the platform seemed a part of him, its hold slipping free from his legs. He looked up and saw birds, fist-sized glyphs trailing streamers as they flew. A thin strand of sigils followed them, caught up in the tree's.

Like the shadow of winter creeping over the horizon, warmth left him in an aching crawl. Muscles trembled in protest, rigid and tender. He could again distinguish his body from the tree, hands from roots, skin from bark. The voice was gone. It left behind an empty silence, like a hollow in his chest. His legs burned from calves to waist, as if he'd knelt for hours. When his hands finally slipped free, he saw their imprints left behind. The ironwood held firm a perfect likeness of their touch.

Others were there to help him. Hands lifted him to his feet, supported his weight. Shoulders were there to guide him in a half embrace at either side. When they turned, he heard relief. Celebration and joy greeted him, a mass of runes and golden *furie*. There were hundreds of them, cheering as a single glyph, touching him as he passed. Their sunlight glow began to fade, a comforting dark closing in on weary eyes. Their happiness settled to a muffled din in the distance. Only memory of the voice lingered.

A whisper in the dark.

# – 3 –

 arr woke the next morning to see Fluora in bed beside him, head on a pillow and watching. Her eyes were dark sapphire stars flecked with topaz, all ringed in midnight black like the waters of the mists. Morning crept through the window and set her crimson curls alight with strands of copper and fiery gold. She smiled at the attention, full lips stained cherry beneath a nose straight and tipped with a pixie's charm. Her pale skin looked of shimmering porcelain, freckled but with a dusting of powdered rainbow and diamond.

"You did it," she said and stroked his hair with a gentle hand. They were beneath a fur blanket, but still he felt warmth from the tree wall at their heads. "You healed the city. And more."

"You've seen it?" he rasped, voice dry from thirst.

He needed water but didn't want to get up, to spoil the moment. When they were together like this, nothing else seemed to matter.

*Welcome back*, Idelle said, perched atop the pens. Aren was fast asleep. *You slept quite a while.*

*I think I could sleep all day.*

"Everyone has seen it." She moved closer and kissed him. Of course she knew what he was thinking. Faeron spoke to each other in thought, and Barr doubted he'd ever learn or even wanted to guard his from Fluora. "You can see it from any window." She put her arms around him, her head now on his pillow. "How did you do it? You shaped the land, as we do on Faeronthalsos."

"Here, the Great Tree is the land," he explained and looked troubled. He recalled seeing runes leave his hands and return to the Niyaen. "Something was different this time, though."

*We couldn't hear you*, Idelle said. *It was like when you first held one of the Emblems.*

"What is it?"

Barr was still puzzling it out for himself. "Either I've never noticed before, when communing with the tree, or yesterday was the first time our spirits merged. I felt lost in it, like it took me over."

Fluora said, "You healed the tree at Karon-Rai. Was it the same?"

"Not at all," he replied. "The other had lost footing in the ley lines long ago. It was dying and the forest with it. This one," Barr shook his head and swallowed to wet his throat, "was scared, terrified of dying. It just has me wondering is all. Have we always merged that way in a Restoration, or was this just the first time I noticed?" Again, he shook his head. "It doesn't really matter. I've just – it feels like I've been seeing more lately, more clearly. Things I thought I knew I'm only now beginning to understand." He laughed and sat up against the wall. "Sorry, I don't mean to ramble."

She sat up as well, pulled the fur blanket with her. She filled a cup with water beside the bed and handed it to him, waited for him to finish and refilled it. She put down the pitcher and took up an ironwood half-mask. It had the look of polished earthen marble with jade veins shot through. Held in place by a leather thong, it was meant to protect the nose, cheeks and forehead, but it had no eyeholes. When Fluora held it to her face, it was a perfect likeness. It was only then he realized she wasn't wearing a blindfold.

"That's amazing," Barr said. He was struck by how fierce it made her look. "A pair of kyan, and only a fool would stand against you."

Fluora put the mask down and tied in place her silken blindfold.

"Lorelei had it made it for me," she said and leaned her head against his shoulder. "We are becoming good friends. I enjoy talking with her. It gives me a better sense of what it was like for you growing up here. I can see why you would have loved her had you stayed." She smiled at his discomfort. "I am only teasing. She does care a great deal for you, and for me that is reason enough to call her friend. What was it like, growing up here? Losing your father Daroth and gaining Tuvrin? Having the responsibilities of a sage while so young?"

*Seems they really did talk,* Idelle said and fought the urge to giggle, *and all about you. I'm off to find a bit of breakfast. Your wall won't affect the animals will it?*

*It covers most of the forest, and only birds migrate out of Darleman.* He considered a moment. *It shouldn't affect anyone but Alixhir. It closes off some minor trade routes.*

*Alright, have fun then!* Idelle was already far above the trees. *I'll be back before Aren wakes.*

Barr put his arm around Fluora and pressed his back against the wall, let its warmth seep in and relax his muscles. It felt as if he'd trained for a week without rest. His chest, legs, even his eyes were sore.

"It was difficult," he said at last. "I didn't know what to think, and I was mad at the world. I felt helpless and small." He let out a deep breath. "Of course I had Aren and Idelle, but I owe much to Tuvrin and Seltruin. I don't know what my life would've been like without them. Being a sage changed me, made it easier to deal with the loss. I took an oath to protect the sylvannis, to put their welfare above my own." He kissed the top of her head, took in the scent of her hair. "There's something freeing about living for others." He was quiet for a time then asked, "What of your father?"

He sensed her wrestle with a sadness long since buried but not forgotten.

"The efreeti wars," she replied. "I am sure you have noticed there are quite more women than men. Three wars in as many decades. It was only in the last that women were allowed and needed to take up arms."

"I'm sorry. I didn't know."

She squeezed his arm tighter. "He was killed in a raid on a settlement close to the southern border. He was a silver leaf general but insisted on joining patrols." She adjusted her blindfold. "He was much like you. He put the needs of others above all else, himself, his family." She cleared her throat and swallowed the rising sorrow in her voice. "He saved hundreds of lives that day but could not save his own."

"Is that what you see?" Barr asked. "My death?" She remained quiet, either thinking of an answer or refusing to give one. He raised her chin gently and kissed her. "I'll teach you anything you want, but waiting to be joined until you can best me..." He tried not to make light of the situation. Whatever the premonition, it had troubled her since the day they first met. "Even if you could, it doesn't mean you can save me from whatever you're seeing."

She turned and faced him. "Do you believe in fate?"

"Yes," he answered after careful thought, "and no. I believe we make our own fate. Our lives are not fixed paths laid out by the gods." He took both her hands in his. It felt as if a revelation hidden inside him, buried by lifetimes of memories, had been set free and given voice. "The higher self, what we call a soul or spirit, guides us toward decisions we've already made. We all have free will. We're just not always aware of the choices we make."

"So you chose. What I see is your choice." Her tone was accusatory, angry and hurt. "I refuse to believe that. I cannot believe that."

He pulled her to him and held her close. He wanted to say all would be well, reassure that premonitions were not set in stone. The truth was he didn't know what to tell her. He hadn't seen the vision, and she wouldn't speak of it. All he could do was trust his own judgment, that whatever choices he makes are the right ones. With Revyn alive, creating new life to attack them from the Dark, there was already too much to worry over.

*Maybe he just wants the gods*, Aren said, yawned and stretched his front legs.

Barr frowned. *How long have you been listening?*

*What? Not long.* He saw Kaela playing with the others and had the urge to go join her – without even waiting for breakfast. Though all the snow and ice had melted last night, a new layer of frost covered the forest. *You should come down and play. It sounds like you both need some fun.*

"I suppose we should get up," Barr said and reached for his leathers. Fluora stayed under the warmth of the blanket. "Aren has a point though. Why target a god, and how did the shiardin kill him so easily?"

"Unther was mortal," Fluora said.

Dressed, Barr stopped to look at her before putting on his boots.

"How can you know that?" He pulled on a boot and added, "Or even know it was Unther?"

Fluora bunched the fur up under her chin. "Toward the end, I was seeing the vision through his eyes." She stared straight ahead, past the silken blindfold. "It was as if I were in danger of being dragged to the Dark with him."

"And the explosion?"

"I was fighting to break free." She looked to Barr, and he sensed fear in her thoughts. For a brief moment he saw what she'd seen, felt her being pulled through a ley line. "I used my powers as Matron. I accessed the mists and drew *furie* from the Dark."

Barr sat beside her as the enormity of her words settled in his mind. Traversing the mists opened a portal to the Dark. Their bodies insubstantial, they slipped between planes. It started to make sense but in a wholly different light that only led to more questions. Where did the mists take them? If Fluora could channel *furie* from the Dark, where even ley lines drew their power, could Revyn do the same but in reverse? Could he force his will across planes and attack without consequence? Barr had been convinced he trapped or even killed Revyn. Now it seemed he might have made the god more powerful than before.

"Can you scry the others?" he asked, still grappling with the notion he had doomed all life. "The gods. Can we warn them?"

"I am sorry," Fluora said and shook her head. "It all happened so fast, and I was afraid for my life." She put a hand on his shoulder, forced him to look at her. "Barr, you did the right thing. If Revyn was still here, all of Taellus, everywhere, would be overrun by shapelings." She was adamant. "You made the right choice. What happens now..."

She left the thought unfinished. Neither of them knew what would come next. Barr could only be certain of one thing.

"What happens now we'll face together."

\* \* \*

Dhar woke for the second time before dawn. The first had been caused by such a magical uproar he thought the world might break apart and explode all around him. Snow and ice had vanished in an instant, rising up in a flash of hissing reverberation. Visible energy had lit up the forest, as if a sunrise had taken root in its soil. Trees shook, the ground thrummed and then the clamor of *furie* had coalesced into a living wall for as far as he could see. He knew Barr had caused it – even considered taking wing to view his friend's handiwork. It had still been dark though, his body tired and the tree wall better viewed by light of day. In the end sleep had won out, and he fell back to the comfort of quiet slumber.

Sera watched him from a distance.

Her back to a tree, knees to chest, it looked as if she were gauging what to do with him. She had been gone when he woke earlier. Scouting or hunting, it had made little difference. Sera could take care of herself as well as he. Most of the blood and dirt had been washed away, no doubt in an icy stream. Her skin was red between the runes, each breath a cloud of frost, yet her body refused to shiver. Stoic, stubborn, she was thin as an ironwood sapling and just as unwavering. For someone who had been forced to submit to another's will, even a god's, she exerted control over her body the only ways left to her – denying sleep, food or drink, comfort of any kind.

Is that what she saw now, with those piercing eyes? An unnecessary comfort? A distracting indulgence? Dhar had a deep respect for her strong will and resolve, but his heart ached at the loneliness she wore like a suit of armor.

"Good morning," he said. He was covered in blood and filth.

"Is it?"

He shifted to a dragon, crushing a few trees behind him, and breathed fire along every inch of gold scale and black talon. Human once more, he was clean. Even his robes were mended. Warmth from his breath lingered in the area, soothing her frigid skin whether she wanted it or not. He was unsure if she meant the giant ironwood wall that had appeared from nowhere or if their intimacy had been a mistake – be it hers or his. He did want to make clear that he was not some farmhand dalliance endangered by her presence. He was the last Patron, a demon hunter in his own right.

To fear for his safety would be an insult.

"It absolutely is," he replied. "It seems Barr has put an end to the war between humans and elves here, and you did not run off during the night." He gave her a warm smile. "I can only assume that means you still wish to accompany me."

Sera got to her feet. "Should I hop on your back now or wait 'til you change?"

"Careful," Dhar warned and shifted. He lowered his neck so she could climb up. "You are perilously close to a smile."

He launched before she could grab hold of a neck ridge, felt her legs tighten and the ground give way. They shot up from a burst of dark soil and splintered branch. Sera laughed, as he knew she would, settled firmly at his shoulders and cheered into the rushing wind. Three more powerful beats put them just under the gray mass of promised snow. Dhar evened out and leaned east, slicing clouds with a wing. He turned fully in air, lifted his head and thrust upward with enough force to break through in a single beat. Sunshine bathed them in warmth, glittered off his belly as they hung suspended for a breathtaking moment. They dropped back into the clouds and swung down in one motion. Dhar caught a warm current heading north and let the wind carry them for a time.

Hours, days, he could have glided forever.

It was quiet that far up. Not the quiet of a still night but the calm of empty thoughts, lulled by steady wind. He felt Sera relax, resting her body against his as she had done the night before. She was free at these heights, or so he wanted to believe. He went out of his way to take them over and across mountains. They were less likely to encounter demons in the rocks far below.

There were certainly none where they were headed. Revyn's second children, demons had once set their eyes upon the peaks of Naerat Sanae. Even now Dhar was sure they would have never reached the top.

Curoch must have felt otherwise.

Dhar recalled those days with a bittersweet pang in his chest. Eoraini had been alive, vibrant as any gold and more beautiful than all the others. She had been made for him, a perfect match, shaped by the hands and will of their father. Eorana had yet to be more than a wishful dream, the unspoken hope still blooming in the hearts of love-struck children.

Time had still been a friend.

"What's wrong?" Sera asked.

They had been flying for hours in silence, yet she sensed a change in his demeanor or movements. He had neither the words nor inclination to be truthful.

"Look straight ahead," he called back.

Naerat Sanae loomed in the distance. Its peaks were frosted with layer upon layer of eternal snow and ice, a biting cold even the sun could not abate. Half again as high as the clouds, the summit city of Naerakeilan now lay still as its mausoleum. Once a place of unbridled joy, it only served as a reminder of how far his kind had fallen. *Their* city, Wyaerakeilan, was half again below the clouds.

He drifted down toward World's Edge, a vast ledge on the southern quarter where dragons of all colors met and sunned their young scales. As if they lived at the very end of the world, because not one of them was able to fly across the frozen peaks at their backs, they watched out over Taellus with undeserved pride – convinced the world had been shaped at their feet. Such arrogance may have stemmed from the sheer size of dragonkind, where they were forced to look down on lesser races to converse. Life from that vantage fostered a delusion of grandeur.

Not all of them were so overly pretentious, but it was commonly believed the rest of Taellus would die out long before dragons grew tired and moved on. It was but one of the flaws their immortality bestowed, a false heady sense of the everlasting. It was true time held no sway, but dragons were every bit as vulnerable to a violent end.

The conclave's answer to the dilemma was isolation, to live far removed from harm's reach. How often had he argued that seclusion was a prison? That sacrificing all the world had to offer – living stale and detached – was not living at all. He and the conclave had parted ways long ago, but there was no escaping who he was or the demands they placed upon him. The only one to roam free, he was least free of all.

Another unforeseen downside to immortality, their collective knowledge had dwindled over the centuries. Without the fear of death ever looming, there had been no pressing desire to leave a mark upon the world, to foster young in a vain attempt at living forever in the memory of others or pen detailed chronicles of all that had passed or been known. Offspring were born of love, taught or trained as need demanded but neither with the impassioned urgency supposed lesser races lived their lives. Seldom had time been a consideration and would have gone unnoticed if not for the changing of seasons. There had always been tomorrow, another sweep of the sun and moon across the sky – two bodies fixed and as endless as they were; there had always been plenty of time.

It seemed the years were now against them.

Dhar landed to roared cheers and skyward jets of flame and lightning. Despite permanent injury and loss, he was still a hero to his people. He let loose his own breath to the sky, a swirling blast of glowing citrine that spread and roiled like a storm cloud and rained liquid fire out away from the ledge.

"You do me great honor," he bellowed in greeting, in the common tongue for Sera's sake. He lowered his neck, allowed her to slip down and added, "Please welcome my guest, demon hunter Sera."

Dragons all across the ledge put one leg forward and bowed their heads. While humans were generally held in disdain, they were descended from the anaire – the first children of Herne, from whom the initial five hunters had been chosen. None would forget or diminish the sacrifice every demon hunter had made on their behalf. It was said Curoch had filled their bodies with the blood of all dragons. Hunters were not long-lived; most died within a year of their Awakening. Yet these mortals were held in high esteem, more akin to dragon than man in the eyes and hearts of those present.

Kaolanni landed before him, bowed her head to Sera. Sunlight glittered off her silver scales and backswept wings. When she looked up at Dhar, her color darkened beneath the eyes with open joy.

"It gladdens my heart to see you." She waited for Dhar's bow and said, "I would be honored to show Sera around the city. The conclave awaits you in the outer sanctum."

It was the only sanctum large enough for him to join them in his natural form and an unspoken request for him to do so. Khrona had never cared for their ability to shift. He considered Dhar's insistence on mimicking the lesser races as a dangerous influence.

"Thank you," he said to Kao, "I shall join them at once." To Sera he added, "I leave you in capable hands. Stay as long as you like, and return here when you wish to leave." He indicated the marble traveler off to the side. The arachon bowed her head, at their disposal should they need it. "I will look for you if we convene early or find you back in Dwendorim when I am able."

Khrona must have posted sentinels in the peaks to alert him as soon as Dhar was within sight. He doubted their meeting would be a short one.

"So soon?" Kao asked. "I thought you might stay for evening meal."

Sera looked from one to the other, far more astute than her few years.

"Don't leave on my account."

She walked away and headed for the main entrance to the city. A couple of hatchlings followed after, a green and a blue. Dhar sighed. He disliked having to explain his every action or worry what others might think of his behavior.

"Revyn is still alive," he said in their native tongue. "The god Unther was slain and taken to the Dark. I must return to help Barr however I can."

"Another god gone?" He saw the growing panic in her demeanor, the wide eyes and trembling wings. Her mind was racing with the very thought that had troubled him when first he learned of the attack. "What of father?"

"Curoch still lives. I am sorry Kao, to burden your thoughts with this news, to keep leaving." He struggled with his emotions, torn between devotion to the memory of the only happiness he had ever known in his long life and the possibility of new joy he simply did not deserve. Duty weighed on his conscience, but the needs of his people would have to wait. "It was never my intention to cause you sorrow."

Kao pressed an eyeridge to his, closed her eyes for a brief moment and fluttered her wings as they parted.

"I will warn others while you speak to the conclave." She lifted off the ground with delicate beats, held aloft more by *furie* than wings. "I will also find and look after our guest. Be safe, dallan Dhar'paogi." *Close friend*, an endearment for courting mates.

"And you."

Dhar leapt and soared east, riding a current to the next peak. He turned and flew straight up, ran the edge of a jagged outcrop and reached the icy summit. His belly scraped the frozen rocks, as he arched over and down the other side. Wind forced his ears back, howling like a demon with every frigid crag narrowly avoided. When the sanctum came into view, a circle of shaped sunstone and molded rock, he raced toward the gathered dragons. He halted his rapid descent at the last moment, buffeting the ground with mighty blasts of his wings, and settled on a rock bed facing east.

The others were already in attendance. They had walked the narrow tunnel up from the temple beneath. Dhar refused to scrape his wings against the walls, as shifting in the temple was strictly forbidden – or so he had been told on his last visit through.

Khronaerrin, the appointed Emissary, lifted his head and gave a curt bow in greeting. Dhar imagined the hot-blooded red did not like to be kept waiting. There had been a time long ago where every breed of dragon sat the conclave, a chosen consul for each caste and hue. Now less than two dozen were given voice, half of which stood for the crafters and various orders. So many were gone, entire bloodlines lost to battle. Even Dhar was last of his kind. Once he passed, never again would a gold take to the skies.

"Good morn, Patron," Ilaenora said in a sincere tone.

She was a green, one of the oldest, with scales like polished emerald and jade highlights on every ridge. One of her wings had a tear in the lower membrane. It did not hamper her flight, so she had refused to have it healed. She wore it as a badge of honor, as did others who had fought beside him at Geilon-Rai.

The all too many who had perished in the battle had already been laid to rest in their house vaults, life deeds and lineage marked and the proper blessings spoken.

"And to you all," Dhar said.

Taenerrin cleared his throat. "We heard a terrible commotion last night. It was quite distressing."

The master shaper wore blue granite rings about the talons of each wing and capstones of equal beauty upon the spines along his back. His scales were a cobalt hue, with a tinge of azure in the morning sun and cerulean ridgelines. A deep gouge across his left eye showed gray scarring where the scales had been damaged, though he had allowed the eye to be saved.

"Distressing," Khrona said and snorted fire. "It woke me from a sound sleep."

"Most distressing," Graenallon agreed with a nervous chuckle. He was an orange, his scales like citrine shot through with amber, and newly made master enchanter. "It shattered four resonance crystals I had just attuned to a ley line."

"We assumed," Khrona said, tufts of black smoke rising from his nostrils, "it was your little human, else we would again be at war."

Dhar pushed the sorrow from his mind, at the same time wondering how he could ask for their help after so many had given their lives. How much blood would it take to finally put Revyn down?

"It was." Dhar took in a deep breath. "He has sealed the elven tree city within the forest."

There was trepidation in Aenorrin's voice, as if she already knew and dreaded the answer but could not keep herself from asking.

"You have more to say?"

Dhar glanced her way, saw sunlight catch the violet of her scales like amethysts kissed by lavender. His eyes touched upon them all before he spoke.

"Revyn is not dead," he said at last, waited for them to settle and grasp what that meant, "and he has taken Unther to the Dark."

"What!" Khrona's outrage was matched by the gasps and startled voices of the conclave. "What did we risk our lives for?" Ilae's pleading for calm went unheard. "How many of us forever lost, and for what! So that Revyn can finally finish what he started, kill us off while we are weak!"

Aetrallin took umbrage. "We are far from weak!" he bellowed, silencing numerous outcries. Master of claw, the gray had seen more combat than the combined years of all the others. "We are still feared and rightly so!" Acid dripped with each word, marring the sunstone at his feet. "How quickly you forget we have faced gods and yet live! If Revyn is not dead," he more snarled than told them, "then we will find him and finish what *we* started!"

"I will fight," said Oranarr, mistress of wing.

"As will I," another said, and two more joined him.

Khrona roared in frustration. "Of course you will fight! We all will," he said with forced calm, "but how can we be sure it is not in vain? He was cast into the Dark and survived!" He shook his head, either in disbelief or despair. "What hope do we have of destroying him?"

Dhar replied, "I did not come here to rally an army. I only wished to give warning. Revyn is still trapped. Until we know more, what he is capable of, we can do little but wait for his next attack."

"We can do more than that," Aetrallin said. "We can prepare ourselves for another battle, with proper armor and enchantment."

Graenallon said, "I admit we were not ready, not fully ready, to fight when we were called. This time we will be."

"What of our future?" Khrona pointedly asked Dhar. "Have you finished with mourning?"

Dhar was quiet as he considered. He would never be done with grieving. The loss of his daughter was a knife in his heart, but Eoraini? A large piece of him had died with her. They were halves of the same whole, incomplete without the other. How could he make these children understand when life and love for them was so different? Grief would forever haunt him; he had been shaped for one and one only.

Ilaenora said, "Perhaps this is no longer the time –"

Dhar raised a claw, indicating he would speak for himself. There was more at stake than his emotions. He had been selfish long enough.

"Once Revyn is dealt with," he said, "I will concede to the will of the conclave. May your choices be better than my own."

With that said Dhar took wing and was gone.

*     *     *

When Sera had imagined a dragon city, she thought of large natural caves or a system of lairs clawed out from the rocks. While her guess had been partly correct, she hadn't expected the scope or sheer artistry put into shaping the tunnels and chambers. Smooth as glass, the walls must have been shaped by dragon fire and magic. They had a mirror-like sheen, polished gray rock flecked with precious metal that stretched up to an arched ceiling at least a thousand feet high. The reflective glow of golden runes lit the darkness far above and must have been used to bolster the passage.

Dragons didn't mill about town either, bustling up and down the main passage, between one another in a hurry to do this or that. No, they flew. Only the young seemed to waddle along the ground. She had to admit, dragons looked far more graceful in air.

Chambers opened at either end along the way, with carved letters she couldn't discern above the entrance. It was strange to see such bulky creatures at work, resting on a hind end the size of a house, fiddling with delicate crystal in claws designed for rending and crushing. There was no wood to be seen, but the semblance of tables and chairs were mimicked in solid blocks of smooth stone. There were even hollowed rock crates used for storage and wide shelves that seemed to grow out from the walls.

No matter the craft, they all used magic. She could feel it prickle her skin and warm the frigid air. Inside the city was much warmer, as if the floor and walls refused to ice over. Her breath no longer frosted; even her meager clothing, if the leather strips could be called that, kept her tolerably warm. Not that she'd complain. After all, it was the intolerable that had kept her sane and lent a small measure of control over her life.

Her stomach grumbled in protest.

Sera ignored it and moved on, into a chamber where a dark purple dragon worked metal with a hammer and anvil, albeit ones of appropriate size. The metal sheet, inches thick, had a luminescent glow. It reminded her of fireflies on a warm summer eve. The dragon turned to see who had entered and bowed her head with an almost reverent respect.

They all did in fact. Never had she been treated so well since... since she had left her family and life behind, the man she might've married, any chance of children or even the freedom to be who she wanted. That's what being a demon hunter had meant for her. The gods had taken her body, melted it down into a slag and poured her into the mold of a monster.

"There you are," a female voice said from behind. It was the silver Dhar had spoken to, the one who fawned like an intended but had deserved no introduction. "I am Kaolanni." Her common was stilted but better than some she'd heard before. "You may call me Kao. It would be my honor to show you about the city."

So what if Dhar was already promised to another? They'd only shared a single night. She had no use for strong drink or the pipe, had no coin or possessions to indulge in, no land or a place to call home. She couldn't risk family or friends and had long ago been resigned to a solitary existence. Coupling was the single pleasure she allowed herself.

It had nothing to do with intimacy.

Besides, even if she did have feelings for him, there was little to be done for it. He could no more stop being a dragon than she could've given up her life as a hunter. Her feelings simply didn't matter.

"Alright," Sera said and let the dragon lead.

They walked on in quiet until the passage split into three directions. Kao was more graceful than the young dragons that had stopped following, had more of a stride to her gait than a waddle.

"Down that way are what you would call homes," Kao said and nodded right. "Ahead are more craft masters, passages to other levels, mining tunnels, crystal fields and our largest temple." She turned left and smiled down at Sera. Could dragons smile? "Up this way is a training chamber I know will please you. It is perhaps less grand than the ones in Naerakeilan but that is true of many –" she paused and furrowed the argent ridges above her eyes. "My apologies, but has Dhar mentioned this is our second city?"

Sera caught herself studying the dragon out of habit, how each muscle moved beneath scales the size of her palm yet the space between them could be measured in hairs; the width and depth of clawprints in the dirt, with talon scrapes the length of a forearm; gauged wingspan and tail reach, heard the rhythm of major arteries.

She looked sharply down at her bare feet, where earth and blood had stained her toes.

"We haven't really talked much."

"You must have flown together for quite some time," Kao noted, her eyes revealing nothing. "His scent is still upon you." The passage had been winding upward and began to grow steeper. "Our ancestors, like Dhar, lived at the very top of Naerat Sanae, far above the clouds. Over time, the air became too thin for us to breathe – at least with any comfort. So centuries ago we were forced to build a new home. Our knowledge has not been kept well," she said with sadness or shame in her voice, possibly both. "This city pales in comparison. Still, we do try. Graenallon, our master enchanter, has learned to create crystal orbs that when crushed in the palm grant us the ability to breathe in any environ, though only for a short time. This allows us to visit Naerakeilan, to search for any lore or clues as to how they managed some of the incredible feats within the city."

"If Dhar is that old," Sera considered aloud, "why not just ask him?"

"Dhar has always had a love for the other races. His life work has been spent studying their cultures. It made him happy," Kao said, breathed oil and flame into a wall sconce that had gone out and continued, "but in the end was not very useful. That was a luxury the firstborn had – they could choose any craft or path they wanted. Those choices have been considerably limited by the conclave. Our numbers are just too few. With so much to be done, there is no time for frivolity, and all must decide on a calling by the end of their first century.

Sera could have done without the endless chatter, but she supposed it helped pass the time as they walked. She did find the bits about Dhar somewhat interesting. It filled in some gaps between stories the other hunters had been sharing – and no doubt wildly exaggerating.

"What did you pick?" Sera asked and immediately wondered why. Was she hoping for some more insight into Dhar by learning about the female he'd chosen to join with?

"I am a gatherer."

There was pride in her tone, as if the title explained all.

"You pick things up?"

Kao laughed. Or snorted. Either way she brightened the passage with a small burst of flame.

"It is much more complicated than that, I can assure you. Gatherers do a variety of tasks, from cultivating crystals to be eaten or enchanted, coaxing ore from the mountain, purifying ice and snow for drinking, keeping a careful tally of all livestock for miles to the south, so the herds are never culled too thin. We also –" She must have construed Sera's quiet for lack of interest and cut her explanation short. "Apologies again. I can sometimes be too... passionate about my calling."

"You eat crystals?"

"And stone and ore," Kao replied. "Our bodies require more than meat and water, to fuel breath, conjure *furie*, enchant – even to fly. You can understand then the great need for skilled gatherers."

Sera shrugged. "Seems you enjoy living for others," she said, as if the notion had become alien to her. "I was like that once too."

"Oh, but you still are." There was no hint of jesting in her voice. "Yours is a sacred calling. Without hunters, the lesser races would be overrun by demons."

"Lesser?" Sera stopped, her brow furrowed.

"No," Kao explained, struggling for words, "that is not what I meant. I seldom get a chance to practice common. Please excuse my mistake."

A curt nod from Sera, and they continued walking. The comment lingered in the air between them, caused her to reconsider whether she approved of Dhar's choice.

She settled on indifference.

"This," Kao said, excited, and moved to a chamber on the left, "is our hatchery."

Warm air struck her like the winds of Danarriden. The shaped room was immense and littered end to end with man-sized eggs of many colors. Their shells had the look of rough leather, like armor without seams. Mounds of rock spewed heat into the air, as if the mountain exhaled into the chamber. Crystals sprung from the ground in clusters of two and three, thick obelisks of cloudy yellow and reflected light from wall sconces – long trenchers of stone filled with oil and set ablaze. Only a handful of dragons tended the dozens of eggs. They gently breathed fire over the tops, causing the shells to glow, or turned the eggs on another side when the heat grew too bright.

"Those are caretakers," Kao said with respect. "There was a time when I thought to be one of them." She bowed her head to them and turned back to the passage. "They spend most of their days in that chamber. I could never bear to be inside for too long. I love to fly, to feel the sun across my wings, warm currents beneath me." The scales under her eyes darkened to a shade of blue, as if she blushed at some thought. "I also imagined I would have a clutch of my own by now, but father has yet to answer my prayers."

Sera quickened her pace, wondering just where this training chamber was and why it was taking so long to find it.

"Gods don't answer prayers," she said flatly.

Kao matched her pace but chose not to respond. She kept her gaze forward as they walked, either confused or hurt. It mattered little either way.

The quiet was a welcomed respite.

With a glance the way they'd come, Sera was about to turn around and head back to the city entrance. Why would she care to see a training room anyway? She'd already seen enough combat to last her a lifetime.

The passage opened up on the left to a wide ledge of shaped stone. They could have gone further, which Kao seemed intent upon, but Sera was done with walking an endless tunnel. She stepped out onto the ledge and into a chamber unlike anything she'd ever seen. The enormity of its size was staggering. Wall sconces below and above were lit in haphazard lines of flickering oil for what may as well have been an eternity. She couldn't see the floor or ceiling, nor were flames visible across the darkness where she imagined the opposite wall must be.

Islands of jagged rock, flat on the surface, floated in midair at varying heights. Golden runes flared across their bottoms in a circle, causing a tingle of *furie* along her spine and a quiet thrum in her ears. Giant pillars of roughly hewn rock, even wider than the great trees in Darleman, rose up from some islands or struck down from others. Their dark stone was lit only by protruding crystals that ran their length. Clusters of thick obelisks, like smoky glass or clouded water, each had a ring of white runes around its base. Some grew longer than others, some spun with jagged arms and a few seemed to lengthen before her eyes. They shone a single color, some red or blue, yellow or green, white or purple, but each set appeared to correspond to a different function.

As a whole the room looked a giant gauntlet, a maze of deadly obstacles and intricate challenges. Through it all flew dozens of dragons, moving with such speed and agility that she found it difficult to follow any one with her eyes. Another thousand feet up and half again to the right was a second ledge. She couldn't tell if there were more, though there seemed to be none below her.

Red crystal exploded on the island straight ahead with enough force to rain shards over the ledge. A gray had flown too close and crashed through the spinning obstruction. The dragon kept on, undaunted and unhurt.

The shards had dissipated into splashes of light across Sera's feet and tickled her skin with their passing. She looked back to the broken cluster, and as fast as it'd been destroyed, it began to grow back.

Upon closer inspection, she noticed a much smaller crystal atop the island. No bigger than a man, a single obelisk, it snapped off in the claw of a black speeding past and remained solid. The dragon then dropped it off at another island further below, where numerous piles had accumulated.

Sera realized they were keeping a tally.

This was the training room, where dragons not only pitted their skills against the gauntlet but competed with one another. She watched a red land on an island just below and to the left, where she could now see rows of white crystals and a single blue in the center. These too were about the size of a man. The dragon had landed on all fours just in front of the formation and breathed a jet of fire that destroyed only the blue. The dragon flew off, and the crystal grew back.

These precision attacks were carried out on other islands as well, though with claw and tail swipes. Sera caught herself smiling and understood why Kao had wanted to bring her here.

"I am glad it pleases you," Kao said and smiled with her. "You seem to find little joy in much else."

Sera's smile faded. "What's that supposed to mean?"

"Just that you are not what I expected." Kao looked out over the ledge, oblivious to the slight. "You are more dour and cynical than the hunters I have heard tale of."

"I've been ankle-deep in blood since the day of my Awakening. Nothing I've done is worthy of story."

An image of the old man returned to haunt her, his white beard consumed by fire, aged flesh withering in her grasp as she devoured his *furie*. She shut tight her eyes, forced the image from her mind. Old man. It was easier to recall him as a stranger, some poor random soul in the wrong place at the wrong time. To allow him a name was to give him a face, to remind her she'd taken the life of someone's uncle. Not just someone, the man who'd fought to save her life, who'd released her from Revyn's hold.

Kao glanced back. "If there is no joy or pride in your calling, why continue?"

"You think I have a choice?!" Sera yelled, far more angry at herself than the dragon.

"I meant no offense," Kao said quickly. "I have the utmost respect for demon hunters, heard stories of their deeds since the time I was hatched. Never have I been told of one unhappy with the blessing." She seemed at a loss for the right words. "You live as we do! In the honor and service of father! I – I just do not understand why you are so unhappy."

Sera fumed. She was also at a loss for words, that anyone for a single instant would think she could be happy as a hunter. Her life had been stripped away. She had nothing left to call her own but the anger. Anger at the gods who'd cursed her, at the demons that plagued her, at the loneliness forced upon her.

Kao sounded as if her childhood dreams had been shattered.

"Do the others feel as you do?"

"Why don't you go ask them," Sera snapped. "They're holed up in that underground city and have no intention of ever again leaving."

"You could join them then," Kao said softly, "be free of your calling."

"I'll never be free."

The truth was Sera needed to keep fighting, to feel the holy fire in her belly, to feed the anger in her heart. It burned away the grief. It wasn't about saving lives. That balance had been forever tipped and could never again be restored. It was the anger. Without it eating at the grief, she'd be left with nothing but despair and a longing for the grave.

Kao had no more words, and the quiet grew between them like a palpable sorrow – an inevitable surrender. That was fine; nothing remained to be said. Talk had never changed anything. There was no reason for it to start now.

Sera turned and left her to the quiet.

\*     \*     \*

*A thousand of them lain in wait around the clearing, hunters every one and alive with the geas. A blessing and a curse, Revyn had made the mistake of imbuing his new children with the shapeling disease. Even though he was mortal, he had still felt it when the Dark claimed Unther. It made sense their fool brother would come for them as well.*

*All that remained was the waiting.*

It was confusing at first, seeing the vision through another's eyes, as she had when the shiardin attacked. Fluora saw them all clearly in the dusk of Greywood, the elite kheos and daumon that had pledged their lives at Halifax. As minotaurs, they were deadly, muscled from hoof to horn. As hunters, with the combined might of three gods, they were the best hope Taellus had in the coming war.

*The clearing was freshly made, trees hewn clean through by enchanted axe or torn free from the frozen ground, broken roots and all. He was there, too, the once god of war. Tempas watched and waited, ready to guard his brother and strike down whatever monster Revyn sent at them.*

*Fluora looked down at her shadow in the moonlight, saw the horns of a stag and realized she saw Herne.*

And how is that? *he asked her in thought.*

So surprised by his voice, she nearly lost hold of the vision. And once again, it was just that, a vision and not premonition.

I am a seeress, *Fluora explained. With great sorrow, she added,* I was with Unther before he passed.

*Herne nodded, drawing a look from Tempas. Long used to battle, his larger brother stood the field with a preternatural calm. Though it shamed him to admit it, Herne was afraid. His immortality stripped away, death was at best an uncertainty. But what would become of him if he was taken to the Dark?*

It is my hope we fare better.

You plan to capture the shiardin, *Fluora surmised,* using yourself as bait.

Tempas as well, *he said.* We realized why Unther was taken first and knew we would be next.

The minotaurs. *Fluora saw in Herne's thoughts what all three of them had done, the ritual at Halifax that had forged a thousand shapeling hunters.* Revyn is brutal and heartless, but he is no fool. When the rift opens, he will see your trap.

*The hollow knock against air, the visible ripples of its resonance, struck in the very center of the clearing.*

He will see, *Herne agreed,* and attack nonetheless.

*Another strike, much louder, shook loose dirt across the earth, rumbled through his middle and rocked the firm of his resolve.*

*Tempas drew both swords.*

*The forest around them became a ring of blue fire and frosted breath, glowing eyes and the mounting thirst for pitched battle.*

*A final strike sent out a shockwave that buffeted hair and eyes with wind like wailing banshees. A rift split the air, like the uncoupling of life and limb, and revealed an empty black so dark it hungered for the light. Violet fire ran the edge of the rift, as if the physical had been set alight and its existence was being devoured.*

I can feel him watching, *Fluora said.* He sees every one of you. He cannot be so –

*A shiardin stepped through.*

*The hunters roared and charged as one, their runic fire scorching earth and rock in their wake. The shiardin eyed Herne and bounded straight for him. He braced for the attack, steeled his nerves and drew his bow.*

The fear, *he said, heart pounding in his chest.* Is this what it means to be mortal?

Fear makes you stronger, *Fluora replied,* if you can hold it to your breast and not give in.

*The shiardin leapt over a clamor of bodies and arcing blades. It sizzled in the moonlight, blows against its chitin plates deflected with bright sparks and a defiant screech of single-minded purpose. Three arrows struck and bounced off in quick succession.*

*The hunters it touched cried out and grayed in their tracks, withered to ashen flakes even as they persisted. They eventually fell like lumps of charred coal, embers burning out and staining the earth. Those the shiardin bit were instantly turned. Their bodies erupted into black streamers and wisps then folded inward to the form of a new child of Revyn. They in turn infected others, like the waters of a plague breaking over the tumult.*

*Herne kept firing but to no avail. Hunters fell or were turned, stopped to fend off their once brethren, had slowed but could not halt the shiardin's advance.*

"Be ready!" *Tempas said and moved to stand before him.* "We will not fall!"

*Bow lowered, Herne put a hand to his shoulder.*

"You were always a good brother."

No, *Fluora urged,* you cannot give up!

We gave up the day we broke our oaths, *Herne said with a wistful laugh in his thoughts.* Father was always strict on keeping oaths.

*The shiardin jumped over a fallen hunter and high into the air. Its body flattened to a blanket of starless night, its edges rippling with the force of its attack. Both blades went through and shredded the inky mass, but even Tempas could not stop its assault.*

*All went dark, numb with cold, as the transformed shiardin enveloped him. Fluora screamed against the pain. It crushed them inward, began pulling them down into the earth. She had no choice but to leave him.*

I am sorry, *she said and wept.*

*Tempas was shouting for the others to hold bodies up into the moonlight.*

No, *Herne told her,* it is I who am sorry.

## – 4 –

arr felt better rested the next morning. They had returned to Dwendorim before nightfall, and he had begged off to go sleep as the runes overhead began to sparkle like starlight. Aren was still with Idelle in the forest. He enjoyed spending time with the other companions, had made new friends among both hounds and bears, but he was especially interested in Kaela – though he would never admit it. Barr felt a flutter in his stomach every time Aren thought of her. Idelle teased her little brother to no end, but there was more to her staying in Darleman than the amusement. There was a longing inside her when she soared over the trees, and she flew further north each time. Barr suspected she wanted to see her homeland or perhaps others like herself. Unique to the Ghaoylens, the large hawks were

just a few hours away by wing. If she truly wanted to go see them, she could have done so and been back before even Aren got hungry.

*I know that,* she said. So long as the rift outside his home remained open to Geilon-Rai, he could still hear them both. *I just don't want to be too far away. In case you need us.*

Aren ran through the snow, dodging arrows and long spears.

*And I don't get hungry all that often,* he complained.

Idelle laughed. *Not since Yuinei started carrying an extra satchel of dried venison.*

*Those are snacks!*

Barr rolled his eyes and went outside.

Yuinei was Kaela's Ballar, a strong girl from House Arraedin. She had survived the forest battle with soldiers from Alixhir, only to be infected upon returning home. Like so many other Ballar, she had been forced by Revyn to slay and consume her companion. The child bonded to Kaela had been killed as well, but the young war hound stayed hidden during the final combat atop the city. She and Yuinei had taken an instant liking to one another, but they would never share the true bond of a Ballar. The thought of it sickened Barr, even frightened him to consider, how he would feel if it'd been him –

"Do not," Fluora said from behind. She took his hand and led him to sit at the fountain. "Such thoughts serve no purpose."

Aren and Idelle were quiet; they too had felt it.

"I know. You're right." He squeezed her hand and managed a smile. Her blindfold was pear green, a touch darker than her dress. "What now? We can't keep waiting for him to strike."

Fluora had told him over breakfast what she'd seen the night before. Coupled with another premonition of her mother dying while giving birth, her sleep had been anything but restful.

"Tempas will be next." She sounded certain. "Herne was convinced the three of them would be attacked first. They did after all create an army of hunters."

He had caught a glimpse of Tempas when she spoke his name, and he wondered if he could find the once god in scry.

"I've seen firsthand what Sera can do," Barr said. "I can't imagine what a thousand like her would be capable of."

*Why make them shapelings?* Idelle asked. *With all those hunters, Revyn can't hope to infect as many people as before.*

"Arrogance?" Fluora replied.

Barr knew she could hear Aren and Idelle in his mind, that his thoughts were unguarded and openly shared. It was only one of several differences between humans and faeron, but it'd been the hardest for him to grow accustomed to. Half-faeron by his mother, he'd still been raised as a human. The elves were much the same. There was a distinct separation of words and thoughts, an innate understanding from birth that the voice in his mind was safe, heard by none but himself.

His bond with Aren and Idelle had changed that to some degree, in that they shared their inner voices with one another. It was the notion that faeron as a race had a similar connection, conversed in images and emotion, thoughts and feeling, which had left him so unnerved when Fluora first explained it. Even with the memories of past lives as a faeron, he found himself anxious around his mother's people. It was a sense of being naked, an uncontrollable lack of privacy.

It could've been the reason he felt more at home in Dwendorim than on Faeronthalsos. Fluora had assured him he could learn to guard his thoughts. Time spent in reflection over any of his faeron lives would've done as much. It didn't seem so important in the underground city. He had no need to hide his thoughts from Fluora and as a result had been spared on numerous occasions the awkward task of expressing his feelings for her.

She smiled and elbowed him in the side, as if trying to wake him from a vision.

It occurred to him he hadn't had a vision since facing Ombreusk. The premonition from a past life, he'd seen a man with all twelve emblems, wearing them as a set of silvery-gold full plate. He once thought that man was Markus, but Revyn's pawn had bled out. Whether it had been a false prophecy or the revenant's tampering, Barr couldn't recall the last time he'd gone a week without a vision – not since they started when he was a child.

"No," Barr said at last. "He was making a point. A single shiardin and they weren't enough to stop it."

"The moonlight did seem to do more damage than their weapons," Fluora agreed. "I recall Tempas shouting for them to hold up bodies to the light."

*Maybe that's why they only attack at night,* Aren guessed. *So far, at least.*

"We should talk to him." Barr stood and brought her to her feet. "Can you show me again what he looks like? Or scry him for me? If we can find him, I can open a rift to his location." He let go her hands and walked toward the house. "I just need to make something before we go."

He heard Fluora begin to scry in the fountain as he searched a drawer for a stone the right size.

*We'll come with you,* Idelle offered, and he felt her turn about with all speed.

*Can I bring Kaela?*

Even from inside, he could hear Fluora's giggle. He grabbed a flat stone the length and width of a fingernail and sat down in the kitchen to begin scrawling runes across both sides.

*We're just going to talk,* Barr told them, *then coming right back. Stop worrying so much, Idelle, and go see your homeland. Who knows? Maybe you'll fall in love like Aren.*

Aren pouted. *That's not funny.*

*Are you sure?* she asked, with no hint of laughter. *We'll be too far apart to hear each other.*

*Just be careful. If we don't hear from you in a few hours, I'll come find you.*

A sigh and Idelle was headed north again. *I wasn't worried about myself.*

Barr finished and found Fluora studying an image in the fountain. It was a human in full plate, his face hid beneath a helm. He stood the center of a large clearing, a stretch of forest where trees had been upended and the frozen earth was scorched. He saw minotaur hunters in the background, their bodies aglow with runes etched into their flesh. A second set of fiery black circled their bodies like enchanted armor, a stark contrast to the holy flames that engulfed them horn to hoof.

"I'm glad they're on our side," Barr said in a solemn tone. "Is that Greywood?"

"Yes," Fluora replied. He assumed the man in armor was Tempas. "He keeps turning his head about, as if he knows he is being watched."

"He was a god, after all. He should at least still be sensitive to magic."

At the other end of the fountain, opposite the rift to Geilon-Rai, Barr began arranging deific runes. The glyph was already completed in his mind. It took only seconds to bring it to realization. Fluora joined him before the cold, and they waited for Tempas to approach.

"I knew you would come," the once war god said in a deep voice. "I have watched you for some time."

"May we come through?" Barr asked, looking up at the towering man. Tempas stepped aside and indicated they should join him at the fire. Tents circled the area, interspersed with cooking pits and the cobalt stares of taur hunters. "I brought you this."

It reminded Barr of Chamal, the troll shamaness he'd saved on his way to Alixhir – shortly after his exile. It was from her gift that he'd gotten the idea for a scrying stone. Tempas removed a gauntlet and took the stone, rubbed his thumb over its surface as if gauging the enchantment and nodded in approval. He slipped it into a leather sack tied at his belt. Armored glove back on, he took off his great helm and set it down beside him at the fire. Barr and Fluora took seats on an adjacent log, grateful for the warmth.

*Should have dressed for the cold,* Aren said, playing at some game with the other hounds.

Barr was surprised they could still hear each other across both rifts. He could scarcely feel Idelle, though, flying high above the trees.

*I didn't think* – he knew better than to finish the thought. *You're right. I've been distracted.*

He conjured warmth to surround him and let it spread to cover Fluora. She pulled his arm around her waist and leaned in close.

"I assume you know what has transpired?" Tempas had long dark hair, a strong jaw and gray eyes like a winter moon. "For what it is worth, I was pleased when you trapped Revyn in the Dark."

Barr shifted focus without thinking. The suddenness with which Tempas' glyph came into view was like an assault on his senses. It didn't give him an immediate headache, as it had when he saw Revyn's, but the sheer complexity of its design, interwoven runes across the three planes, far larger than his physical body, was both staggering and humbling. So much more intricate than his own, it left him feeling small, almost insignificant by comparison.

Tempas was still a god.

Nothing had been stripped away, only masked. The runes in the astral were somehow faded, as if dormant or blocked. A lesser portion in the ether was also affected. Each rune was still part of a larger whole, but they no longer turned in place within the spinning pattern. Once alive with *furie*, they were now obscured by shadow, like a frozen wasteland out of reach of the sun.

He began to wonder if the runes could be restored, if given enough time he could –

Fluora squeezed his hand hard.

Barr blinked away the vision and cleared his throat, a poor apology for the length of his silence.

"Thank you," he said quickly to fill the quiet. "I've been struggling lately with the thought that I'd made a mistake."

"Nonsense. All would have been lost had you not acted as you did." Tempas reached over and clapped him on the back. Even if Barr could return him to godhood, it wasn't his place to make that choice. "Nothing short of removing Revyn would have ended his plague. He was the true fuel of the disease."

"Could he return?" Fluora asked, giving voice to the unspoken fear Barr refused to think on. "And if he did, what would happen to all those who were infected?"

Tempas considered, the hard set to his features softened as if he recalled a painful sorrow. He too must have wrestled with the notion.

"I cannot say for certain," he relented. "I can only promise to stand against him –" he looked out at the gathered hunters, at the cairns of those who had already fallen and the taurs who had arrived to replace them – "for as long as I am able."

"The stone," Barr said. "You can use it to contact me if anything should happen."

"I guessed as much, and I thank you for it. I must admit this being mortal has unsettled me." Tempas gave a weak smile. "It is not death that troubles me; it is the thought of going without a fight."

Fluora said, "We should leave the rift open. I will ask Hanar to send what help they can."

"The arachon golems?" Tempas asked. He looked as if he might decline the aid, either to suggest the golems would fare no better or to spare them the inevitable loss. "Alright," he said and nodded, "any help is appreciated. Perhaps together we can find a weakness, kill or even capture one."

When they stood, he shook forearms with Barr. To Fluora he bowed with fingertips to forehead, a respectful farewell – and greeting – for a faeron.

Once back in Dwendorim, Barr said, "I'm going to see if I can meet with the arbiters. We can't have rifts lying about unprotected. This is exactly what the portalis was intended for."

Fluora kissed him, a soft lingering touch of lips that calmed him for the moment.

"I will look for Uinahd then," she said. "Hanar should still be at shapers circle."

With a furrowed brow, "Why would she be there?"

"Have you forgotten already?" Fluora straightened his shirt and shook her head with a *tsk*. "The point of teaching them to shape was not to change themselves," she reminded him. "They want children of their own.

"And Hanar wants a son."

\*   \*   \*

Dhar flew down to the third level below the surface of Dwendorim, where new forests had been planted days ago. Already full grown, they filled the cavern with fresh air. The scent of rich soil reached up on a warm wind, while sunlight caressed his wings like a summer blanket. The craggy ceilings here were a mixture of thick quartz and lush moss a claw-length deep. He had yet to ask how the system functioned, but he knew the crystals were ice clear by night and bright as molten gold by day, when the sunlight stored within them was released. Water was funneled down from dozens of aquifers along runic paths of shaped stone, formed a small lake and a handful of streams. When moisture within the cavern saturated the ceiling moss, it let fall the excess water in a semblance of rain.

He had only experienced the flash rain once, and while it felt somewhat refreshing he much preferred the grip of storm clouds, the heady scent of a thunderclap and the charged air before lightning lit up the skies. Still, the arachon had done all they could to make their city into a home others might love as much as they did. He admired them for that, felt proud to call them friends.

Dhar swept left and kept searching.

The soil he knew had been painstakingly collected and mixed in with the existing earth. Each tree, a great redwood, had been coaxed by hand from sapling to aged bole. Even now, hundreds of feet below, he spied arachon tending the forest with an endless diligence and patience he had never seen in another race. They had become so much more than first intended, when families –

Her scent broke his reverie, brought him up short in midair. She sat against a tree, hidden from view. Only by shifting his vision could he see the heat of her body, a blend of red and yellow encased in fiery white. She was alone, as the champion had told him.

When Dhar had returned to Dwendorim, he could not find Sera at her house or any other spot he thought she fancied. He had spent hours in a leisurely search, was disappointed when she did not show for dinner at the main square and eventually fell to sleep in his own home close to Barr's. This morning had been much the same. He had eaten breakfast with the other hunters, but none of them had seen or heard from her in days. More searching had led only to frustration. He had finally relented and asked an arachon. The champion was no longer a part of the protectorate, but he had worn an enchanted necklace that allowed him to speak with all the others.

It had taken only a moment for them to find her.

Now that she was in sight, he hesitated. Why did she go to such lengths to be alone? Especially when there were other hunters in the city she could talk with. No demon would ever find its way in – not without help, he added, and recalled being told of the group of chaodyn that had infected her. Though he had no memory of carrying them through the mists, the attack was his fault as much as Revyn's. She bore him no ill will for the part he played in the mad scheme, but he knew the resulting murder weighed heavy on her conscience.

The resulting murder... Dhar could barely say the man's name, let alone picture his face without the threat of inner turmoil. It was foolish to feel responsible for his death, but the heart had no use for logic or rationale. It was a child crying out, screaming its every impulse.

And what of Sera? His actions at the Mirror Pool, his loss of memory and weakened body, allowing himself to be marked, all had led to shattering what little peace of mind the geas afforded her. Could be that was why she avoided the other hunters. They were a reminder of her time as a shapeling – the only time in her few years she had taken life other than a demon's.

Solitude would not heal her heart nor assuage any guilt; of that much he was certain.

Unless it was merely the privacy she sought. Being here in the city, far away from any demons, might be the first time since her Awakening she had time to herself. If such were true, should he interrupt?

Why did he want to spend time with her anyway? Their encounter had been purely physical, as far as he knew. He had no real feelings for her; she was just easier to be with than... others. She had no expectations. She wanted nothing from him nor needed him to do anything but be who he wanted. They had somewhat in common, at least where killing demons was concerned, and she did seem to enjoy hearing of his time on Danarriden.

Was that why he sought her out? Because she was genuinely interested in him, in what he had done, and not because she had fallen in love with some glorified ideal of who he was supposed to be?

He closed in and searched for a place to land. The trees had all grown in a uniform fashion, but the space between them was haphazard at best. He managed a spot not too far off from where she sat. In the dark soil and soft underbrush, back flat against a tree, eyes closed beneath the song of blue finch and chestnut sparrow, she breathed deep and even.

"You've been hovering for minutes," she said in a soft voice, knowing he would hear. "You scared away all the birds."

"Not to worry," he replied, his deep voice louder than he wished to be, "they cannot go very far."

Dhar remained a dragon. Why? He could shift with a thought, go sit by her side, share in the forest calm. Did some part of him hope she would come to him first, ask to go hunting or just fly through the caverns? Or was it a test to see if she preferred him as a man and not as he truly was? He frowned at the notion and settled his bulk into the cool earth.

Since when did he spend so much time in thought, caring about the wants or motivations of another? Not since Eorana, he admitted, and the sorrow returned like a mountain across his chest. His blatant stupidity, his selfish despair, had cost him a daughter when all he wanted was an end to his suffering.

Sera touched him, and he opened his eyes. He had not realized they were closed, that the buried memories had resurfaced with such ease. She reached out to wipe the moisture from the scales beneath an eye, caught sight of her dirtied hand with the ever present stains of blood, and resisted. She sat with legs crossed before him instead.

Neither one said a word for some time.

"Tell me," he said at last, struck by an odd thought, "why do you suppose there are still so many demons upon Taellus?"

That seemed to brighten her mood. As a human who had spent a good part of her life under the geas, demons were probably one of the few topics she could speak on – or so Dhar imagined.

"Some are powerful enough to open brief portals," she explained, "usually near a ley stone." She must have seen him raise an eyeridge. "Summoners. They create the stones. They're like physical anchors to a ley line. Makes it easier to summon demons, I guess."

"I have heard of them used for many things before but not for calling demons."

Sera shrugged. "I'm not compelled to destroy them, but I do it anyway. I'd probably kill a summoner, too, if I ever met one." She looked up to gauge his reaction, to maybe see if he was judging her. "Not that they live long. Imps and hatchlings are never enough. They always want more. Soon all that's left is the bloodied stone and a charred corpse."

"And the demon."

"Right." She let a handful of dark earth fall away like sand from an hourglass. "They don't live long either."

He watched her pass the time in awkward silence, plucking stems one by one from a bush. Dhar expected to hear more but waited until she was ready. He knew she did not enjoy conversations the way he did, had said as much when they first met, so he let her choose the pace of their discourse.

"Then there's the mushroom portals," she went on, turning a leaf over and thumbing its veins. "Those go to Faeronthalsos. They're not like ley stones, though. They kill plants and nearby trees – even the dirt."

"Why would faeron need portals when they can use the mists?" Dhar wondered aloud.

"Only faeron and nymphs can do that. After dryads were banished south, the Matron refused them access. Besides," she added with a little quirk of her mouth, as if he should already know what she was about to say, "there're dozens of other races on Faeronthalsos, not the least of which are efreeti."

Dhar was impressed. She knew more than he had presumed, and he felt sheepish for misjudging her.

"With so many ways to Faeronthalsos, it is a wonder Aranadir has not yet been overrun."

"Most demons give in to the bloodlust," she said and crumpled the leaf. "They feed and feed until the change comes. Older demons are stronger than that." She wiped the debris from her hands. "They resist and seek out portals to Faeron. They want to open the rift from the other side, give Danarriden a new feeding ground."

Dhar had studied other cultures for most of his life, and even with his atonement on Danarriden, she seemed to know more of demon lore than he did.

"How do you know so much about them?" he asked. "Or what happens on Faeronthalsos? Have you ever been there?"

"No." She had a faraway look to her eyes, as if she could see the enchanted realm in her mind. She shook her head and said, "Some comes from observation, from having survived this long. Most comes to me in times of quiet or in dreams when I let myself sleep." She looked up at him, as if she knew her words would affect him. "He speaks to me. Curoch. Not to me directly, like we're talking right now, but... to my soul. If that makes any sense."

Sera got to her feet and indicated with a short laugh how little sense it made to her.

He could not recall the last time father had spoken to him, to any of them. Dhar supposed it was the battle at the foot of Naerat Sanae, when Revyn had sent his new children to destroy all dragonkind – but even of that he could not be sure. Curoch was not angry with them, or at least made no show of it. The god had simply stopped speaking with them. He no longer witnessed hatchings, made his presence known in the temples, blessed the bond of new mates or gave any sign he heard their prayers. They were left with nothing but faith, the trust he still listened, the conviction he still cared. So long as they loved him, believed with all their hearts he was still with them, the hope endured that he too loved them in return.

The world erupted beneath his head. *Furie* roared so loud it drowned out all else, tore through his senses with a violent clamor and vibrations that shook him to the core of his spirit. The once gentle hum had expanded in an instant, increased a thousandfold and dwarfed him with its presence. Flames licked at his scales, the warm breeze now a scalding tempest that threatened to erode him, wear away his body as so much sand beneath the tides. The translucent aura of fire had become a blinding inferno, a white-hot blaze of incandescence that masked all sight with its ire.

"Arch... Demon!" she cried, voice hoarse in his ear, and dug fingers in his scales. Pain faltered beneath the tumult as she climbed, lost to the maelstrom of pale fire and gold smoke. "Fly!"

Legs crushed him into moving, hands gripped scale and flesh, and the forest fell away into the fading crackle of its own flames and spreading char. Moss withered and rained ash, amidst a shower of crystal and broken rocks against his head. His bellow was overwhelmed, a whisper in the gale. Fingers tightened their hold on his neck and forced him onward, flying blind through the torment like a pyre given wing.

Thought escaped him, battered into the remnants of primal urgency. There was only anguish and the closing dark, the brand that drove him forward, wings clawing through air in a futile effort to douse their fires. Breath came in ragged gasps, scorched his lungs with the fading effort of each intake, until the struggle to press on was no longer a choice. He flew by magic alone, the leathery membrane of both wings all but consumed.

They soared through the cavern, over forests and turned fields, endless rows of ripened crop, lakes that mirrored the flames of a passing phoenix and a shallow stream that rose higher with the promise of salvation.

Dhar gritted his teeth and beat the fiery remains of skeletal wings. He refused to give in, not again. Not ever.

This time his roar stifled the din of *furie*. It shook rocks from the walls as they climbed to the next level, tore marble in great swathes from a quarry as they passed and resounded throughout the city like a harbinger of doom. Death was not the answer to the pains crippling his spirit. A false savior, an empty oath, it was the fiction of despair. Life was the true redeemer, the seat of hope and absolution. It was reason enough to persist, to make amends, to cherish love, to share and be shared with.

More than ever he was determined to survive, to fight tooth and claw for both himself and those who depended on him. He endured the pain, knew Sera was wracked by an agony even greater, and followed her lead toward the Arch Demon.

As fast as it had come, the fires died away. The *furie* abated to a dull thrum, the wail of its fervor just an echo in his mind. Sera collapsed against him. With the onset of sudden calm, his strength began to waver. Barely able to stay conscious, let alone in air, Dhar searched for a place to land through bleary eyes. Exhaustion left him few options, but he did what he could to avoid rocks and shaped stone. He tried with all his might to slow their descent. The best he could manage was to shoulder the impact.

They crashed into hard earth, upending mounds of dark soil and rock in a trench three hundred feet long. He caught Sera as she slipped from his neck, placed her gently beside him and rested his head against the pillow of earth.

"Sera."

His eyelids grew heavy. A rasped breath and he called again. She slowly began to stir, the luminous fire about her weak but steady. He knew the geas would heal her, but he needed to be certain.

"Are you –" his eyes closed for a long moment then fluttered opened, as one who labored to stay awake. "Are you hurt?"

She forced herself up with a groan and shook the dirt from her front. She was covered in blood, the dusky crimson of a dragon. A look his way left her speechless, mouth open without sound, eyes wide in tearful horror, body trembling with the rise of panic. She was up and running so fast, she slid to a stop at his face.

"Dhar! You stay awake!" She looked around for help, her voice and body frantic. "I – I'll find help. I'll get an eldarath." She swallowed her fear, determined as he had been. "I'll get Barr. You *don't* fall asleep!" Tears ran freely down her cheeks. "You hear me? I'll bring help."

He realized he must have looked a mess. Blood ran from a dozen wounds in rivulets across his body, where the scales had been burned or torn away. Muscle and tendon were exposed, scorched by fire or tattered from his exertions. His wings were gone. Only their outline remained, blackened bones in a web with stubborn flesh still clinging on.

"Stay," he pleaded. "I can heal. It just… takes time."

Sera caressed his eyeridge with hands calloused from a thousand battles. They were gentle, caring.

"What can I do?"

"Keep… me focused." He worked to steady his breath as he summoned *furie* from within. "If I pass out… I will die."

"Alright," she said and nodded, "I can do that." She sniffled and wiped her eyes with the back of a hand. "I'll be right here."

She looked into his eye as he willed his body to mend itself. They were the blue of deep sapphires, the autumn sky at break of day. Warmth flecked with hope, they held him in a state of wonder. *You're alright*, they whispered softly, fingers trailing the grooves between scales. She laid her head against his, stroked the ridges of his face, but never left his gaze.

When the first wound began to close, she caught sight of it and smiled. Tears flowed anew, but they were tears of joy and relief. New scales began to form, and Sera laughed with delight. All the tension had fled her body. Though it took minutes of concentration, focusing his mind on each injury in turn, breath started to come easier and no longer pained him. The fresh scales were pale citrine and malleable as heated gold. It would take some time for them to harden to their natural density. He lifted a wing, testing the flexibility of its new membrane. Light shone through and highlighted each tender bone and vein. It was still sensitive to the touch, but it too would thicken over time.

All the while, Sera's eyes never left his.

"Thank you," he said, "for keeping me focused."

He was tired through and through, but there was something comforting in the way she leaned against him.

"You're strong." She sounded almost as surprised as he was. He had never been so close to death. "So much stronger than I thought. And stubborn!" She smiled and looked away, wiping her eyes as if ashamed. "We have that in common too."

"You are not to blame." His tone was insistent. "This was not your fault."

She kissed his eyelid and wept.

Whether from guilt or shame, the helplessness of her situation, she cried as if she had not shed a tear since her Awakening. He wanted to hold her, to tell her she would be alright, to be there for her as she had been for him.

He shifted without thinking, and she fell against his chest, into his arms. She looked up at him in shock at the sudden jolt, at the *whoops* look on his face, and the two of them burst into laughter.

"Perhaps I could have done that with more grace," he said and wiped the tears from her cheek.

Her laughter faded, but she still smiled. She seemed glad of his touch.

"I'm truly sorry," she said. "I never meant to hurt – I'd never intend you harm."

He traced the outline of runes beneath the stubble atop her ear, studied her features as if seeing them for the first time.

"You are beautiful."

He did not mean her appearance but who she was beneath the geas. She gave a small nod, and he knew she understood. He imagined it was something she had needed to hear for a long time, that the geas did not define her; she was more than what the gods had made her, and she was worthy of love. She touched her fingers to his lips.

"Thank you," she mouthed, too choked for words.

She laid her head against his chest, arms beneath his neck, and let him hold her. They stayed together that way until daylight began to fade.

\*   \*   \*

Fluora stepped through and into the portalis, once envisioned by the first arachon but only recently come to pass. The grand chamber was immense, thrumming with *furie* and alight with a myriad of runes. Its design was intended to safeguard the city, should the hall somehow be overtaken. It was completely isolated, with no way in or out but for the portals. The Aegis, bloodstone arachon specialized in defensive magic, already kept vigil though no portals were left open. They might have been there solely for her sake.

Hanar walked beside her as they headed across the chamber to a waiting traveler and several Aegis. Each city to be offered a portal had already been decided upon and their placement carefully mapped to avoid conflict between long-standing adversaries. The arachon were to remain neutral. Any violence in the portalis would be met with a swift and harsh punishment – even exclusion from its use. Fluora eyed the alcoves where destroyers would line the walls. Kingdoms would not be allowed to abuse the portals to wage war, but a time was soon coming when all of Taellus must band together to face a common enemy.

The portalis would be instrumental in that endeavor.

Barr had met with the arbiters. His plan to rebuild and unite Taellus was already underway. Hence her visit to Alixhir, while he helped Tempas prepare for nightfall. She knew the true reason he had asked her to go in his stead. Despite how many sylvannis had been killed, the plan was more important than vengeance or grief. They would need every city, and that meant putting aside any differences that would undermine the necessary peace.

She was glad of his trust, to be given such a delicate undertaking, but she was also aware how his appearance might offend – even more so than her own. Despite his heritage, he dressed like an elf and had their accent on his tongue. Barr would not lie either, if asked where his loyalties lay, and she doubted the new king would want to deal with the man who had sealed Darleman from his grasp.

Uinahd touched her shoulder.

"Are you ready?" she asked.

A bloodstone golem, once part of the Aegis, Uinahd had fought beside Barr at Faith's Spire, the Brotherhood stronghold at Garand. She led a command of arachon, Protectors remade by their own hands. Like eight of the twelve with her, Uinahd was a champion, a weapons master devoted to the Art of Melee. They wore full suits of enchanted blue steel plate, a sight to which Fluora had yet to grow accustomed.

Two more were enchanters. One of them, Kalar, had introduced himself earlier. Like his counterpart, he wore heavy robes reinforced with leather and blue steel, but it was the rosewood staff he bore that had caught her attention. No runes marred its polished surface, but either end was capped in silver. It was there, around the metal casings, where cerulean runes circled in air.

It had reminded her of faeron jewelry, the living flames and water crystals, *furie* splashing down across a shoulder like sunlight through a waterfall. It had made her long for home, to see and hold her mother.

"My lady?" Qilahd prompted, as if wondering if she were ill.

"I am fine," she assured him. The eldarath had a kind spirit, but she supposed that could be said of most healers. To Uinahd, she replied, "Yes, I am ready."

Fluora straightened her silken blindfold as the portal was conjured. As much as she would have liked to wear her new ironwood mask, Alixhir was no place for elven artistry.

Though another wove the portal, Uinahd's command had a traveler of its own. An arachon of striking blue granite, Aerahd lent her *furie* to the weaving. Two Aegis accompanied them. A dozen more stood ready to rush through if the need arose. Within moments the portal was complete.

Before Fluora could take a step, a tear appeared before her as if the very air had been forced apart. It looked much like the rift between her home and

Danarriden, the demon plane, but this was a deep crimson with paler shades stretching out. Champions reached for their swords and moved to surround it as the Arch Demon Fezuul stepped through. She held up a hand to set them at ease.

He looked much the same as when she saw him last at Starshrine, a tall faeron with ebon skin, thick muscles and a ready smile marred by fangs. His eyes were the black of starless night, saw all and revealed nothing of his thoughts. The scales at either side of his neck and arms, both legs and broad chest, had the sheen of blackberry wine. She felt more than saw the change, the power that emanated from his dark frame. It coursed through his veins like molten *furie*.

She saw it then, the brief flash of a vision, of Fezuul and Verran struggling against Revyn's disease and what the Arch Demon had done to survive it.

"Asaen Fezuul," she said in way of greeting.

He inclined his head, as much respect as could be expected from a demigod.

"Apologies for the intrusion," he said, eyes glancing toward the portal, across the arachon beside her, "but there is a pressing matter that cannot wait."

A roar in the distance echoed dully throughout the chamber.

"You risk much in the telling," she said, fearful of the destruction being wrought within the city. "All five demon hunters are here in Dwendorim."

"I am aware of the danger." He looked up toward the east, as if he could sense them as well. "However, Ariana would not forgive me if I did not at least try. You must convince your mother to accept my aid. Without it she will be lost giving birth."

"I am also aware," Fluora replied, "but my mother will not see reason in this matter. What offer of aid has she refused?"

"My blood." He seemed to gauge her demeanor before saying more. "If she consumes small amounts, at a steady–"

"Demon blood is caustic! You would kill her as surely as the creature inside her."

She had not meant to disparage his race or reveal her true feelings toward the monster growing in her mother's womb, but she could see in his reaction she had done both. Another roar, much louder, told them time was running short. Even without a way in, the hunters would claw through stone and earth to destroy him.

"I am no ordinary demon," he said with calm. "I can temper my blood so that it causes her no harm while sustaining the child." Again he studied her reaction." I could also end its life, with no one the wiser. If you ask."

Fluora hesitated, considering, and hated herself for it. As much as she wanted to save her mother, to rid her of the abomination that will tear her apart as its born, she had no right to make that decision.

"You must leave."

"And your mother?" Fezuul pressed.

Fluora blinked away the vision of death she had been forced to watch time and again. "I will speak with her once more, but she will not change her mind."

"You have my sympathy," he said and turned back to the rift. "She means a great deal to your Queen."

She reached out a hand to stop him, felt his skin burn with power.

"With Verran gone," she began, a warning meant as thanks, "the other Arch Demons..."

"Will try to kill me," he finished for her and smiled back. "They will find the task an unpleasant one and not easily accomplished."

With that he was gone, and the rift closed to the sound of crimson fires dying out.

"He should not have been able to enter the portalis," Kalar noted in a grave tone.

"Indeed," Uinahd agreed. "The arbiters must be made aware." The clear crystal upon her necklace began to glow, thrum briefly and then fade. "We may go now."

"Have you considered," Fluora asked as they walked toward the portal, "constructing a second set of runes about the body, like Sera's, rather than wear scry crystals?"

Ilear, their other enchanter, replied, "We have not," in a manner that seemed to say, *Until now.*

They stepped through into the courtyard of King's Keep in Alixhir. Royal guardsmen surrounded the portal, polearms to bear, liveries torn and bloodied. All of them looked weary and worn, ragged from grief and stained by the labors of burying dead and rebuilding homes. She saw fear in their eyes as well, a slight shaking in the hands that showed more than tired bodies or flagging spirits. Worry was plain upon their brows, as if they were faced with yet another invasion.

The yard was in shambles, carts overturned, broken and burned. Flames had marred the icy stones as well, left ashen streaks across cobbles and licked up along the walls, devouring ivy in a webwork of devastation. Dried blood soiled all, from mere spatters at the entryway to several pools with thick trails that told of bodies dragged away. The very air was afflicted, each intake of breath an assault. Heavy with the acrid pall of death, a coppery miasma of char and sickly sweet that stung both heart and lungs, each chilling breeze brought a new wave of revulsion. It was a nightmarish scene, made all the more horrid by the light of waking day.

Though the arachon tried to appear peaceful, it was difficult at best for living statues to seem unimposing to a people raised with fear of magic. Even Fluora must have looked a story book character come to life. Her hands were open at either side for all to see, as Barr had instructed, a show of respect and good faith on the part of a weaver. So many things could go wrong with this single encounter, the first of many that day, she felt uncertain just where to begin.

Other soldiers began to arrive, men in the black robes and heavy cloaks of justiciars. Guardians, deadly hunters of magic, she had felt firsthand how they treated weavers and had hoped to avoid meeting them again. Ten in all, they rushed forward with eyes wide at the bane of their existence. Only a sharp command from one in back kept them in check.

He stood taller than most, broad of shoulder and thick limbs, with a dark beard and darker eyes. A heavy axe against his shoulder, he looked one at ease felling trees and men alike. He considered the sight before him with nostrils flared and a piercing gaze, noted each golem but rested that hateful stare upon Fluora. From what she knew of Guardians, they answered only to Herne. This commander, however, seemed reluctant to act.

"Wait for the King," he ordered, as others moved past to fill the yard.

"Is she an elf child?" one asked in a whisper.

"Fairy, I think," another replied and was elbowed to silence for the trouble.

A dozen in heavy plate and battle robes were from the Brotherhood, holy warriors and priests who had bled the field in Curoch's name. They alone seemed at ease, as if word of the arachon who had fought to liberate

Faith's Spire had reached them here at Hope's End. The knight who led them stood in stark contrast to the dark Guardian, his armor battered and dirty, chain links slashed beneath an arm where a wound tarnished the steel. Tawny hair and stubbled chin, he carried his helm in one hand and rested the other on his belt.

His eyes were kinder, Fluora noted.

The rest were city watch, men more familiar with a cudgel than a sword. The knight approached her first, two men at either side.

"I am Knight Commander Balinor," he said with a bow of his head. "To what do we owe the pleasure of your unusual company?"

Fluora greeted him in the faeron fashion and replied, "I am Fluoralandylae of Faeronthalsos, an Oracle of Saernol, Matron of the Guiding Mists and emissary for the arachon at Dwendorim. I apologize for our abrupt arrival, but it is the fastest way to traverse such a great distance and render aid. We have come in peace and wish only to speak with your king."

The Guardian shook his head. "Aid from a blind child and her cadre of magic statues? I think not." Some of his men laughed at the quip. Others remained nervously vigil, waiting to draw swords. "Besides, you're too late to help in this war. The elves have used their foul sorcery to blockade the entire forest."

Fluora regarded him from behind her blindfold. "I meant help in dealing with the effects of war with Revyn and his shapelings."

Another three men stepped into the yard, dressed in fine clothes and unmarked by hardship. Both at either side were somewhat aged, grayed at the temples, faces lined by time. The other, she surmised, would be the king. A bit younger than expected, he looked no older than she, though he did carry himself with a noble bearing. He surveyed the courtyard, listened to the whispers in his ear and stepped forward without hesitation or fear.

"I am King Tamyr," he said to Fluora, a safe length from her entourage. The Guardian moved to his side and spoke briefly, drawing out a frown that soon smoothed itself away. With a nod, he added, "You've met Knight Commander Balinor. This gentleman," he indicated the lead Guardian, "is Marshal Hunter Naero. You'll have to excuse me if I seem unaccustomed to dealing with foreign realms. I have not been King long. My cousin Garrick was slain by Revyn's puppet, Markus."

"Many have suffered at those cruel hands," she said with deep sympathy, "myself included. I am pleased to say it was my blade that brought him to an end."

While Balinor raised a brow in admiration, Naero openly laughed in disbelief. The king leveled a disapproving look his way and was promptly ignored. Whether out of true interest in the portal or an attempt at apology, Tamyr stepped closer and asked how it worked.

"My liege," Naero warned and reached out a hand to restrain. "It's not safe."

Balinor gave a warning of his own. "That's enough, Marshal Hunter. Stand down."

It was the king's turn to ignore Naero, and he stepped further out of reach as Fluora began to explain that the arachon were responsible for creating a system of portals that allowed instant transport from one city to another.

Naero nodded to one of his men.

The Guardian pulled forth a rusted iron bell and struck it with an equally worn mallet. Each Guardian drew their sword as the spell reverberated out, a ringing drone that dampened the courtyard of all magic. Their armor flared with the runes of a protective ward, while the runes of every arachon came to life with a weak glow, a dull glimmer as if each struggled to survive. The other men clapped hands over their ears, strained against the assault and fought just to see. The Knight Commander fell to one knee and screamed.

The portal instantly collapsed.

Fluora desperately covered her ears from the noise, but the invasive thrum pulsed through her body and thoughts, shook the world all around and brought her down to her knees. The incessant ringing and terrible vibrations reminded her of being imprisoned by Markus, of the torture she and loved ones had endured for days, when she had helplessly watched on as Barr nearly killed himself trying to break free. She had been terrified all throughout the ordeal, pushed to the edge of despair, to the verge of losing herself in the fear.

But she was no longer that scared girl and had endured far worse since. She had faced down her fears and came away the stronger for it. She was Matron of the Guiding Mists, with power from the Dark at her disposal. Any fright she might once have felt had boiled away and left behind a bitter anger. It grew within her middle, pushed away the buzzing until it was but a bothersome din. She raised her head and glared at the Guardians, dark *furie* running the tips of her fingers. They had no idea what she was capable of. She could end every one of them in a maelstrom of magic, tear the city down to its foundation stone by stone, unleash *furie* the likes of which none of them had ever seen or imagined in their worst dreams!

Hanar slammed her hands together. A sphere of blue light went up around them, blocked the dampening spell and released all from its grip. Ilear clenched the air with a fist, crushed the ringing artifact by will alone and sent

Guardians sprawling from the ensuing explosion. Uinahd drew her sword with a deadly intent and eyed those who dared to attack.

"You should *not* have done that," she said, as the other champions pulled free their swords in unison.

The arachon spread out to face the Guardians and protect Fluora. Aerahd was already conjuring a new portal for reinforcements, as Kalar and Ilear called fire to their hands. Qilahd helped Fluora stand, sent soothing warmth through her arms that assuaged her spirit and lessened her outrage. With the assault passed, Fluora breathed more easily and quelled the remaining anger deep within. The black wisps of dark *furie* fell away from her frame.

"Hold!" Balinor ordered his men, prevented them from drawing their weapons. To Fluora he said, "Don't let the foolishness of one stand in the way of helping so many others. Attack now and whatever good will you sought here will be gone. Regardless of who is in the right."

She nodded, her anger fully gone. "Please," she asked of Uinahd. "Do not attack them."

A new portal flashed open, and a dozen Aegis rushed through. Balinor had got to his feet and pulled the king away. He stood firm between Tamyr and the golems with knights at his side, while priests invoked the blessings of Curoch. All ten Guardians were poised to strike, certain cold steel would prevail where magic had not. Fluora placed a gentle hand upon Uinahd's sword arm. The golem forced her gaze away from the foolish men, blinked away her justified ire and nodded assent.

"As you wish," she agreed and lowered her weapon.

Fluora thanked her and let out a breath. Their offer of peace had nearly sparked a new war.

Any anger she felt toward the Guardians served no
one, despite her gut reaction to the attack. She was not
like Barr when it came to magic. It was not a tool nor a
weapon, a means or an end. It was a part of her, who she
was, her body and spirit. From birth to passing, faeron
and the land lived together in a shared harmony. She
could no more take magic from the land than light from
the sun. Both were simply there, for her to share in or
not. When the Guardian struck the bell, it had angered
her deeply. It was because of their intolerance, of people
like them, that Barr had lived his life as an outcast, was
forced from his childhood home and lost his father.

She did her best to put all that aside.

To the king she said, "We wish only to offer aid, to
help rebuild the city, feed and clothe those who need it,
provide shelter and warmth while homes are mended. We
are obviously very different, but not all weavers would do
harm."

Naero sneered, "Magic rots the soul! It eats away at
the resolve until all that matters is the drunkenness. The
power over life and death is an intoxication no man can
resist for long."

"What of you then?" Fluora asked. "Do Guardians
not wield magic?"

"It's not the same," he protested. "Ours is not magic
but divine blessings from Herne." She did not have the
heart to tell him Herne was dead. "There's no pleasure in
what we do. We don't crave power. We live only to serve."

"I see," she said and wondered at his motivations
and who truly ruled here. *Why is Tamyr not enraged by
the attack?* "What of a ruler then? Kings have the power
of life and death over their subjects. Are all kings evil as
well, destined to be corrupt?"

King Tamyr took especial interest in the question
and waited with arms crossed for Naero's answer.

"That's completely different!"

"I've heard enough," the king said and stepped out from behind the knights. To Fluora, he asked, "Why would you do this? We've never had dealings before or even knew of your existence. Why put yourself at risk to help us?"

She smiled then, one of understanding and relief. She knew in that moment they had accomplished their task, that Alixhir would accept their help and join in the portalis.

"It is the arachon who offer aid," she replied. "I am only here on their behalf."

He approached Hanar, studied her with a sense of wonder and esteem. "They are magnificent. Can they all speak?"

"We can," Hanar answered, "but we have had limited contact with the outside world, since our creators were killed by a disease of Revyn's making."

He reached out to touch her and was surprised when she lifted a hand to meet his.

"It's soft!" he said and laughed. He caught Balinor's bemused look at the unkingly display but paid the Knight Commander no mind. "Sheathe your swords," he ordered the Guardians. "The arachon are my guests and shall be treated as such."

"Tell me," Balinor began, as weapons were put aside and the tension somewhat eased, "did any of you fight to defend Faith's Spire?"

"I was there," Uinahd said, wordlessly calling for her command to put away their blades. "Many of us died that day, but it was an honor to fight beside Commander Vaumont and his men." Her voice grew wistful, almost reverent. "I watched High Priest Dalwyn wield Vereu on the field, destroy the revenant Isdael and scatter the orcish tribes."

Naero said, "You speak of honor as if a statue can know of such things. You speak words and mimic actions, no more."

"Enough, Marshal." King Tamyr indicated the keep doors, inviting the arachon to enter. "Please, let's go inside where it's a bit warmer." He led the way and said, "I don't suppose you eat or drink. Is there anything I can offer you?"

Hanar walked beside him. "We require only good company and conversation."

Tamyr chuckled. "I can assure you the former," he said as they entered the keep, "but make no promise as to the last!"

The Marshal Hunter and his Guardians declined to join them.

**– 5 –**

 he next morning, Barr woke early and headed for the park near home. More trees had been planted, stood mature and boughs full over handcrafted paths of white stones. Moisture clung to grass and flowers, wet his legs when he sat, but soon dried in the warmth of runic sunrise. Legs crossed, eyes closed, he took in deep breaths and let his tensions slip away with each steady exhalation.

The arbiters had seemed relieved when he offered to help secure the portalis and speak on their behalf with kingdoms across Taellus. With the University reopened, it was their hope other races would visit Dwendorim, enjoy the fruits of their labor and learn from one another. Numerous arachon were already preparing to teach a wide variety of subjects, from language to history, trade skills to theology, as well as medicine and art.

Callahd, the first arachon remade with a focus on gathering and furthering knowledge, had been named Headmaster after little discussion. His first official act, to revive the Academy, had caused a bit of a stir. Their creators had shut down the military school to pursue more productive endeavors, had decided resources were better used on more practical vocations. War had never breached their underground city; studying tactics and war strategy, combat and martial discipline, had become outdated pursuits, a hobby at best.

It was his firm belief, however, that all knowledge was worth pursuing and had reminded the arbiters that the need to protect themselves and others would only grow. Revyn's attacks had made that abundantly clear. The god had proven he could strike anywhere, at anyone, without a moment of notice. So long as Revyn and his shiardin remained, no one in Dwendorim was safe.

He had asked Barr to head the school.

*It would be a good opportunity*, he thought, *to train new Valar.*

*You did promise Teldein*, Idelle said. She'd been quiet since her return from the Ghaoylens, happier, more at ease, but definitely quieter. He wondered if she'd made a new male friend – *Never mind about that*, she warned playfully. More somber, she added, *Seltruin would've wanted you to.*

Aren grumbled. *Don't you two ever sleep? It's still dark out!*

*It's been light out for whole minutes*, she teased. *You have to open your eyes to see it, though.*

More than training a new generation of Sages for each elven nation, he could teach the Art to any who wished to learn, offer a place of safety and understanding away from the Guardians. He could take away the fear of magic, show it was just a tool no more dangerous than any other. Magic could once again be enjoyed, shared for the betterment of all. Weavers the world over would have a home where neighbors didn't fear them, where friends knew what they were and saw them no differently. What would he have given to have such a place when he was a child in Alixhir, when the visions first came upon him?

Visions, he reminded himself, the reason he'd come to the park in the first place. They no longer came of their own accord, so he'd decided to draw them out one by one. He hoped calling up specific past lives and studying them at length might give him some insight as to what his final lesson might truly be. He wasn't sure what enlightenment would bring or even if he wanted it. Would he live out the rest of his life with some sort of divine knowledge, or would his spirit ascend the moment he knew clarity?

*You're not concentrating*, Idelle said.

*Shush. I am too.*

He needed to choose a life to focus on, but there were far too many for him to see them all clearly. Like studying divine runes for the first time, it made his head spin as he struggled to pick a single voice from the maelstrom in his mind. It was overwhelming and painful to look upon, like trying to see the details of a single leaf in a whirlwind of forest all about him. He took in deep breaths to relax his thoughts, attempted to give in to the swirling visions and let one come to fore. The voices would have none of it. Either he chose one from the clamor, or they'd persist until he fell beneath the chaos.

The previous night's losses led his thoughts toward minotaurs, of the stoic daumon clans in their longhouses upon the plains, the dutiful kheos families and factions in walled cities within the mountains. The storm about him subsided to a mere din, as thousands of lives fell away like rain into the black far below. Dozens spun in a panorama, all his taur lives in a single dream that went on without end, melded together in a haphazard pool of images that overlapped, touched death to birth with no space between. He reached out to touch...

*... her cheek, felt the warmth of her beneath his fingers, and was overcome by joy and stabbing pain in the same breath.*

*"How could I have forgotten," Barr said with heartfelt regret that he'd let memory of their love fade with his lost life.*

*Dawncry smiled up at him, her eyes liquid honey lit by sunlight and vibrant youth.*

*"You did not," she replied gently and kissed him. She slipped his union ring on, where he never should have taken it off. "You simply misplaced it."*

*He felt lost in her gaze and was glad for it, but no matter how much he tried not to look away, his attention was forcibly drawn to the line of mourners headed for the pyre. It struck him then, when and where he was.*

*"My father," he began with sudden realization. Dawn squeezed his hand in comfort. "No, I don't want to remember this."*

*She pulled him toward the others, where they'd be waiting for him to send his father to the Great Lands.*

*But in a moment of fear, he let grief rule his heart and pulled away from her grasp. The look of sadness in her eyes...*

...as the image fled from his mind, left him only with the heartache of sorrow and remorse, was like no pain he'd ever experienced in a vision. It felt as if he'd been physically there, standing once more upon the sundering plains, holding hands with the love of his life, the day after his father had fallen to an orcish blade – and reliving the crushing guilt of knowing he was to blame. In those fleeting moments of joy and grief, he'd *been* Bhorok Stonefist, just as surely as at this instant he was Barr.

He looked down at his hands, hairless and small, no scars or ring, human.

"Is everything alright?" Fluora asked. She regarded him from a short distance from behind the silken sheen of her ironwood mask. She stepped closer and knelt beside him. "What is it?"

Idelle was perched in an aged oak not far away but said nothing. She already knew what he was feeling. Even Aren, who was now awake and sunning by the fountain, chose to remain quiet in the wake of those emotions.

"Nothing," he said, took her offered hand and stood. "It's just going to take a lot more practice than I thought." He noticed she carried sparring swords. "Do we have time for that?"

She kissed him and slipped one into his hand. "We must make time for what matters most." Barr gave a dubious look, wondered if she meant spending time together or training in the hopes of one day saving him from certain death. She poked him in the middle with the blunted end of her sword. "Both."

Aren yawned. *I'm going to see Kaela while you two play.*

*And skip breakfast?* Idelle said in true amazement.

He was already headed for the rift. *Don't be silly. They'll have food there. Besides*, he added as he passed through to Darleman, *I woke up early and had a light snack before going back to sleep.*

"That light snack," Fluora said with a wry smile and squared off against Barr, "was meant to be our morning meal."

Memories of his minotaur life still clung to the back of his mind. The sword in his hand felt wrong, small and unbalanced. He longed for the haft of an axe.

"Just as well," he said and did his best to shake off the strange sense that he was not himself. "After what happened last night, I'm not very hungry."

She was on the offensive, forcing him to block, to engage in any way. A sideways feint and jab nearly scored a hit, but Barr fought with lifetimes of training that had become second nature, an instinct that required no more thought than taking breath.

"We had no way of knowing."

The detachment clouding his mind gave way to a growing anger. That they had no way of knowing where or when Revyn would strike was exactly the point. Once again he felt helpless, or worse, inadequate. He'd spent hours weaving a glyph he was sure would trap and hold a shiardin. Tempas and his hunters had worked for the better part of a day preparing the field, carefully digging oil trenches to encircle them, crafting nets and snares of steel and magic. All their work and readiness had been for naught. By nightfall, hours away in either direction, Revyn had sent two separate shiardin to take Celene and Kierna.

Revyn was growing stronger, and there was nothing Barr could do to stop it. What choices were left? Gather the remaining gods, risk them all at once, and wait for an attack? Isolate and try to protect them individually? As much as he hated to admit it, they were fighting a defensive battle with no hope of winning back what was lost.

*You can't think that way,* Idelle said, her voice a soothing calm in the growing worry of despair. *All we can do is our best.*

*And when our best isn't good enough?*

Fluora lowered her sword. "We may lose battles, but we *will* win the war." She stepped in close, kissed him and hooked a foot behind his. A push and she was atop him, wooden sword across his throat. With a grin, she added, "No matter the cost."

Barr's sword was flush against her, between her breasts. Had they truly been fighting, he would've slipped his blade up under her ribs and into her heart. She would've died before they struck the ground. Sometimes grim determination and a willingness to do anything just wasn't enough.

He gave a wan smile and nod of assent, as if her good sense had won out. She kissed him, a lingering touch of warmth and affection. What remnants of lost love had clung to heart once again faded to the shadows of distant lifetimes and memory.

\*  \*  \*

Barr had taken a few moments to gather himself and his thoughts once Fluora had left to go visit her mother on Faeron. He was headed back home, the morning light warm upon his back, when he caught sight of Hanar down the cobbled road. She knelt before a much smaller arachon, one of ebon stone struck through with veins of cobalt and paler blues. Its silver runes seemed large for one so small, and there was a certain frailty in the way he held onto Hanar's hands.

*The child she always wanted.* Barr had stopped to watch them together, felt the pang of longing in his chest for a family his own. He wanted to go talk with them but didn't want to intrude. There was also work still left to be done in Greywood, where Tempas and his hunters would be waiting. *She looks happy.*

*They're beautiful,* Idelle said, her voice betraying the shared longing for her own offspring. *You should at least congratulate her.*

Hanar caught sight of him watching and beckoned, every bit the proud new mother.

"Good morning!" Barr called as he approached, glad to see such happiness in a friend so deserving of it. His eyes went to the young arachon, studying its features from foot to naming sigil. "I see there's a new addition to the protectorate."

*Hmm.* There was something familiar about the child, but Barr couldn't quite put his finger on it.

*What is it?* Idelle asked. She ruffled her feathers and began cleaning a wing. *You seem puzzled.*

*No, I don't know. It's just –* As he drew close, the boy's features became clearer. He was certain he'd seen that face before, or at the least one very like it.

"Yes, there is," Hanar said proudly, with a light touch to her son's chin that elicited a giggle.

*I think I've seen him before.*

Idelle said, *He's newly made. How could you have? Maybe he just looks like someone you've met before, when you were an arachon.*

He was steps away when the realization finally hit, and the dawning of it sent him reeling back in time to another life, to the crushing heartache of a past loss.

"Master, I present to you Fanar."

Barr blinked away the memories that flooded his mind and stole away his breath, of his life long ago as a shaper. It felt strange to see such a visage from this point of view, as if he'd stepped out of himself and caught a glimpse back in time. Though the features were far smoother, youthful at the eyes and cheeks, there was no denying their familiarity.

"He looks like me," Barr said, still coming to grips with the notion. "I mean, like Fanarin."

"Mostly, yes, though a bit also like myself." Hanar stood and smiled down at her handiwork, as if there was little need of explanation. When moments passed without Barr speaking a word, she added, "We are family, Master. You shaped me with your own hands. I could think of no better way to honor that gift."

*Aww*, Idelle said, *that's so sweet of her. It's like he's your grandson.*

*No it's not.*

Barr didn't mean to sound offended, but he couldn't help feeling somehow betrayed. He knew he should be grateful for the gesture, that it was meant as a show of love, but all it did was remind him of the wife and daughter he'd never again see.

"Are you upset, Master?" Hanar asked. "I meant no disrespect. I truly thought it would please you, to see your family line live on through me."

Idelle said, *I'm sure she had the best intentions.*

"No," he said gently and felt a fool for ruining Hanar's moment. "I'm not upset with you. Or you," he said to Fanar. The boy's attention was elsewhere, on a butterfly of sea blue and speckled black flying by. "Seeing him just reminds me of all we've lost."

She put a hand to his shoulder, both warm and caring. "There was more to their lives than how they were taken. To recall only their end would be a disservice, to their memory and to you." A stream of golden *furie* slipped down her cheek. "I loved Shanaran with all I had, and I do still miss her. It is now time to feel love like that again, in my son, and I hope you too will one day feel the same."

119

Barr put a hand over hers. "I'm sure I will." He shook his head and gave a small laugh. "You even named him for me."

Fanar left to chase the fluttering wings, his gait still unsure. He didn't move quite as fast as an arachon child but was full of the same wonder every youth shared with the world.

*He doesn't say much, does he?* Idelle chuckled when the boy nearly tripped in his eagerness with a poorly timed leap. He laughed in that unabashed way only children can and gave chase with an even greater zeal. *Aren will love playing with him.*

Barr brought Hanar to a stone bench beside the road and took a seat. She sat down beside him and watched her son play.

"Has he spoken at all?"

"No," Hanar replied without a hint of worry. "He is one of our first. Of this size," she amended. "We have no way of knowing how he will progress."

"What of the destroyers?" Barr asked.

Hanar shook her head. A thought seemed to occur, and her mood grew somewhat somber. "Do you think they are flawed?"

He knew what she was really asking. If they had made a mistake in the crafting, then what of Fanar?

"I think they're everything they were meant to be," he replied and found himself smiling wider, as the boy tried and tried again. His tenacity was unending and his laughter infectious.

"When he is old enough," Hanar said, "he will be given an adult body and taught the craft of his choosing. By then a whole new generation of arachon will be there to join him."

*It's amazing, when you think about it,* Idelle said, her voice wistful. *What they've accomplished. They've made life out of nothing but stone, metal and sheer will, just as their makers had. Do you think the original arachon would be proud?*

*I know they would,* Barr said, *because I am.*

Thought of Fanarin and his other lives here within the city brought his mind back to the task at hand, to the need for mastery of his past. Without full control of his visions, he had no hope of reconciling them. He just needed more time, but there was always a new pressing matter. He sighed at the futility of it all.

*How am I supposed to reduce an entire life to a handful of lessons, let alone glean a single truth from it all?*

*Maybe you're overthinking it,* Idelle offered. *Then again, nothing truly worth having is easy.*

He turned to Hanar. "If you had to pick the single greatest lesson you've learned in your lifetime, what would it be?"

She regarded him for but a moment.

"Master, there is no single greatest lesson. They are all equally important and make us who we are. Life," she added, "is a series of choices, with new insight at every step. No one decision holds more value than another, because none would be possible without the many that came before."

*She's going to be a great mother,* Idelle said, with newfound admiration.

Barr watched Fanar lose interest in the butterfly and try his hand at climbing a tree. The boy's runes hadn't been made smaller to account for his size, which meant much less space to work with. Barr wasn't sure there would've been enough room to make him a part of the protectorate, let alone the Oath, and certainly not much else. Fanar leapt at the bottom branch, tried to grab hold, but fell short of the mark again and again. He then did something that surprised Barr, something that should not have been possible yet. Fanar clumsily dragged a large decorative stone over to the tree, stepped up, jumped and caught hold of the branch.

Fanar had *learned* from his failed attempts.

"How did he do that?" Barr wondered aloud. When Hanar looked at him in askance, he said, "He figured out how to climb that tree without being told or shown how."

"Every obstacle is an opportunity to learn."

Barr said, "Yes, but *how* did he learn?"

"He chose to," Hanar answered, in a matter of fact tone. She saw Barr still unconvinced and further explained, "Our craftsmen know all the arachon did at the time of their passing, yet we have greatly improved upon their knowledge and techniques. We are more than our instruction runes. We uphold the Oath, whether it is carved into our bodies or not, because we choose to do so. We are no longer forced to. It is a decision." She seemed surprised at the need to tell him these simple truths. "We have free will."

Idelle flew over to the boy and landed a few branches above him. *They've been learning new things since we first met them. Why's this any different?*

*Because he isn't sentient yet,* Barr replied, *or at least he shouldn't be. It takes a long time for magic to become aware.*

*I thought he was alive, though.* Idelle studied the boy as he climbed higher and grinned up at her as if she'd set him a challenge.

*Protectors were never alive,* Barr said, *just animated by a very complex runic structure. They can't die. They can only be destroyed or unmade.*

*I don't see the difference.*

"I know you have free will," Barr said, apologetic. "It's just surprising to see him, to see Fanar, pick up on things so quickly. It makes me wonder where it is he's storing all he learns."

Hanar considered and said, "You have memory of past lives your physical body has not lived."

Barr nodded. "I have a spirit, separate from my body, with a memory of its own."

"Then that is your answer."

*They have souls?* Idelle asked.

He shifted focus and saw Hanar's glyph come into view, a myriad of runes that spanned the three planes. How had he never noticed this before? It made perfect sense but went against what he'd been taught over numerous lifetimes. He looked over at Fanar and saw the same, though the structure was much smaller in the physical.

*If magic doesn't grow sentient,* Barr surmised, *then at some point a soul must choose it as a vessel, just as they would which lives to experience next.*

Idelle hopped away from the grasping hand beneath her. *Have you ever...?*

*No,* he replied, *but I've never been a dragon either. Maybe that's why it took me so long to see it. It just never occurred to me to even look.*

The understanding of it all led him to another train of thought he hadn't yet considered. His soul was the one thing all his lives had in common. Maybe he had been overthinking things. He smiled as the task began to feel less pressing, as a sense of relief eased both his body and mind.

Though he still had far to go, Barr was one step closer to unraveling his final lesson.

\*　　\*　　\*

Fluora thanked the traveler and stepped through to her mother's home on Faeronthalsos. The portal closed behind as she headed for the spiral staircase. Sunlight shone through the crystal walls and cast azure shadows across the tiles like thorny tendrils. That glow from within pulsed in a semblance of life but was born of faeron magic. Its vibrant hum was a reminder of home and followed her up the stairs.

When she reached the top, she found the Queen and Fezuul waiting outside her mother's bedchamber. Ariana wore a bright dress the colors of springtime but looked as if she already mourned a friend. The Arch Demon wore black leathers with crimson edging and a look of deep concern, but Fluora knew his only worry was for the Queen. Ariana's demeanor brightened at the sight of Fluora, and she immediately embraced her in what felt like consolation.

"Dear child," she said, "I am so glad to see you well." She studied Fluora at arm's length, as if waiting for an emotional response. "I just wish it was a happier occasion."

From the hall Fluora saw her mother in bed and was shocked at the alarming turn for the worse. Gray and frail, hair damp and clinging, cheeks sunken and bereft of their usual color, she looked gravely ill. The High Healer sat beside her, weaving warmth and nourishment, as two more tended other needs. It tugged at Fluora's heart with a flashed reminder of the vision that haunted her sleep. Unconsciously, she reached at the knot of her blindfold and found it secure. She took a deep breath and found the courage to step inside, to sit beside her mother in such a state.

The Grand Seeress Elaedraoni, Oracle of Saernol, opened weary eyes and smiled with joyous pride at her only daughter. Though it elicited tears, Fluora was glad for that smile and returned it without pause. She felt a fragile hand take her own in a trembling grip, and it was all she could do to keep from sobbing. Fluora looked to the High Healer in askance.

"The child has grown too fast," Naedrilla explained, "for her body to adjust to the demand. It has sapped her strength and drained her essence beyond repair."

Fluora placed a hand on her mother's belly. It was firm but not overly swollen, nowhere near to full. The demon child moved beneath her touch, but there was no joy in the exchange. To her, the unborn creature offered nothing but death and the pain of loss.

Naedrilla said in a somber tone, "She will not survive for much longer. Her only hope is to accept Fezuul's aid."

Fluora glared at the Arch Demon, for not telling her how close her mother was to death and for the simple need to place blame, for any way to vent her frustration and helpless anger.

His dark eyes gave her nothing.

"I did stress the urgency," Fezuul said. "I am happy to lend assistance should it be required." He made it clear all fault lay with Elaedraoni. "I am afraid it must be soon. The child will undergo its first transformation in the womb. There will be no birth as you know it. It will tear her apart from within."

"You do not know that!" Ariana chided. "There has never before been a faeron cambion." Fluora could hear the unspoken thought, *that has survived this long.* "We have no idea what will happen."

Fluora grew angry with them both.

"Why are you standing in the hall instead of trying to help?" Fluora refused to blame her mother, stubborn though she may be. Elae was in no shape to argue or refuse. "Just do what needs be done!"

"We are not welcome inside," Fezuul replied, with a hint of satisfaction, as if death were a just punishment for rejecting his aid. "And it is not so simple a task."

"She must accept freely," the Queen said. She looked as one who had already frayed both ends of this argument and could do nothing more to change its outcome. "The attempt is for naught if she resists, and she wants nothing to do with demons, or me for that matter. Elae greatly disapproves of our pairing."

Fluora saw them clasp hands. Apparently they had decided to make their intention toward one another public.

"Mother, why?" Fluora pleaded more than asked. "Would you rather die than have demon blood in your veins? The *child* is a demon. Do you hold it with an equal disdain?"

"No," her mother rasped through dry and cracked lips. Naedrilla held a cup of water for her to drink, but all Elae could manage was a few sips before her body was wracked with coughing. When she could finally breathe, she said, "He is not a demon. He is *good*, a true faeron with a truer heart. I can feel it in him and in my spirit. He will grow to one of virtue and high esteem." She squeezed Fluora's hand. "He is my blood, your brother, and he has the whole of my love." She coughed again, but this time dark blood flecked her lips. "He must survive," she said, pleading in turn, "no matter the cost."

Her own words to Barr, they echoed back in a taunt that brought with it understanding. Some costs were simply too high to pay.

Elae took in a sharp breath with eyes widened and looked to Naedrilla with an unspoken assertion. This was the moment Fluora had been forced to witness, that her heart would not accept. She shook her head with firm refusal, willed it not to be, but no force or desire could undo her mother's decision. Fluora's premonition was at hand, and she was helpless to stop it.

"Promise me," her mother said, with grace and great calm, "promise you will care for him." Fluora wept and again refused, fought just to breathe. "Promise."

Naedrilla moved the sheets aside, tears streaming down her cheeks. She drew a blade from beneath her apron and cut across Elae's middle with swift precision.

"No!" Fluora yelled in impotent fury, flailing against the vision unfolding before her eyes.

Her mother gasped, eyes clenched and jaw tight, as the child was torn from her body. Held in both hands, a palm-sized creature of ropy limb and fiery scale, it let loose a watery keen that grew to an infant's cry in the same breath its body expanded and took the form of a normal faeron child. Elae, body tensed against the pain and sundered flesh, relaxed of a sudden, laid back and breathed her last.

Overwhelming sorrow set in with a crushing despair, left Fluora broken, without words, unable to convey – let alone cope – with the depth of her loss. She had watched her mother die countless times in seer sight, but only now did she truly feel the grief rake across her soul and hollow out her existence.

*Why!* Fluora screamed in her mind. *Why did you not listen!*

Though it made no difference, it felt better to rail, to give her grief any outlet it could find. She wanted escape from the anguish, and only anger stood ready to fill the void. She got to her feet and backed away from the bed.

As Fluora fought for breath between sobs, her pale skin became alight with dark *furie*. Wisps of translucent black fire, it licked up and down her frame, danced along her arms and shrouded her heart in a haze of growing rage. It beckoned, gave her ease, and the more she gave in, the better she felt. More than solace, it offered power, a vibrant thrumming in her chest that fought back the dejection, made room for steady breath and prickled her entire being with its allure.

The baby's cries drew her attention. A healer had taken it across the room and held it protectively. Its wailing was incessant, like a death knell with no end. Though all of them mourned, openly cried, confusion and fear was plainly writ upon their faces. Naedrilla tried in vain to calm her, but Fluora's gaze upon the child turned hateful.

"You killed her!"

Fezuul left Ariana weeping and was through the door in an instant. He stood between Fluora and the baby like a protective father. His eyes were pools of black, bereft of emotion, but warned against harming the child. She met his look with grim defiance from behind her blindfold. The flames about her held no heat, did not burn cloth or flesh, but were a glimpse of her true power and a warning all their own. They flared even stronger, set the room in flickering shadow, and caused Fezuul to narrow his eyes in either caution or maybe fear. She knew he could sense it, the magic emanating from within her, distorting the air between them. She grinned at the minor triumph and knew if she but gave further into the anger, it would grant her the means to strike down even an Arch Demon.

Ariana stepped past him. She spoke softly, as a mother, her voice and touch a soothing balm against the raging pyre that swelled in Fluora's heart.

"Do not dishonor her dying wish," the Queen said with flowing tears, in a tone so soft Fluora had to focus to hear it, "or the sacrifice she made so that the child may live." With each word, Fluora's rage diminished. "Her passing will pain me for the rest of my days, but know this. Her child is an innocent and undeserving of your ire."

Fluora allowed herself to calm, to face the reality of her grief, and the dark *furie* all about her began to wane. She looked at her mother's body, a torn and empty shell. Tears fell freely once more, but no longer would she be consoled. She pulled away, drawing a pained look from the Queen.

"That creature is not innocent," Fluora said. "They are *all* monsters." She looked pointedly at Fezuul and felt disgusted that Ariana could care for him. "Every one of them."

At his nod, Naedrilla and the two healers left with the baby. Its cries echoed back for a short moment and were gone.

"Can you not see?" the Arch Demon asked. "He is the key to bridging our two peoples."

Fluora sneered, "There can be no bridge. Your *people* offer nothing but death."

Ariana asked, "How long has this been happening? How long have you been channeling the Dark?"

Fluora wiped her eyes with the back of a hand. It felt wrong to speak of anything else at this moment, when her mother's spirit was gone but body still warm.

"Just recently." She looked away from her mother, suddenly wanted to leave. There was nothing more she could do and had no desire to take part in the passing rite. "I did not know a Matron held this power. I have yet to grow used to it. My anger seems to get the best of me when I draw it out."

"It is not your anger that draws it out," the Queen said, "quite the opposite. This is no gift of the mists but a rare effect of being joined with its spirit. Only once before has this occurred, where the bond was so strong that the Matron became attuned with the Dark." Her mourning had given way to a deep concern for Fluora, but her demeanor shifted to ominous fear at the memory. "Many lives were lost, entire bloodlines forever gone. It is not something I would see us endure again."

Despite Ariana's sincerity, Fluora saw no harm in at least trying to master her new power. Just because one Matron failed long ago did not mean she would as well. Ariana must have seen the doubt.

The Queen insisted, "You must remove yourself from its touch."

Her grief momentarily in check, tears dried upon her cheeks, Fluora was firm in her resolve, confident the power was better used than thrown away. Neither was there a guarantee that her replacement would not face the same fate.

"I cannot think about this right now."

"Fluora, please," Ariana said. "Heed my advice. If you do not relinquish to another, the Dark will consume you from within. There is no other way, and the longer you delay, the harder it will be to break free its grasp."

Fluora's jaw tightened as she held back a bitter reply. The Queen could not fully know what it was to be Matron. Only Fluora understood the true extent of her own power – with the exception of Barr's mother.

*But she was weak*, Fluora thought to herself, hiding her mind from Ariana, *her spirit frail and will broken. Daesidaoli should never have given in. She should have embraced her calling to its bitter end. Better to die fighting than to shirk duty and let another shoulder the burden.*

Fluora could not help but feel insulted that the Queen thought her too feeble to control the rare gift. She had barely enough time to realize it was there, let alone try to conquer its potential.

"When I have done with mourning," she finally said, "I will consider your counsel."

Before Ariana could say anything further, Fluora disappeared into the mists to grieve alone, without a care for the threat of Revyn attempting to break through. If he should dare to try, she was more than happy to deal with him on her own terms.

In the realm where *she* ruled supreme.

\*   \*   \*

It was snowing in Greywood, a gentle flurry that in time would blanket all with its embrace. Prepared for the cold this visit, Barr wore a suit of furred leathers and looked out beneath the hood of a heavy cloak. Kaela by his side, Aren shook off the snow and sat patiently with the other war hounds. Half a dozen Ballar had come through the portal an hour earlier, just before two full companies of arachon.

*Still nothing,* Idelle said from her vantage in the storm laden skies, *and we're about to lose what little daylight is left.*

Dozens of campfires had already been set, and large pyres circled the immediate area in anticipation of the coming fight. No longer a thousand strong, the gathered hunters were still an unearthly force. The runes on their flesh glowed cobalt beneath plates of steel and chain armor, accompanied by the ghostly pall of holy fire. Weapons in hand, they too stood waiting in the quiet storm.

"He has returned," Ellaena noted, unaffected by the chill wind or the snow in her long braids. Like the Ballar with her, she was scarcely clad in sylvannis armor and looked wholly out of place among the taur. "They are hidden from sight but not scent, most likely magic."

Barr had heard it as well, though until then it barely carried on the wind. When the enchantment fell away in a shower of luminous silver, Tempas and a much smaller companion were revealed.

*That's cheating,* Idelle said in complaint. *No wonder I couldn't find him.*

*This is taking too long,* Aren said with impatience. *What kind of hunters don't hunt or have anything to eat?* Kaela rolled her eyes. *What, I'm the only one growing hungry?*

*Growing,* Kaela said, *would imply you are ever sated.*

*I can be,* Aren said with a sullen frown. *It's not my fault I'm hungry more than not.*

She and Idelle shared a giggle. When the brooding persisted, Kaela playfully nudged him until he too gave a laugh.

Cloaks weighted by frost, Tempas and a female trudged toward camp, careful to avoid the myriad of traps and pitfalls in their way. The once war god gave commands to two hunters and headed for Barr. Though her face was concealed in shadow, Barr was certain the woman Tempas had left to find and brought back could be none other than –

"Saernol," Barr said, voice betraying emotion. It had been a very long time since the goddess of magic stood before him, not since his first life as an illuminaire. He smiled despite the dire circumstance of their meeting and took her hand in formal greeting. "I'm glad you're unharmed."

"I have my young brother to thank for that," she said and smiled.

Her time as a mortal had not been kind, evidenced by the fatigue in her voice and bearing, but her dark eyes were still bright with the light of hope and perseverance.

Tempas folded his great arms. "It is early for thanks, yet I remain cautiously optimistic."

"I recall you as Serce," she said with what sounded to Barr like pride, and pulled her cloak more tightly about her.

"I was," Barr replied with a wistful laugh, "strange as that is to say. Are you here to help fend off the attack or…"

"Bait the trap?" Her smile somewhat faded. "No, I am here to capture, if I can, and hopefully discover a way to either stop or undo these new darkspawn."

"If he sends one at all," Tempas said and grumbled at nightfall swift approaching.

"It stands to reason," Barr said, "that he'll come for you next. That's why I'm here."

Saernol agreed. "Revyn would sooner part with a limb than a grudge."

"He is a fool and a coward." Tempas spat and said, "Even now, he sends children to fight in his stead, never once sullying his own hands. He tried to destroy all life on Taellus, yet somehow it is I who slighted him."

"Rarely is madness taxed," she said sagely and with a hint of humor, "by the burden of sound reason."

The snow was unrelenting and made it difficult to see across camp, let alone the surrounding trees. Barr saw her shiver despite the cloak and suggested they wait by the main fire. The shapeling hunters, sustained by their geas, had no need of food or drink, so Barr offered what few supplies he had brought. They shared cinnamon half-loaves with sliced apple and dried venison from Darleman. Both former deities took drink from a small cask of dark ale. It seemed though the taur could go without, they chose not to part with their homeland stout. Barr politely declined, in favor of a skin of Renahd's melon water.

*That smells good*, Aren noted, unexpectedly close to Barr's shoulder.

133

*Here you go*, Barr said and offered two halves.

The hound gingerly took them in his mouth and carried both back to Kaela. He placed one before her, lay back down by her side and chewed his piece in quiet. Aren looked content, more so than the brief sating of his incurable hunger. Surprised to see him share food, neither Barr nor Idelle wanted to spoil the moment with teasing.

Long hours passed in numbing cold before the storm gave a respite. Face hidden from the wind beneath his hood, Barr fought to stay awake in a losing battle with heavy lids. A hollow, distant knock sounded off in the distance and reverberated through the trees with enough force to shake snow free from their limbs. Familiar with that noise, the connecting with a ley line, Barr quickly stirred and readied to face off against the shiardin.

He wove a glyph about each kyan, tracing runes in a pattern memorized the night before. By Fluora's account, a shiardin was the twisted corruption of an umbral, a creature unaffected by Barr's ironwood blades. Luckily, he already knew what caused harm and might destroy them. When the weaving was done, both weapons began to radiate absorbed moonlight. Faint at first, their yellow glow would grow stronger with each moment, even more so by light of day. Unfortunately, the enchantment was unstable and would not last.

Another knock sounded in the distance, and a rift finally appeared at the center of camp, a fiery violet breach between realms. Tempas was first to move, heavy axes in hand and calling orders as he rushed to stand before it. The hunters executed his plan with practiced precision, took up positions in a fanned circle around the rift and lit the oiled trenches between. Spiked bulwarks were lifted and secured in place, each with a half-dozen archers set to loose enchanted barbs. Split tree covers were pulled back from the closest pitfalls, revealing a tangle of steel wire. If a shiardin fell in, climbing out would be the least of its worries. Luminous runes and holy fire set alight the entire area. All was silence but for the crackles of surrounding campfires.

Though nothing passed through, all could feel upon them the angry gaze of a god weigh their worth.

Barr moved closer to study the rift, to determine how Revyn wove them. Saernol fell in step beside him, but Tempas held her back at a dozen paces. Close enough to feel the otherworldly warmth of its flames, Barr felt more than saw the enormous flow of raw *furie* bleeding out and sustaining the glyph. With vision shifted, he saw the runes spiral through a series of broken spheres and half rings, their silvery flames awash in the light of a full moon. He followed their path into the ether, where they spun and swirled against the backdrop of clouded pale blue. From flames to a shimmer, each rune continued on its set course through adjoining wards, pieces of a bigger puzzle taking shape. Into the starry black and settling embers of the astral, runes left off their luster for a wan hue and frosted trail. Despite its complexity, there were just too many missing segments and connections, empty spaces that should have held whole wards and breaks within the conduits lacking form or even logic.

The entire structure was flawed.

Barr had no hope of making sense of it, let alone find the means to close it from this side. He had almost given up when a strange rune caught his eye. Its argent sheen was blackened and sizzled beneath the moon, as if its surface had been corroded by strong acid. More troubling was its shape, foreign and unfamiliar. With his lifetimes of knowledge, combined centuries spent in study and woven glyphs numbering in the thousands, never had he seen such a rune. It was akin to discovering a new letter in the alphabet, one used in forming words outside his vocabulary.

As quickly as it appeared, the unusual rune spun away but not into the ether. Lengthy moments went by, as Barr waited for its return. He scoured the pattern in the physical until his eyes burned, both afraid to shift focus to another plane or blink and miss its passing. He spotted it immediately upon its return, tried following its path, to no avail, and was rewarded with a splitting headache for his pains.

*Och!* He pressed the back of his hand against his forehead. *What the blazes was that?*

*What's wrong?* Idelle asked, perched and waiting to swoop in. *And why do you sound like a dwarf?*

*It's just a headache.* He tried to shake the stabbing behind his eyes and whichever past life had pushed its way to the surface. Again, he searched for the rune. *There's something here I've never seen, and if I can –*

It appeared once more, and this time Barr forcefully latched onto it with his mind. When it twirled forward to the next plane, he was prepared to follow along but not for the shift into an entirely different realm. His vision swam in an ocean of deep violet, within the haze of a lavender misted sky. Dizziness and nausea overwhelmed his footing and sent him to his knees, where he retched the better part of dinner onto the snow. Entire wards of alien runes swam above him, a massive runic structure like a clockwork of blackened cogs.

"Kraug's balls!"

He had no other words, nor the time to explain.

A shiardin stepped forth with a pained keen and eyes aglow the verdant shade of Tarrandor foxfire. The chill air and pale moonlight assaulted its body without delay, set its chitin to hiss and smoke a fetid odor like burning pitch. At the first touch of its claws, snow vanished in a billow of rising steam. Dormant grass and nettles were stripped of life in an instant, wilted beneath its step by a slow spreading corruption. Soil gave way and cracked in a halo of encroaching death, as the blight advanced both outward and below. It was only a matter of time before it depleted all in its path, until its grasp reached downward into the arteries of Taellus and choked the very life from this world.

Tempas was there in the span of a breath, pulled Barr to his feet and a safe distance away. The once war god slipped free the axes from his belt and rushed in to swing first against the darkspawn. A nightmarish cross between man and umbral, it moved with great speed and gauged its prey with equal cunning.

One swing struck a glancing blow against its rune-strewn body plates, lit the night with sparks born of enchantment at work, but did little to slow its advance. Tempas dodged a rapid series of claw swipes that would have taken his head or raked his chest wide open had he been a lesser being, but he was the embodiment of battle, brought to existence in the hearts and minds of countless soldiers come before. His next swing was exact, with the full weight of strength and skill directed to a single point. It took full on the center plate, where thorax met middle, and with enough force to send the creature a step back. It slid for a brief moment, cut short by thick claws gripping deep into ruined earth, while the axe was utterly destroyed. The steel head shattered like glass in an explosion of jagged shards. The wooden haft followed suit, splintered in an outburst half down its length.

Weaponless and exposed, Tempas would have fallen if not for the score of barbed arrows swiftly loosed. They caused no harm to the shiardin, did little more than elicit sparks, but they gave Tempas enough time to recover his senses.

"Tempas!" Barr shouted and tossed both kyan.

The former god caught them without thought and followed through to a low spin in the same motion. He swept the ironwood blades beneath an outstretched claw and slashed their sunny glow across a leg plate. Chitin fractured and hissed along the score mark. The resulting wound exposed an inner luminescence, like the stoking of a purple ember, and loosed ichor in a thick trail the same hue.

With a high pitched keen that pierced the ears and left a ringing in their wake, the shiardin leapt back. It looked to the sunlit blades with a baleful disdain then dashed away and around Tempas with incredible speed. Wisps of smoke followed behind, its chitinous body still besieged by moonlight. Hunters attacked as it sped past, tried to force it through or into traps on its relentless course toward Saernol. Those the shiardin clawed or bit on the way fell instantly sick, either dropped to all fours or cried out in agony as the corruption overtook them. Flesh and fur shriveled to black, sloughed off into ooze, left exposed bones and hardening organs to be remade in divine runes.

Soon hunters were too busy fending off their turned brethren to give chase or bar the shiardin. Saernol called *furie* to her hands in spectral blue fire, as Barr hurried to weave his new spell about the wooden spikes of a near bulwark. Tempas rushed to intervene as his sister let loose a barrage of ghastly flame. In streaks the length of a man, and just as thick, her magic struck against the shiardin to no avail. The onslaught splashed upon its shell and fell away as so much water upon the rocks of a shore.

Worse still, the conjured *furie* healed its wounds.

Hunters abandoned their heavy axes and spears in favor of sunlit spikes and hefted the shorn trees with both hands. Divine enchantment ran their length at the touch of a hunter, coupled with and strengthened Barr's spell.

With the chaos of taur fighting one another behind, the shiardin bounded into the air and transformed into a rippling inky blanket. An arachon snatched it midair, before it could reach Saernol, and drove the shiardin down with enough strength to crater snow, ice and earth. Golems were already keeping at bay turned hunters, but many more stood ready to cleave or pummel this new foe. The creature returned to its previous form and flailed beneath the stony grip at its neck. Corrosion took hold within the blue steel, ate away at the enchantment and dimmed its luster to a brittle gray. It took less time to spread into and up the arachon's arm than it did for realization to set in. Gauntlet and hand turned to ash upon the wind, quickly followed by the bloodstone and silver runes of its arm, before the rest of its body had fully succumbed.

"Galahd!" a female voice cried out in horror. Elehna, his mate, fell dumbstruck to her knees.

The golems beside her stood shocked into stillness, were quieted by the enormity and seemed to Barr for the first time to show fear.

The shiardin was up and past them when the Ballar intervened. Long used to loss, the sylvannis had struck without pause and scorched the shiardin with half a dozen wounds. One of their sunlit spears had even broken the carapace at its shoulder. Turned hunters had been held down by each limb and impaled to the ground with spelled spikes. Only the shiardin remained a threat, and all eyes were upon it.

Aren was first of the war hounds to charge, sent the darkspawn into a backpedal with the full force of his massive head into its thorax.

*Don't bite!* he warned the others, not wanting to risk affliction or being turned, if that was possible. *Don't let it claw or bite you, either!*

Three more battered the shiardin in a chain of blows to the middle by giant paw or thick skull. Kaela sprang high into the air after them and bounded off the shiardin with a kick of her hind legs. It tried to claw her but lost footing and fell back into a pit. The steel wire did little to slow the shiardin. In no time, it scrambled up along a side and was free.

*I don't think so!*

Idelle dove with all speed, swept across camp and took the shiardin in her talons by a chitinous arm. It tried to rake her leg, but the swiftness with which she ascended and looped around left it careening and off balance, barely able to focus. She beat her wings in great strides, hastened them ever downward, and soared at the last before flinging the shiardin with all the strength she could summon. It sped toward icy snow like a kindled bolt, smoking a trail from the divine arbalest that had loosed it.

Elehna stood waiting with an uprooted birch in her wide hands, soiled roots behind, leafless branches to fore. Barr had just enough time to finish weaving his enchantment, to bathe the timber in a sunlight glow, as the shiardin was met with the business end of a tree. It looked an unwieldy weapon, but she had swung the unearthed wood with a terrible precision, smashed the shiardin through snow and frozen earth, past rock and root, and crushed its body into a mass of broken shell and burning flesh.

When the fractured tree was pulled aside, Tempas jumped down into the impact, held still the darkspawn with a boot to its throat and drove a sunlit spike straight through what was left of its shattered thorax, deep into frozen ground, where it remained pinned and keening in untold pain.

Barr hurried to study the original shiardin, as the newly turned were already breaking apart into spent embers. Saernol climbed down beside him and placed a hand into the air above the dying creature, as if touching upon the runes would give a better sense how they were formed.

"It's too small," Barr said of the glyph and searched for any runes he didn't recognize.

"You see them?" Saernol paused her inspection and gave a look of wondrous surprise. "All of them?"

"No," he replied, distracted and voice trailing off with his search. He found one and latched on, followed it to the Dark, and let go his hold. He pulled back his focus to take in the entire glyph. With narrowed eyes, he added, "Not all of them."

The pattern was complex but no more so than other life. It followed the same rules, used similar defining arrangements – at least in form – and stood a fluid system organized by equal logic. Though all the runes remained foreign, he began to discern functions, saw channeling runes link to conduits, augment runes to structural wards, energy runes to power wards, anchor runes to protection wards. Most started to make sense, but there were missing pieces he couldn't account for.

*Even if the runes are different*, he surmised, *the glyph still behaves like ours. So what am I missing?*

*Are you missing something?* Idelle asked. *Or is there something hidden?*

Barr pursed his lips, watched on in consternation as wards interacted, spun around and through one another, in a sequenced dance of sigils. It was a mirror image of countless other glyphs he'd woven before, albeit grander in scope and needlessly convoluted. The shiardin's wail had faded to a clacking struggle to draw breath, and its ruined body began crumbling to ashen flakes. Barr was running out of time, and he was no closer –

*Wait*, he thought abruptly. *Mirror image. That's it!*

He seized a rune and followed it along each ward, watched it tumble through the glyph until it passed to another plane, then again to a third before slipping back to the Light. As expected, both realms had three planes, a physical, ethereal and astral. Two halves of a whole, they coexisted at either ends of the same spectrum.

His smile must have betrayed the discovery.

"What do you see?" Saernol pressed and appeared frustrated at her own lack of progress.

*The rift's closing*, Aren said. *I guess that means we won?*

Idelle let out a weary breath. *With all those we lost, it doesn't feel much like winning.*

"I'm not entirely sure," Barr said, wary of her intent, "but I think its true weakness is its link to the Dark."

As if on cue, the rift closed with an inward rush of chill air, its violet flames dashed out in an instant. The shiardin collapsed into a pile of ash, which decayed further into dusky motes and lastly into naught but a blackened imprint in the scarred earth. Nothing of it remained to study, and Barr was left with no way to see back into the Dark.

*   *   *

Sera ran fingertips across his back as he slept, a languid caress that curved the shoulder and trailed ever downward. She felt the small hairs beneath her touch, so fine as to seem pale, but only caught sight of them when the candlelight flickered. His skin radiated warmth, like a ray of dawn upon the cheek, and much softer than she expected. He was lean and muscled, hardened by years of battle, yet her tender strokes had discovered no scars. Once afraid he'd recoil at her calloused hands upon him, Sera no longer kept at bay her desire to be close, to press against and envelop him. Though he was too weary from healing for another bout, she was sure his longing had endured into dream, even risked his slumber for the feel of certainty.

Thought of it caused an impish grin, but she quickly stifled that bit of mirth before it built to a giggle.

With a somewhat serious demeanor, she sat further up and propped the pillow at her back. Down feathers and silken cloth, a bed like sturdy clouds and a cozy woolen blanket soft as a kitten, rare comforts were all around.

They were a constant irritation.

She had conceded to indulgence and lain with Dhar, but every moment of idle rest weighed heavily upon her. The task that tried to rule her existence was not without merit or need. Effort wasted on anything but hunting demons was yet a chance of another likely death.

She looked down at her arm, at the runes etched in perfect lines, as if the story of her life had been plainly writ upon her flesh. Down to the wrist, over the hand, up each finger to the tip, she was stained by earth and blood, by divine will and a mortal resolve. It didn't matter how clean the surface or how often she scrubbed at it. The stains could not be hidden from her sight. They went deeper than flesh, were carved into bones and embedded in her spirit. Try as she might, she'd never be free of them, and in times of dark quiet, at moments like these, the troubling thoughts rose to plague her, that neither did she deserve or even want such release.

"You stayed," Dhar said with a sleepy grin, freshly woken and still weary.

"I thought leaving too predictable," she said in a wry tone and playfully kneed his side. He winced, rolled onto his back and stretched visibly sore muscles. She glanced at his bare chest, down the contours to his waist, where the blanket poorly hid any modesty. She fought the urge to let her gaze linger. "I wouldn't want to risk any air of mystery I have left."

"No worry of that," he said in a lighthearted tone. He waited a short time, patient smile upon his lips, until she met and was caught in the open admiration of his golden eyes, until she relented with a smile of her own. "Did you sleep at all?"

Sera dismissed the notion. "I don't need it. Besides, rest makes me uneasy."

"We could hunt," he offered and hazarded a hand within hers.

She rewarded the gamble with a squeeze.

As much as she would've loved to take to the skies and satisfy the geas, to rid herself of the growing knot of restlessness and anxiety tightening her middle, she knew it was too soon.

"You almost died." She gave a stern look, silenced his protest before he could draw breath to speak it. "You're not going to rush into battle because I'm fidgety. You haven't even eaten yet."

"I could grab a cow or two on the way."

Sera was about to berate his awful humor when she realized he'd meant as a dragon. For the first time in so long she couldn't remember when last it happened, she let out a genuine burst of laughter. Imagining him swoop down as they flew together and snatch up a full grown cow in his mouth, accompanied by its mooing objection, only served to send her further into a fit.

"Clearly, you have a more discerning taste than I," Dhar said with feigned indignation. "I prefer deer, given a choice, but cows are more plentiful and convenient." He mimicked a fearful wide-eyed stare. "They just mill about in packs, waiting to be eaten. I suppose the pens make it easier."

She left off laughing for a gasp of surprise. "You steal them?"

"Not always."

Another round took hold, before the rare and fleeting moments of amusement had fully passed. A deep breath eased the aching remnants from her sides, and a single shake of mock disappointment relayed her view on his petty thievery. To see him laugh without a care, body whole and mended through and through, as if he hadn't recently suffered multiple injuries that would have killed anyone else, set her thoughts to the other dragons that had fought and died at the elven tree city.

Sera asked, "How did you heal like that, your wings and scales, when so many others at the forest battle were killed or permanently scarred?"

"We were created," Dhar explained, "with an innate ability to heal ourselves. We could choose not to, could keep scars as trophies –" his tone grew somber – "or even pass on." He propped himself up on an elbow, hand once more in hers. "Over time, through disuse, this ability in younger generations has waned."

Reminded of his considerable years, she couldn't help but wonder at the differences between them. He was able to do as he wanted, at any given time; she'd forever be bound by the geas, her only choice to hunt demons or die in agony resisting. She answered to none but the holy fire in her belly; he had unbreakable ties to his people, with obligations to fulfill.

She wasn't like his silver dragon, open and cheerful, affectionate and obliging. Sera's life had been a hard one, and it had hardened her in turn.

"What about Kaolanni," she asked, "will you give her the children she desires?"

Dhar paused to consider, either unsure of an answer or searching for words to spare her feelings. Not that he needed to. He and Sera had no arrangement, spoken or otherwise. They barely knew one another, despite lying naked in bed. Besides, what did she really have to offer that anyone else couldn't give twice over?

"I told the conclave," he replied at last, "once Revyn is dealt with, I will do as they ask. If we should live to see the day, I have few doubts they will select Kaolanni." He rubbed his thumb along the back of Sera's hand. "It will be awkward. I do not feel as she does."

Sera blew a quiet puff of air out her nose in a single, derisive snort.

"Isn't that the way of love?" Though she sounded sarcastic and bitter, she couldn't help but feel a twinge of hope. "We always want what we can't have or don't see what's been there all along." She wistfully thought back to life before her Awakening. "There was a time when I would've given anything to bear a child."

"And now?"

She felt his eyes upon her, warm, caring, intruding. It was fruitless to think on the impossible, to dredge up old desires and dress them in dreams. It left her sad, hurt and achingly aware she was alone.

"It can never be," she replied, disheartened and long resigned. "The gods won't allow it."

"I have lived long enough to know, with a dreadful certainty, the gods do not know all, do not control all." He persisted and asked, "If by some magic or miracle, to which I have born witness many times, it did become possible. What then?"

Sera stared into the distance, gradually lost in the prospect, no matter how absurd. For long moments she

146

allowed the musing, at the wonder of giving life to a child, to give all her love and hope, every effort and good fortune, to see that child grow into the wondrous person she'd always wished to be. She found herself smiling, and at least for the moment kept the weight of reality from crashing in all around her.

"Then what use would I have of a dragon?" She gave a spirited grin, pushed him to his back and climbed atop. She pinned his arms and tightened her legs around his middle. He may have been stronger, but she had the benefit of leverage. "Hmm?"

Dhar narrowed his eyes. "I can think of –"

Her body arched in tremendous pain, every muscle tensed against the strain of an unseen force crushing from within. Her skin flushed and grew darker in quiet torture, as long moments passed one into another with her unable to take a breath.

Dhar panicked and called out, but his voice went unheard beneath the rhythm swelling in her ears. He took her by the arms, turned over and eased her to one side. He cradled her head in a hand, brushed lips against her with muffled words and struggled to find any means to help.

Still caught in the endless throe of an unforgiving spasm, it felt to Sera as if her bones would shatter from the tension. Eyes clinched into blinding flashes, the dull tingle of numbed flesh spreading inward from hands and feet, she was too long without breath and in desperate need of a reprieve.

As abruptly as it had begun, the convulsion passed of a sudden. Her body eased and let in air with a horrid gasp. Blood resumed its course with a stinging rush, the deadened prickle of her flesh now a stabbing ache. Her muscles screamed in complaint, chest wracked with each breath, and the pounding behind her eyes had finally settled to a violent thrum.

It was all she could do to stay conscious, to fend off the lull of darkness at the edge of her vision. The warm void tried to claim her senses, but his voice brought her back.

"Deep breaths," Dhar said and did all he could to calm her gasping. He still cradled her in one hand and soothed her chest with the other, all the while his eyes locked with hers. "You are fine now. Whatever it was is gone from the city."

The holy fire about her body subsided into nothing.

"It wasn't a demon," she said, voice choked and tears welling. She shook her head, refused the awful truth. "It wasn't..."

The runes floating just above her skin winked out in a flutter of dying light.

Helpless, confused and concerned, Dhar could only watch as the *furie* fled her body.

"What is happening!" he pleaded, more to the gods than to Sera.

The runes on her flesh began to fade.

When they lost all color and disappeared, she knew the geas had been broken. She was free, of the cursed blessing that had taken from her every hope of a happy life. She was free, set loose and adrift into a maelstrom of uncertainty, of empty joy and the ashes of sorrow in her mouth. She was free, her naked body no longer marred by its divine touch. She was free, of the silent voice that had spoken to her soul, of the strength that sustained her spirit, of the power that coursed through every fiber of her being.

She was free.

"He's gone." Her voice caught in her throat, told the depth of a misery and remorse that could never fully be revealed.

Dhar would not hear it, shook his head in a weak show of denial.

"No," he said, implored, and the sound of it broke her heart. "Please, no."

Sera spared him the words, would not be the one to deliver such pain. She pulled him to her breast, hugged him with all the strength her starved and frail body could muster. But they knew, deep inside where the hollowed chasm of their spirits would never again hear his voice; they both knew.

Curoch was gone forever.

# – 6 –

 arr woke with the dawn, a habit long fixed from his time with the sylvannis, one born more of duty and its ever pressing weight than any rustic commitment to the rising sun. The few hours had afforded solid rest, but the singed haze of weariness still slowed his rise. A ceramic pitcher of water chilled on the bedstand, runes etched along its bottom eliciting the cerulean blush of an enchantment. He drank two cups to ease his throat and wash clean the bitter taste of battle remnants from his mouth. He put on clean breeches but was forced to endure the shirt another day, until the others could be mended. A plate of sweet breads and cinnamon butter awaited him at the dining table, with a mixed bowl of berries, salted ham and a decanter of goat milk. He ate enough to quiet the rumbling in his middle, wrapped a

fair amount into napkins for later and stuffed them in either pocket.

He'd been careful not to wake Fluora, planned to practice recalling past lives at the park, but when he reached the doorway, he paused for a look back down the hall. The house felt oddly quiet. Idelle was asleep in her favorite perch outside. He sensed nothing of Aren, which meant another night spent at Geilon-Rai. Barr let go the latch and went lightly toward her bedroom. When he eased the door open, he was surprised to find the bed empty and unused.

Barr knew her mother, Elaedraoni, had a difficult time ahead. Her decision to keep the demon child forced upon her was not welcomed by all, risking her life with a stubborn refusal of Fezuul's aid even less so. He hoped Fluora could sway her mother's mind and attributed her absence to that end.

He closed the bedroom door and headed out.

Seated at the fountain in a short dress, gauzy layers of soft blue and faded cobalt, Saernol trailed fingertips over the splashing water. Sable hair tied at the neck in a gossamer bow, waves of curl and silken petals spilled down her back in the semblance of a nighttime fall. Pale skin and slight frame, she cast a shadow far less than her station once granted. Her beauty was unquestioned but not defined by the delicate cheeks, slender nose or full lips. She possessed a grace of movement and artful touch, the tenderness of unspoiled youth and the vigor of a strong will with a stronger mind. Her presence inspired warmth and the aspiration to grow worthy.

She saw him approach and offered a wan smile. All notion of divine charm fled his thoughts at the sight of her dark eyes, reddened and overwrought with the stains of sorrow. A closed palm ended the scry, and she faced him with trembling hands clasped in her lap.

"What is it?" he asked

"I have been searching," she said, "for my brothers and sisters, those that yet live."

She took a deep breath to steady her voice.

Barr said, "We don't know they're dead, just they've been taken. If Revyn meant to kill them –"

"No," Saernol said, as if appreciative of the attempt but not at all comforted, "it is something else. I have searched tirelessly and can find no trace of Curoch or Kraug." She looked once more on the brink of tears. "They must have fallen last night while we fought. We could have protected them."

"Maybe," he said, with no desire to diminish the loss, "but I don't think we would've fared as well against three shiardin."

The once goddess shook her head and looked away, whether in grief, shame or reluctant agreement, Barr couldn't say – most likely a measure of each. When she turned back there was an edge to her voice.

"What did you see?" she asked.

The intent with which she gauged his reaction left him uncomfortable, like a child caught beneath the gaze of a disapproving parent who fully expected a lie. The best he could offer was a half-truth.

"You mean its glyph." At her nod, Barr went on, "It was much less complex than I've seen in other life." His turn to study her, "What about you?"

He could see she had hoped for more, kept searching his eyes for unspoken truths. After a few quiet moments, she relented.

"I agree it was far more sparse than it should have been. I could only guess that my brother has learned to hide certain aspects of his work, or the creature itself is fundamentally different from anything in this realm." Her look was then one of askance. "But you had clearly seen more than I, of that much I am certain. Do you yet trust me enough to share?"

Barr considered, knew what the revelation would stir but saw no way to avoid it.

"I saw runes in the Dark," he said at last, watched her initial doubt turn to surprise and the speculation he was afraid of. "More so, the realm is a mirror image of our own, with three corresponding planes of existence."

Saernol was quiet for a few moments, eyes lost in her trail of thought, then let out a short laugh.

"You knew," she said in lighthearted accusation. "Go on, then. Or would you rather I ask?"

*Was I wrong about her?* he wondered.

*It wouldn't surprise me,* Idelle said and yawned, had apparently just woken and was in a feisty mood. *Seems common among men.* She stretched her legs and ruffled. *Who were you wrong about?*

*Saernol. And I didn't say I was wrong.*

Barr took in a deep breath, leaned back and shifted his focus. Saernol's glyph came into view, a staggering work of intricacy.

*The goddess? Oh, there you are.* Idelle landed atop the fountain. *What are you looking at?*

*Shush, I'm thinking.*

As with Revyn and Tempas, it was much larger than his own, though more elegant than the war god's. Whole wards and several runes in the astral were dormant, dim and unmoving within the continual flow. It was the same in the ether, less so in the physical, but there seemed to be nothing amiss. The inactive pieces were masked, their inner *furie* somehow doused, and no longer replenished within the cycle. Could restoring her godhood be as easy as reactivating the runes?

*I'm off to fish then,* Idelle said and took wing. *Enjoy the awkward silence.*

153

He began to wonder if the children gods were a natural occurrence, as opposed to what they had told the first races, or if they truly were formed by the same being who had forged the known realms.

The more he studied her glyph, the many differences in scope and detail between gods and mortals, the better he grasped the full meaning and potential of deific runes, the language of creation.

If only there was more time.

Barr took in a deep breath and let it out with the trepidation of one about to disappoint a friend. He was certain he could restore her and the others, given enough time and patience, but didn't think it wise or his place to do so. The challenge intrigued him, but he felt it crossed a line he didn't fully understand. If the gods were unable to set right their own glyphs, then perhaps it was best they remained mortal.

"I'm sorry," was all he said.

He hoped she would take the apology as surrender to an impossible task, rather than the truth of his refusal to help.

Saernol patted his hand. "Not to worry, child. Even if it could be done, I would not risk your ascension." She looked up at the runic imitation of morn, down the path toward an arachon tending fig trees and bright flowers. "You should be careful."

"Of what?" Barr asked.

"Creating life," she replied. "If you can see the divine runes, you can manipulate them as well, remake them or even start anew. No matter the urge, you must not." Her look grew somber, haunted. "Our children upon Taellus were not the first. What we wove from nothing became twisted, ravenous, fed on Light and Dark alike, and in the end we were forced to return them from whence they came, to the nothingness of the Void."

Barr had never read or heard of such a place, in any of his lifetimes. Could there be a third realm?

"What is it?"

"A place between what is and is not," she said, "an empty black bereft of sound or sight, warmth or love. It is where my brothers, sisters and I were given life." Saernol regarded him as an innocent, one as yet unsullied. "Be thankful you will never know its touch." As if the dark moment had passed, her manner brightened to a smile. "Am I to understand you will be teaching the Art, here in the city? I think I should very much like to see that."

"You're welcome to stay, of course," he said, "for as long as you like. There's plenty of room. There aren't any students yet, or the time to teach if there were, but I'd be glad of any chance to learn from you."

"So long as we can keep my brother from stealing me away." She turned toward the house, as if something had caught her eye. "It would give me the chance to study you as well."

Barr heard it before he saw her, the whisper of magic that accompanied the mists, and turned to see Fluora step from their front doorway.

Usually vibrant, with a ready smile, she looked on the edge of exhaustion. Strands of hair had slipped loose their gold spiral binds, fell listless over ears and damp along her jaw. Her eyes, red-rimmed with lack of sleep, narrowed at the sight of Barr's company. He realized she wasn't wearing a blindfold and the thought caused her to look his way. With reluctance, she pulled it free from her sash and secured it unnecessarily tight.

By the ire in her demeanor and irritation in her voice, he guessed Elaedraoni would not be swayed.

"Are you alright?" he asked and knew she wasn't.

She walked over and embraced him, pulled him in much closer than a single night apart would warrant. His body began to react before his mind could rein in the sudden longing.

"It is now," she said and kissed him, soft at first but then deeper. Her brief but rough touch left his lower lip in a throb and moist from the attention. "I am just tired from dealing with my mother."

When she eased her pull against his lower back, he felt keenly aware how inappropriate the display must've seemed to Saernol. Fluora had never shown such a level of affection in front of others, as if she were jealous or laying claim.

"Why risk the mists then?" Barr was more than just concerned of her odd behavior. "I thought we agreed –"

"I am more than capable of holding Revyn at bay," she fairly snapped, then added as an afterthought, "so long as I am the only one traversing the mists. I was there most of last night, exploring my new strengths and abilities as Matron."

"Strength or no," Saernol said in a worried but caring tone, "there remains the possibility he might –"

"I appreciate the concern," Fluora interrupted, "but I really do know what I am doing." She gave the smaller woman a cursory glance. "And one irksome mother is quite enough, thank you." Barr barely opened his mouth to offer Saernol an apology, when Fluora said, "I also had some unwelcome visions. The attack on Tempas was a ruse, a distraction from the true targets."

Barr still struggled to make sense of her manner, the obvious anger and undeserved bitterness toward their guest.

Voice heavy with sadness and regret, Saernol said, "We know, child. I am sorry you had to witness such a terrible sight." Fluora visibly angered, as if weight of her news had been lessened by the foreknowledge. She said nothing but continued to seethe. "Are you sure you are alright, dear? Your Barr and I were about to engage in a lengthy talk of magic. Perhaps you would care to join?"

The sound of his name shook his attention.

"I think Fluora needs to rest," he said, more worried than disapproving, and hoped a good sleep would set her right.

"Nonsense." Fluora took a firm hold of his hand, turned and walked toward the house with him in tow. "He can play later," she said, without a second glance to the once goddess. "Right now, we have a few things of our own to discuss."

Barr looked back to give a sincere apology but saw Saernol amused rather than offended. He had to hurry to close the door behind them, as Fluora pulled him toward her bedroom. Still concerned and now confused, though admittedly a bit excited, he wasn't sure just what she intended. They'd talked about being intimate on a few occasions, but both decided it was best to wait. When they reached the bed, Fluora let go and slipped free her dress.

Something had clearly changed her mind.

\*　　\*　　\*

Dhar caught scent of him as first light crested the upper passes and cast uneven shadows across the basin. A thick crescent of lush greenery, mottled by ash trees wide as any dragon, even a dense blanket of snow could not fully mask the verdant wonder stretched out below. Edges scarred by drawn stone, gentle slopes and a placid lake, bathed in the warmth of a ley line forced up toward its surface, the enclosed valley looked a paradise rudely woken by its clash with Naerat Sanae. Tenfold greater in size, by any measure given, the dragon home jutted up from the lesser mountain like a triumphant brother.

On a hunt of his own, the Emissary had scant looked skyward as he stalked, let alone gave any indication he had scented another. It was the way of reds, so bold as to seem reckless, more assured than was warranted, forced to claw free by brute strength the inexorable dilemmas of their own making.

Khronaerrin drew up short from a tight spiral, used the trees and their great height to veil his presence. He was largest of his kind, a trait only recently cherished by ever smaller hatchlings, but looked a stunted child in contrast to his forebears. The Patron and Matron reds Dhar had emerged from broken shell beside were noble of mind and body, bore a brazen love of life, held a deep respect for their ken and calling, were worthy of true praise and loath to hear it. While Khrona possessed physical attributes of the lines that preceded him, the blackened eyeridges and upturned horns, nostril plates and jaw barbs, reverse wing talons and double spine blades, beveled scales and coarse grooves, – also the swooping ear creases from a past pairing with a blue, though he would never openly admit it – he had nothing of their mindful bearing, no impassioned aspirations beyond political or social standing, no use for love apart from mating, no want of beauty outside his own and worse had never shown an inclination to change.

As evidenced by his hunting for mere sport.

Dhar watched from below deepening storm clouds, as Khrona fell upon his prey, a full party of seasoned and grisly augryn. An offshoot of ogres, distant remnants of the titans, the dark-haired and gray-skinned brutes were more rancor than reason. They spent most of their lives in crude dwellings beneath the mountain, in the damp chill and somber dark of all-encompassing bitter stone. Though unused to the sting of sunlight and had long ago brought down pigs and goats to sustain them, the dark ogres occasionally sent out hunters to the surface for the meat and pelts of dire bear and caribou.

Khrona gave a roar of challenge, dispensing with the foolishness of stealth or surprise, sped down and over their readied spears and thrown hooks of hardened iron. He swept them aside by the sheer force of his passing, caught one with a tail barb and tossed the lifeless body back at them, like a stone from a catapult. Molten flame dripped from his fangs as he laughed at their aimless scurry, even paused his attack to revel in the chaos.

His next pass was not as successful. Though only half the augryn had found footing, one managed to snag a leg with his hook and heavy chain. He was carried off with Khrona, swung wildly through the air and smashed against a tree. It was unlikely the hook had done any damage, but the augryn and chain got entangled in the branches, threw Khrona askew and fighting to right his course. Spears struck against his underside, bounced off and away without harm, though a flinch may have meant one scored a touch between scales.

Seething with anger, the Emissary leveled fire and claw against them, crushed one underfoot as he landed and set aflame another three. A hook wrapped an arm with expert precision, then one around his broad neck and another at a wing. Khrona may have thought he was at play with lesser creatures, but Dhar recognized the sudden danger the stubborn youth was now in.

Not since the Descent, when dragons came down from their mountain home to deal with the gathered hordes of feralkin sent against them, had Dhar put wing to assailing the basin. He landed heavily beside Khrona, his great golden bulk enough to scatter the augryn in a wide circle of flailing bodies through the air. Earth and snow rose all about them, in a corona of fearful screams and ringing ears. His bellow shook stones loose from the mountain, cracked snow laden branches at the bole and sent augryn running for the relative safety of home.

When Khrona moved to give chase, Dhar held him back with the restraining touch of an elder. He removed the hook from Khrona's wing. Had the obstinate red gone after them, he would have risked pulling the iron claw down the delicate membrane.

"Let them be," Dhar said, voice weighted by recent loss and unwilling to shed innocent blood.

Khrona scowled back, his fun and demeanor clearly spoiled.

"I was honing my skills," he said in complaint, but his manner visibly changed when he saw how greatly Dhar was troubled. "What has happened?

Dhar lowered his head, found it difficult to convey the words. Speaking them aloud was akin to admitting the awful truth.

"Curoch has been taken," he replied, fending off the imagined scene that would not relent, "into the Dark, and is gone from us forever."

Khrona was silent as the terrible news settled in, as the brunt of its meaning, the full weight of its import, worked through thought and gave rise to emotion upon his face. The vehement denial, unwanted consideration, reluctant acceptance and inevitable anger played out across his features, blossomed into a rage on the verge of eruption.

A swipe of his tail left two ash trees cut in twain, cloven straight through, into an explosion of splintered wood and snowy ice in an outward arc. He clawed deep gouges in the sheer rock face of an outcrop, sent rock and debris spilling out to the distance in great heaps of hewn earth. Stones slipped free and rained down in the wake of those tremors, threatening to bring with them the entire mountain.

With heavy breath and unchecked fury, he let loose a lengthy blast of molten fire that ate away at the outcrop, melted it to the core and caused the perilous overhang to give way in an avalanche. The liquid flames consumed all, tore through the stonefall with ravenous hunger and was not sated when the last bits had tumbled down. When Khrona finally succumbed, dropped to his knees with strength expended, all that remained was a morass of slag and flitting embers.

Dhar abided the outburst in patient understanding, barely able to keep his own sorrow from turning, but he had fallen prey to the allure of rage many times before. It offered no solutions, was nothing more than an outlet without meaning or purpose. It was easy to let emotion rule, to forego the burden of fault or need of reason. As with most aspects of life, so it was with trying times.

Rarely was easy the best choice.

Far better to channel such anger and anguish to a focused goal. For Dhar, that was the utter destruction of Revyn.

"It was him," Khrona stated more than asked, "the changeling god."

With a calm he did not feel, Dhar said, "It was."

He knew any attempt at consolation would be lost in the turmoil. Khrona was young, brash and prideful, but no less a heartbroken child than himself. If Dhar could scarcely still his own grief, what hope did he have to offer?

To his credit, the red steadied his ragged breathing and pulled himself up, with the stoic bearing and firm resolve befitting an Emissary. With no show of conceit or shame, he deferred to the wisdom and experience of the last living Patron.

"What would you have me do?"

Dhar appreciated what it took for Khrona to admit he was lost in the conflict of inner turmoil, to seek and accept aid without the fear of seeming weak.

"Tell the others," he said, not with authority but the firm desire of vengeance equal to their injury, "and ready for my call." With a hint of growl and bitter promise, he added, "You will know when the time comes, for it will shake the very footing of all Taellus."

Khrona gave a stalwart nod, the need for words given way to the want of action. He lifted off and sped toward home.

Dhar looked skyward, uncertain where to go or what to do next. His thoughts were of vengeance, of tearing Revyn to pieces by claw and tooth. He knew such thoughts would only lead to impatient anger and soon after certain madness, so he put them aside and took wing.

There was no escape from the loss of father, but he could assuage it, at least for now, by enjoying the innate gifts bestowed upon him and all his kind.

With powerful thrusts, Dhar headed for the clouds

\*     \*     \*

Half the day was gone by the time Sera woke, eyes gummed and head throbbing to every beat of her heart, like the echoes of an unsteady drum. Her body trembled with fatigue and the burning ache of neglect, tightened her chest so that even drawing breath was a chore. It was a struggle to sit up, to let the waves of dizziness and nausea pass, without slipping back into the empty black of collapse. Every muscle punished her with agony, as she reached for the set of clothes left on the chair beside her bed. There was a walking staff as well, a length of knotted ash with a leather grip at its middle. Loath as she was to use it, she knew she'd never make it out the door on her own.

Sera took hold of it and growled against the strain of getting to her feet. Sweat formed on her brow, wet the back of her fresh tunic and made her palms slick upon the leather. One painful, laborious step at a time, she made her way to the living area and dropped heavily into a wooden chair at the table. Morning meal had been set out, the bread and sausages gone cold, the diced fruit and pitcher of milk now warm but not unpleasant. Each bite went untasted beneath the bitterness in her mouth, each swallow forced down out of necessity. When her stomach could hold no more, she waited patiently in the quiet for any semblance of strength to return, focused mind and body on merely breathing.

She knew Dhar had to leave, to tell the other dragons what had happened, but for the first time in a long while, she didn't want to be left alone. There was a desperate need within her to share the pain and grief with someone who understood it, to split the burden weighing down her every thought, to ease in any measure the overwhelming despair threatening to crush the air from her body, the light from her spirit. The other hunters would offer no such comfort. They had been content to languish in idle excess and now probably reveled in the loss. No, there was only one she'd let see her pain, allow and welcome in her heart.

And he was off consoling another.

Sera gripped the staff hard and stood, ignored the resulting torment and headed out the door. The cobbled road outside her home was empty, quiet but for the few birds and insects about the flowerbeds. Determined, she made it as far as the wide hazelnut tree, where another road intersected, before succumbing to a bout of ragged breath. Her frailty and limited strength only served as a harsh reminder of what was lost.

It wasn't the power the geas afforded, the divine will and potent magic coursing through her every being in its endless aim to change her. It was the struggle against it that defined her, showed the true nature of her spirit. What was she without the strife, the daily trials she'd endured, the raging conflict that ruled each waking moment and spurred her to greater heights? She was nothing without the turmoil, the shadow remnants of a weapon steeped in holy fire, doused in the acrid blood of a thousand demons, stripped of identity and self-worth, with no value to the world. The fight was all she had left, of life before and after her Awakening.

The geas, now gone, had taken that too.

She leveled a punch against the tree with every bit of anger and frustration pent up inside, set it free upon the unforgiving bole and found a great sense of satisfaction in watching the bark crack. A tearful laugh escaped her lips, as she found pained relief once again in a fight she couldn't win. Again and again, she struck amidst a haze of wrathful numb. Smeared in blood, the wood splintered but left her hand in utter ruin. A welcome distraction, the shattered bones and torn flesh were tangible proof of her control, an injury of her own making.

Sera looked down at both arms and felt the geas upon them, knew without a doubt the runes were still there, carved into her bones, burned into her flesh. Like tinder, they just needed a spark to set the flame. She wiped her eyes and took a deliberate, calming breath. If she could feel the runes, then so could the others.

She found an eldarath to heal her hand but gave little in way of explanation. The jade golem performed the task and wished Sera well, with an unspoken concern in her eyes that the hunter take better care.

What would have taken minutes before had now cost an hour, but Sera found them exactly where she had expected. The teahouse now served as a makeshift tavern for the other four, and as usual they were lazing about, laughing with one another over stories not worth telling. All manner of food and drink spoiled the tables and bar, spilled onto the floor and went unnoticed beneath the din. The arachon were patient and generous hosts, but she couldn't imagine them tolerating such boisterous buffoonery for much longer.

"A bit early for drink," Sera said loudly.

The four held up their mugs and cheered in unison, as if she'd come to join the celebration. Ale-stained and unshaven, raucous and unwashed, they were oblivious to the discontent in her voice. Her contempt was plain to see by any but damned fools, which admittedly explained their unwitting disregard.

"I've come to ask about the geas," she went on and gave one – Talbor, Talburn or some other nonsense name from the southern isles – a kick to his chair, to gain his attention. The sun-scarred clod spilled his drink, which caused the others to laugh all the more. "Can you feel it?"

"Feel what?" Carem replied, laughing but growing annoyed by her sober interruption.

"The geas," she said, more emphatically. "It's still there. It's just dormant."

Maelor tore a leg from one of the cooked hens before him, bit off a mouthful and said, "Don't make no matter. We've no intention of leaving, and neither should you." He spit a piece of gristle onto the table. "The way you been walking around with that face, like you stepped in it but good –" Carem laughed an explosion of ale at that "– it's a wonder you can even see us from up there!"

More snickers and howling. Sera had a mind to beat some sense into them with her walking staff but didn't think she could muster the effort. Unlike her, they were far from starved and had been feasting since the day they arrived.

Sera glared at them in turn. "There's a war coming. Everyone will need to fight if we're to survive."

"Not likely," Tal-something said. The rest agreed with a nod and took a swig. "Wars are fought every day, and not a one has come knocking."

Carem crossed his arms, spilling on himself. "Never will I fight again. Especially not one I didn't ask for."

Up until then, Hamon had quietly gone along with the others. Or was it Hamor? Sera's frown deepened. Not a one's name was worth remembering. But this one was just a boy, barely a month Awakened.

"What of you?" she asked him.

The lad cleared his throat, ill at ease at the eyes upon him.

"I wouldn't be much use," he said meekly. "Better if someone else did the fighting."

"Then all of you will die!" Sera fumed.

Maelor poured another drink. "All the more reason to live as much as we can now!"

Sera gritted her teeth and swatted the mug from his hand with her staff.

"Hey now!" he shouted, but she was already back out the door. "Someone's got to clean that up, you know."

Carem chuckled. "Well it won't be me!"

Their laughter followed her down the road, haunted her steps as she wracked her mind for what to do.

*Barr,* she thought, *the one who brought me here. He used magic. Maybe he could find a way to fix the geas, wake it up again.*

He and others had been visiting major cities across Taellus, offering use of the portalis, but Sera knew what they were really doing.

*They're forming an alliance, preparing for the war when, not if, Revyn returns.* The details of her argument began to take shape, readying to convince Barr. *They're going to need us, all five of us, if they want to stand any chance at winning.*

There was no denying her logic. It was in everyone's best interest that Barr somehow give them back the geas, even if Curoch was gone for good. It was just a matter of whether Barr was able to help, and if not him, then some other. The golems had magic too, maybe stronger than his. No matter what it took, what the cost, there had to be a way.

And Sera was resolved to find it.

\*　　\*　　\*

Barr opened his eyes and let fall the remembered life, like a thin veil shaken loose from his senses. He sat in the comfort of thick grass, with the warmth of afternoon upon his shoulders, and heard wind chimes from nearby homes play in time a lazy rhythm. It continued to grow easier, recalling his numerous pasts, less painful and more clear with each attempt. Similar to the memories of his current incarnation, his preceding lives were no more than a jumble of images and emotions, until he focused on something – or someone – that had happened to him. Once within that frame of mind, it took little effort to expand further, to move back and forth throughout the recollection, to jump from one to the next as each memory sparked another.

In a sense, it was akin to opening a history book and reading about a significant event, then paging to related incidents in the notes. It still took concentration to stay within a single life, when recalling a lost love for instance might lead to a string of similar heartbreaks in any one of the others, but he was growing more adept at that as well.

*That was much longer than the last,* Idelle noted. She was meticulously preening her feathers of any fish scales left over from lunch.

Kaela was asleep, her head in Barr's lap. Aren had tried to nudge her away hours ago but left off to sun on the flat of a warm decorative boulder. The park was alive with birdsong in boughs, the buzz of industrious bees, the flutter of butterflies among the wildflowers and the general scents of an ever-present spring. While beautiful, comfortable and undeniably lovely, his hours spent at the park often left him longing for the brisk winds and rich colors of autumn.

*I should wake her,* Aren said but didn't move a paw.

*Don't you dare!* Idelle warned, mirroring Barr's own thoughts. *There's no need to be so jealous.*

Barr chuckled. He loved Aren with all his heart, but the big war hound could be such a puppy at times.

*You're too big to lie in my lap, anyway.*

*Am not,* Aren muttered then remained quiet.

*You know you're lucky, right?* Barr asked, stroked the tip of her soft ear. The steady rise and fall of her deep slumber was calming. When Aren didn't answer, he said, *She is too.*

His thoughts turned to Fluora, of her sudden and unusual relent to desires. Their bout of lovemaking, their very first, had lasted hours before they both fell asleep in a shared embrace. He'd never felt closer to her than in those moments after, head nestled in her nape, the scent of her in his nose.

*Enough,* Idelle said, *or I'll need a bath to cool off.* She ruffled her whole body, shook off downy tufts. *I may need another visit to the Ghaoylens now.*

Aren looked over at them, confused, but soon closed his eyes and went back to feigning disinterest.

Barr didn't want to wake Kaela, but he was eager to learn more of the Dark runes he'd seen in the shiardin. He could weave a portal to the other realm but thought it too dangerous, wasn't sure he could keep at bay any of the creatures who might seek to pass through. What he needed was a way to observe one, preferably in its own environment, or else it would die too quickly.

*Maybe I can scry one,* he thought and got to his feet. Kaela stirred but didn't wake. *Not sure I can pierce the Dark, though. Saernol said she wasn't able to.* With a sigh of frustration, he worried his lower lip. *It'd be a lot easier if I didn't need something created in the Dark to see those runes again.*

*Just scribble some in the air,* Aren suggested.

Barr shook his head. *I can only recall a few, and I have no idea what they do. Any glyph I make with them won't work.*

*Does it need to?* Idelle asked. *Maybe writing out the ones you know will help you remember the others.*

*It's worth a try, I suppose.*

He drew the first one that came to mind. It hung in the air, lifeless and unmoving, and immediately began to wither in the Light. Its surface bubbled, and the edges appeared to dissolve. From the rate of decay, it would be gone within minutes. Curious, he conjured *furie* and fed the rune a small amount. To his surprise, it began to erode at a faster pace, as if eaten away from the inside out.

Within moments, the rune was gone.

*That makes no sense,* he said and wondered what it could mean. *Runes need* furie *to work. Why did this one react like it was poison?*

Barr traced the rune again then added to it the few others he recalled. It seemed a pointless endeavor, like scrawling letters on a scroll in the hope of accidentally forming a word. Worse than inactive, they were under assault, suspended motionless and dwindling with every moment. He tried linking them one at a time, to gauge their interaction, but without power they served no real purpose – intended or otherwise.

*This is pointless!* He discarded the runes with a wave of his hand, like motes of ash carried off into nothing.

"Trouble with a glyph?" Saernol asked.

He hadn't heard her approach from behind, barefoot in the grass and enjoying the aroma of a daffodil. Her smile was infectious, despite his disheartened demeanor. Pale nose and cheeks slightly reddened, she looked in danger of freckling but paid it no mind.

*She's pretty,* Aren said. His desire for a closer sniff was palpable.

*Please, don't.* Idelle's warning held mirth. *Unless you want to be turned into a squirrel, that is. Come to think of it, I am a bit peckish.*

"Of a sort," Barr admitted. "I was trying to recreate some of the Dark runes I saw last night and hopefully figure out how they work. It's not going so well, though. I need another shiardin to study –" a thought occurred "– or something like it."

"You will work it out," Saernol said, confident, "all in good time." More somber, she added, "I am loath to ruin such a beautiful day, well, any more than it already has, but I fear I bring poor tidings. Both Wynter and Veralnon have fallen."

"Since this morning?" He was shocked, to say the least, and felt a sense of dread at the implications. "In midday sun? He's either getting stronger, bolder or more reckless. I don't know which is worst."

"None of those options bode well for us," she said in a forced attempt to lighten the dire turn. "All that is left of us who were made mortal are Balsina and I. It is only a matter of time before we too are taken, no matter where or with whom we hide."

*What about the Watcher?* Idelle asked. *You'd think he'd want to save his brothers and sisters from a terrible death. Well, the sisters anyway.*

Aren refused the bait.

"Why doesn't Laeryk do something?" Barr passed on Idelle's question, wondered at it himself. "I understand he's never been one to meddle, but to stand idly by while his family is destroyed. It's unconscionable."

"I doubt he will risk his godhood," Saernol replied, "might see this as just reward for breaking our oath. No, he will not intervene. We are on our own."

Barr considered. "Has Revyn taken any of the other gods, those born after you? I thought for certain he'd go for Tempas, to punish him for the shapeling hunters."

"My brother has a clever mind and a cruel heart. He could be saving the war god for last, to cherish those final moments, or he is using our expectations against us." There was fear in her voice but also a subtle sense of resignation, as if her fate had been sealed long ago. "He will come for me soon, but I will make him pay dearly for it if I can."

"I have an idea that may help," Barr said, thought again about the plan hatching at the back of his mind. He just needed Fluora to grant him use of the mists. "I wonder why Fluora didn't come tell me what happened. She must have seen it."

Saernol looked across the park and down the road to their home. With eyes squinted ever so slightly, it was as if she tried to see Fluora through a great distance.

"She is not there," the once goddess said simply. "Perhaps she returned to the mists to further explore her new powers."

Barr caught the hint of skepticism, but his concern for Fluora took precedent. He'd been out here for hours, but she wouldn't have left without talking to him first. Especially since –

"I am sure there is no need for alarm." Saernol put a hand to his arm in a gesture of comfort. "Tell me, what will you do now?"

*Fluora's fine*, Idelle said, though with little insistence. *She probably just needed some time alone.*

*Why?* Aren asked, genuinely interested. *Why won't you tell me what happened?*

*I* did *tell you*, Idelle answered.

*Shush!* Barr told them.

"To be honest," Barr said with some reluctance, "I think I can do more by figuring out how to deal with the shiardin than I can in protecting Tempas."

"And me." Her tone was not accusatory but matter of fact. "I agree, of course. If there is anything I can do to help, you need but ask."

"Come to think of it, there may be. Do you recall the sunlight spell?" At her nod, he continued, "I taught it to the arachon enchanters with Tempas. It should help a great deal, but it's unstable. The conduits begin to fail after absorbing light for about an hour."

"You could limit the intake," she suggested, "though that would weaken its potency. Are you familiar with substructures? Perhaps you could use one within the conduits to bolster their resilience."

Barr thought back to Fezuul's glyph at Starshrine, how the conduit had collapsed to a protection node when he tried to tamper with it.

"I could make it so when they collapse, they become storage nodes."

"Hmm, that is clever." She saw the inherent flaw as well as he. "It is not a perfect solution, however."

"No," Barr agreed, "it'll only extend the duration. The enchantment will continue to grow weaker after the first collapse, until it completely fades away."

*I really need to get into the mists*, he thought. *Maybe I should scry Fluora, so I can ask –*

*Leave her be*, Idelle said sternly. *If she wanted to talk, she'd be here.*

*Pfft*, Aren scoffed. *You don't know that.*

Idelle sounded annoyed. *I speak from experience. You wouldn't understand.*

*I understood just fine*, Aren said. *I just don't see what all the fuss is about.*

Saernol must have seen he was distracted.

"Could you show me the runes you saw last night?" she asked. "Maybe together we can sort them out, or at least gain a better grasp of how they work."

"Alright," Barr said and smiled, "I'd be happy to."

* * *

Fluora knelt in the waters of the mists, felt its gentle touch lap against her, envelop her spirit, and soothe the tumult of emotions that swirled within her. Head hung low, blindfold gone, through the veil of tired, teary eyes, she saw the expanse of starlight overhead twinkle back across the ripples. Those gleaming pinpoints of light were not the same bodies housed in heavenly constellations. They were souls connected to the mists, to her, in any measure, descendants of Saernol's first who shared in the wondrous gift.

None had a deeper bond with the mists than she, held sway over its use or kept at bay the encroaching Dark. This was her domain, her burden, and she bore it for them. Altogether they lent her a modicum of strength, bolstered when her spirit flagged, renewed when her body waned, but the full of their efficacy was but a pale whisper in a ferocious gale when held against the utter power her unfettered link bestowed upon her. It spanned worlds in an instant, bridged realms without effort, cured the sick, mended wounds and held time in place. Its reach had no bounds, its potency no restraint, its living conduit, the Matron, absolute. As in all exchanges, there was a price.

And Fluora's was slowly killing her.

Bit by angry bit, shred by tattered shred, her spirit was besieged and giving way to a wasting rage. Though she fought to remain whole, to withstand the unrelenting assault and preserve her inner light, deep within the core of her all was the resigned awareness this struggle had no happy end. There was no amount of perseverance to suffice, no triumph to be had, nothing but the cost. It was their salvation and her doom, a bargain made with no regret, and for him she would gladly do it, over and again.

The irksome itches had become rashes, inflamed further each time she conjured the dark fires and let them ride roughshod across her flesh. Up her arms, down her legs, the damage to her spirit manifested as spreading burns. The waters cooled with their touch, but her relief was short-lived. The injury was from within and would never abate so long as she persisted.

Fluora wiped her eyes and stood. It was time to put aside grief and shame, to endure for the sake of others.

She waved her hand and pulled through a wooden armor stand, its pegs adorned by a full suit of polished steel. It was identical to those worn by Guardians of old, because it was from them she had taken it. Each piece had been enchanted by powerful wards from long ago, from a time when the magic hunters used a magic all their own. The runic protection woven along and into every plate was intended not only to defend against turners but inhibit their abilities as well.

She conjured faeron magic, the rainbow light and silver sparkle of a soul at one with nature. It swirled in her palm, a flickering and fading shadow of what was once a healthy shimmer. Like tossing a stone, she flung it toward the armor and directed her *furie* by will alone. In a splash of dying color, like the wispy blooms of a dandelion, her magic struck and burst away into failing motes.

The reverberation swelled out with enough force to sway her hair and dampened dress, battered her senses and left a pounding in her ears reminiscent of a time in shackles. Suppressed beneath the onslaught, her magic was no longer of any use. She could barely hear the echo of her own thoughts, let alone summon light *furie* to her will.

Patience ended, her body erupted in a furor of ebon waves and a translucent corona of shadow fire. The din receded from one beat to the next, dispersed to a deadly quiet and brimming ire. Grim defiance and baleful gaze, her hatred gave rise to a palpable force, an inferno of dark *furie* that whirled out and around the ancient magic safeguarding the armor. Her fevered will stripped it bare, corroded runes and wards in a bubbling flash of dusky wildfire.

Once the Guardian enchantment was eaten away, the shining steel beneath dulled and blackened with the stain of an unforgiving decay. An unstoppable blight, it rotted the alloy with terrible speed, cracked its surface in fine lines and thick breaks, left a wake of deterioration with no hope of escape. Steel crumbled as it passed, fell apart as brittle flakes, consumed and corrupted beyond the limits of existence. Within moments, it was all gone, bright armor and wooden stand alike.

All that remained was her fury and the intense need to spread it further.

She sent her will through to Danarriden and pulled a young demon from its hatchery. The leathery whelp let out a snarl of surprise, a throaty rumble that ended in narrowed eyes and a barbed tail poised to strike. Liquid fire dripped from the extended prong, a caustic poison no doubt, and was ringed by smaller spines that spiraled down to a prickly patch across its abdomen. A thick layer of mucus ran the edge of its snout, fell over a gapping maw with jagged teeth three rows deep. Its brutish arms were bristled with pale bone as well, from the tufts of wiry black hair at its shoulders to the curved talons at the end of both fingers and thumb. There were no legs to be seen, just the bottom of its plated torso in the waters.

Like a wild animal, it shook its head with a furious challenge and charged.

Her first impulse was to use the mists, to speed her body out and back in just behind it. She had practiced for hours against weapons and armor of various shape, size and material. This was her first living target, and though fear fluttered at her insides, the angry fires rising up from within pushed it aside. She quelled the urge to pull blades through to either hand and attack, instead steadied her nerves with a breath, brought will to bear and loosed the dark *furie* in a torrent of flame.

The first instant smashed the demon into stillness, stopped dead its momentum and held fast its seething mass, like a sparrow flown headlong to a storm. The next moment came the wailing, the torturous outcry of one in the clutches of death. Its spines eroded to blunted nubs, hair fizzled outward to ash, mucus bubbled over flesh in the midst of a crumbling wither and ridged plates began to crack beneath the strain. The third and final moment saw complete disintegration, a spreading burst of ember in collapse carried onward in the gale. The lasting echo of its passing endured and faded in a downfall of flaking remnants.

A premonition broke her focus, let fall her hold upon the fire and sent her to all fours. The dark *furie* had left, but the burning inside her kept on. The waters hissed and bubbled as they cooled her, sent up fading wisps of smoke and lent her strength while she struggled with the pain she had chosen and the glimpse of a likely fate she had not.

*It stepped through from the Dark, another creature of his making, small like an umbral but spiderlike in many ways. With no understanding of how or why, she knew it to be a valkstrun, loosely translated as spirit anchor and burrowing fear.*

*It had four concaved pits for eyes, atop a cavity that served as both ears and nose. Its mouth was hidden in a pocket beneath a chitin beak, with three short tendrils of midnight black on either side. Eight legs, like an arachnid, jutted upward and back down, protected by thick plates and layered in coarse, beryl hairs. Its bulbous, fleshy body was sheathed in a ridged carapace. Small runes glowed violet across every chitin surface, up each length in steady rows and round each curve in finished rings.*

*The valkstrun dropped its middle to the ground with great force and plunged pincer legs deep into the sphere of earth corrupted by its touch. The halo of blight crept inexorably further out but spread downward at a much faster pace. When it touched upon the intersecting ley lines, the creature began to gorge on golden* furie *with an insatiable lust. Its runes grew brighter, a piercing glow of violet doom, until at last it could take in no more. Cracks spread along its carapace, spilled lilac phosphorescence into a trail of pooling blood. It let out a prolonged shriek that trembled its changing frame, split open to a dire quiet and transformed into a living ley stone.*

*The darkstone thrummed and shot out a nimbus of violet* furie *in a sluggish, steady rhythm that continually fed the rift, caused it to gradually grow in size. Six more valkstrun came through, surrounded the first in a wider pattern and began to fuel their metamorphosis with a sickening voracity. When their conversion was complete, the violet pulse grew, brightened and quickened its pace, sounded like the vibrations of an unearthly heartbeat. The rift expanded four times taller and half again as wide, large enough for a dragon to pass through unimpeded.*

*An immense creature lumbered through, shook the ruined ground with its bulk, and bellowed a clarion cry for the many waiting in its wake.*

*She knew Revyn was amassing an army, to secure that foothold and others like it. She had no way to be certain when the premonition would come to pass, only that it would mark the start of a terrible end. Her vision rose up and viewed the landscape from above. The blight continued to spread in all directions at a steady pace. It would be just a matter of time before it reached villages and towns, entire cities, the whole of Taellus, before it threatened to take from her the one she held most dear.*

Despite the fresh lesions beginning to fleck both her arms, Fluora stood with renewed purpose and returned to her task. She would master the dark *furie* or die in the trying.

Grimly determined, she practiced all the harder.

\*   \*   \*

It was late when Barr sat down at the fountain to scry Fluora in its water. The shimmer of nighttime runic light reflected off the surface in gentle eddies, a stark contrast to the worried turmoil that'd been churning his middle with each hour passed and her still gone.

*You're making my stomach nervous*, Idelle said and left off picking at her stonefish. A dozen or more warblers and finches, who'd been patiently waiting, descended with all speed to finish off what remained. *You're more anxious than Aren before morning meal.* Fortunately, he and Kaela had returned to Geilon-Rai to sleep in the pens, else his feelings might've been hurt. *And lunchtime, supper, snacks, the occasional second supper or when anyone mentions honeycakes.*

*Be nice.* Barr had been trying for long minutes but was unable to pierce the veil protecting the mists. Unless Fluora was elsewhere, hidden by powerful wards. *I can't help being concerned when she's been gone for this long. She didn't even say she was leaving.*

*Does she need to?*

He knew better than to step into that one. *Of course not, but it would've been nice, polite. She'd be upset if I just up and left without a word.*

Idelle scoffed. *You do that all the time! To me as well!*

Barr ended the scry. *Is that why you're suddenly on her side in everything?*

*There are no sides, you dolt.* She laughed, and her tone softened. *Nothing's changed. She's still the same Fluora.*

*That's just it*, he said. *Plenty has changed. It's not safe for her to be off all alone. With Revyn attacking more and more... It's just reckless and unnecessary.*

179

*She must have her reasons,* Idelle said. *Besides, she couldn't be anywhere safer than the mists.*

Barr wasn't so sure about that, since it depended on what exactly she was doing there. He'd been wondering about the mists lately, in light of recent discoveries, like what set it apart from other places. Was it another plane of existence or a realm all its own? If it existed here in the Light, did it have an equivalent in the Dark? His mother had called it a gift from Saernol, a place between realms and a source of great magic. She'd spoken as if it were meant only for the faeron, but others were able to use it at will – when permitted by the Matron.

That was another issue that bothered him. Why was there need for an emissary of sorts, and why has it always been a woman? From what he'd been told, the Matron kept at bay any umbrals that sought to break free of the Dark by way of rifts opened momentarily when anyone traversed the mists. That's quite the design flaw, considering who had created it.

What if Saernol *hadn't* created the mists, though, but had merely shared her discovery of it and called for a Matron to prevent other races from using it? He could ask her, he supposed, but doubted her answer would be forthright. The notion of it having existed before the children gods led him to another.

*What if the mists weren't an actual place,* he began to ponder, *but a shared construct of the mind or a living conduit like the Mirror Pool?*

*But you've been there,* Idelle pointed out. *How could it not be a place? The Mirror Pool is a place.*

*I meant not an actual, physical place,* he replied.

*But you've* been *there.*

Barr let out a heavy breath, as he tried to explain. *I've been to the ether and astral, but neither of those are physical places. The environment of another plane alters the body of those who enter, changes its very nature – or at least tries to, which may or may not cause damage. That's what I think happened to Revyn, when I forced him into the Dark. It didn't unmake him, like with the shiardin who come here and burn. It remade him instead, as if he were now like one born to that realm.* Barr shook his head at the multitude of new questions rising up but put them aside for now. *I don't think he's trapped there at all, but I also think returning here won't change him to what he was. That body is forever gone.*

*So he can come back whenever he wants?* Idelle then asked a more troubling question. *What happens when he does?*

*I can't say for certain,* Barr answered. *Whatever his plan, I suspect he's been taking his brothers and sisters, one by one, not out of vengeance but necessity, to remove any hindrance. They're all that could have stood in his way.*

*Not all,* Idelle disagreed. *You'll find a way to stop him. I know you will. You can be plenty a hindrance when you want to.* He laughed at that. *What about the mists then?*

Their discussion had gone off path, but he recalled the original line of thought. If the mists were a magical construct, he should be able to see its glyph. He just needed to know where to look. On the other hand, if it were like the Mirror Pool, a conduit grown sentient over time, he could figure a way to make contact and reason with it.

*Just that I don't think it's the mists protecting her from scry,* he replied. *I think Fluora's purposely hiding.* Before she could start another argument, he added, *Not from me, in particular, but whatever she's doing there, she doesn't want anyone to know about it. You saw how strangely she behaved.*

"There you are!"

It took him a moment before he realized it was Sera, the demon hunter. In homespun clothing, unmarked by divine runes, bereft of holy fire, she seemed so much smaller than the fierce woman he'd once seen faced off against a demon. She looked exhausted, weakened and somewhat defeated. He'd been a hunter before, knew well the pains she'd endured since her Awakening, but she was free now, set loose when Curoch passed. He should have felt glad for her, and yet he couldn't help but share in the remorse reflected back in her eyes.

*She doesn't look so well,* Idelle said, *like she hasn't eaten in... ever.*

"Evening," Barr said, friendly but solemn. This was not the time for pleasant smiles. "Were you looking for me?"

They hadn't spoken much, not since she'd killed his uncle Therol, while under Revyn's thrall. Heavy breath and shaky legs, she must have been searching for some time. Whatever the dilemma, she certainly appeared in earnest.

"You weren't here when I first checked," she said, still winded but settling. "Good thing I circled back." The way she worried the ends of her shirt, looked away and down from his gaze when it held her eyes for too long, gave the impression of nervous guilt. He began to wonder if she'd done something wrong. "It's about the geas..."

*Ah,* Barr said, *that's why she's so anxious.*

*What do you mean?*

*She's going to ask if I –*

"Can you bring it back?" Sera must have noticed she was fidgeting, balled up her hands in tight fists to stop. "I – I want it back." She held out both forearms for him to see. "It's still there, I can feel it. I'm guessing you can see it too. It's just... asleep, and I want to know if you can wake it up again."

Idelle's surprise matched his own. *Is she serious? I thought being a hunter was a terrible curse.*

*She's afraid*, Barr replied, *would rather the pain she knows than the uncertainty of what's ahead.*

"I know it's difficult right now," he said, "but things will get better. You just need time to adjust."

"To what," she said bitterly, "being normal? I know what I am, what I've become, and nothing will change that. I'm telling you the runes are still here. Will you just look!"

Barr glanced down at her arms but didn't need the bare flesh to see the runes of her glyph. A large portion in the ether was dormant, like that of the children gods made mortal. The geas wasn't a blessing or a curse, not a spell or an enchantment, not divine will or some grand magic inflicted upon her. It was a fundamental part of her being, like the immortality of gods. It could no more be taken away than it could be given to another. It was simply in her nature, from birth to the grave.

Unlike the gods, however, her grayed runes weren't masked. They were emptied of all *furie*, passed through to the Dark and returned without change. It was Curoch who'd fueled the geas, with *furie* drawn directly from his spirit, and connected all five hunters together. With their link to him severed, there was nothing to be done for it but find another source.

He looked more closely at the overall collection of wards and spinning runes, wondered if the geas could be linked to another spirit or possibly to the ley lines. It also meant the other hunters would be reawakened. Perhaps that's what she'd seemed so nervous about.

It was then he caught sight of a second glyph, one faint, much smaller, but there all the same. The way it folded out and within almost made it indistinguishable from her own, but Barr had grown used to discerning complex glyphs, recognized what should and should not be there.

"Well?" Sera said, her patience wearing thin.

"It's possible," he replied with reluctance. "I'm not sure how long it would take me to figure a way, but I'd have to talk with the other hunters." At her deepening frown, he added, "You're all linked. I can't reactivate yours without affecting theirs. It means the geas will carry on past your lifetimes." He paused to let that sink in a moment. "You'd be condemning future hunters."

"There's no need for talk," she said firmly. "I'm here on their behalf, after a lengthy discussion. I'd not have come looking if we weren't all in agreement and ready to aid in the fight against Revyn." It was her turn to pause for effect. "You *need* us," she said, fervent but plain. "If you hope to stand any chance of surviving this next war, you'll do what's right. We hunters have saved countless lives since the first, scouring Taellus of any and all demons. We're not *condemned*. We're needed!"

*She's right*, Idelle agreed, *we could use all the help we can find.* She could sense Barr's unwillingness. *Would it be so wrong?*

He sighed inwardly. *It's not our place to make that decision for people not yet even born, no more than it was Curoch's. Those he put in harm's way had no say in the matter.*

*But these five do,* she insisted. *They've already made their choice.*

*It's not them I'm concerned for.* "Alright," he said, "let me take another look."

Barr took a step back and seemed to focus at the space above her head. His eyes trailed over runes she couldn't see, through a circuit of wards within the glyph of her life. Again, he saw the second set, a dimmer pairing that looked both a part and separate all at once, as if a piece of Sera had pulled away to form an entirely new glyph.

*What?* Realization dawned, but he was shocked, too disbelieving, to give it voice. *It can't be...*

"What's wrong," Sera said more than asked, her tone suspicious. "You said you could do it."

Idelle asked, *What is it?*

"You're with child."

Sera blinked, taken aback, but then narrowed her eyes as if insulted.

"I'm not stupid!" she said and nearly growled. "I've been barren since my Awakening. Hunters can't have children!" She took a threatening step forward, as if she might strike him, but visibly forced herself to calm. "If you don't want to do it, fine. I'll ask one of the arachon –"

"No," Barr said, "I'm not saying I can't or won't do it. I'm telling you there's a child, and I have no idea what activating the geas will do to it." He saw tears well at what should've been happy tidings but knew the inner turmoil she now faced. "Inflicting the geas on hunters yet Awakened is one thing. Are you willing to risk the life of your unborn child as well?"

Sera was quiet and looked away, conflicted emotions plainly writ upon her face. After moments, she shook her head and swallowed hard, as if forcing down a decision she was loath to speak.

"I've always wanted a child," she said, let tears fall unabated, "but the battle with Revyn is lost without us."

Idelle said softly, *Barr. You know whose child it is.*

*I know.* He fought back his own emotions. *It's not my choice to make.* As much as it pained him to say, *Nor is it his.*

"There'd be no world left," she went on, with a dread finality to her tone, "for a child to be raised in."

Sera wiped her eyes and squared her shoulders. Her mind was made up, body tensed but ready. She took a deep breath and let it go, shaky as her resolve, and gave Barr a firm nod of understanding.

"Do it."

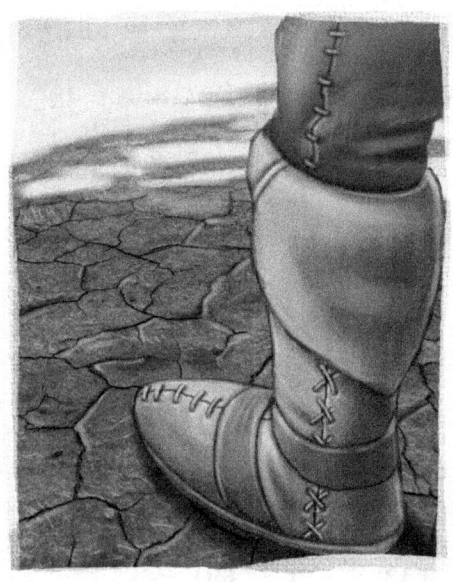

# – 7 –

arr and Saernol returned through a portal in early morn, from biting winter and bleak loss to springtide warmth and a bitter truth. She was all who remained of the children gods made mortal and likely would not last the day. Shiardin had poured from the rift in dark waves, a midnight tide that crashed against and through waiting hunters. For every darkspawn brought down by sunlight weapon or spelled defense, two had taken its place and twice again turned. No amount of power or preparation, pitfalls or perseverance, could have held at bay such an onslaught. Death and anguish had filled the air, drowned out the din of battle, for terrible hours on end until at last Balsina fell. Once she had passed, no more shiardin came through, and the rift left them all to the growing stillness of aching failure. There were no wounds to tend,

187

only those who had survived and the dying ashes of their brethren.

All had suffered loss, the Ballar and their hounds, the arachon and shapeling hunters, but he imagined none had felt it quite so keen as the once goddess. She openly showed a measure of sorrow and frustration, but what she held back, the many lifetimes worth of love for her family, the horrible fear of what had become them and the certainty she was next, left Barr wordless at even trying to comprehend it.

They sat together in quiet solace, as he waved the portal closed.

Idelle had gone back to Geilon-Rai with Aren and Kaela. Three Ballar and four war hounds had died in the battle. She knew he needed comfort, though he would never admit it. Barr had felt Aren's loss as well, wanted nothing more than to lie beside him in the pens until he slept, but deep worry over Fluora had won out. Not only did Barr want to be sure she was alright, he needed her to allow him into the mists. Every moment spent at any task but understanding the Dark runes, learning to undo the shiardin or close the rifts, was yet another chance for Revyn to strike. There was precious little time left before Saernol was taken, when what Barr believed was just a step in a mad scheme was complete.

He dreaded to think what followed after.

The need to act rose up within him, an urgent pull without direction. He had only one plan in mind, and it hinged on the mists.

"I should go check on Fluora," he said and felt even worse that such a small moment of respite could not be spared.

Saernol put a hand to his shoulder. "She is not yet home. I would offer to help scry, but we both know where she is."

Caught off guard at the remark, Barr wondered if she meant there was no need to look or that neither of them could pierce the mists. It seemed as good a time as any to find out just what Saernol truly knew about her gift.

"Are you able to allow me in?"

She regarded him with those dark eyes and relented with a smile.

"You are far too clever, child," she said, and her gaze seemed to drift for a brief time into the past. "Though I wish it were otherwise, you know I cannot."

Barr considered. "Could you go there yourself, right now? Do you need her permission?"

The question seemed to upset her, as if he'd aired a painful memory.

"In my current state? No more so than you." Her voice was tinged with sorrow and regret. "At my best, I could not force my way in, but there are other less artful measures I might have taken."

"Such as," Barr prompted, tried not to sound quite so dubious.

Again, the guarded look that both gauged his worth of the knowledge and the inner scrutiny that seemed to question if it should even remain hidden.

At last she replied, "I might have usurped her bond with its spirit or forged a new one of my own. Neither of which is a pleasant prospect, I assure you."

*So it is like the Mirror Pool.*

"Is there a way to contact its spirit directly?" Barr asked. "If I could explain –"

"No," she said in gentle interruption, as a mother to a child discussing issues meant for adults, "not in any way you or I converse." She appeared to be searching for the right words. "To do what you ask requires first having an open dialogue with your own."

"I – you can talk with your spirit?"

Saernol closed her eyes, gave a remorseful smile and single shake of her head.

"At one time, yes. Not anymore. It would seem that connection has gone with my immortality."

Barr wondered at the correlation. Was contact with the soul a right reserved for the gods? He'd never before considered trying, had no idea it was possible.

"I'm sorry," he said, found it difficult to imagine such a loss. "There has to be a simpler way. I need into the mists, sooner the better. You know what I plan to do." At her nod, he added, "I thought as much. We have no time left, and I don't see any other way to stop Revyn." Loath as he was to say, let alone admit its necessity, he said, "If the only way into the mists right now is to wrest control away from Fluora –" he hated himself for thinking it "– then that's what I'll have to do."

"Easier said than done," the once goddess warned, in a tone that seemed to say she did not envy him should he try.

Fluora appeared amidst streamers of pale wisp. She looked ragged, exhausted and once again haunted by the horrors of premonition. He felt power emanate from her body like never before, a thrum that touched his middle and set both ears to tingle with a slight ring. The noise faded at the same moment he noticed she was without a blindfold. He couldn't help but wonder if this newfound interest in exploring the depths of her abilities as Matron had anything to do with her stubborn insistence on saving him from a vague, uncertain death.

Her timely arrival made him wonder if she'd heard.

"You've been gone a long time," he said and walked over to hold her close. "Are you alright?"

She pulled away and regarded him with an oddly angered scrutiny, as if he had insulted her somehow.

"Why would I not be?" She adjusted the sleeves of her dress, further annoyed. "Because of the blindfold? I decide when to wear it."

He didn't understand her behavior but assumed it had to do with her mother and a distinct lack of sleep. He reached out to take hold of her arms, to offer comfort and support, but again she pulled away.

"I know this is a difficult time," he said, did his best to understand. "You had me worried is all. I didn't know for sure where you were and couldn't reach you in scry."

Somewhat mollified, her frown lessened and body eased. She looked away, as if ashamed at her reaction. Barr leaned in and kissed her softly.

"I missed you." Another kiss, and he said, "Don't tell me you wouldn't be mad if I left without a word."

Fluora pursed her lips in consideration. "I can recall quite a few times, actually."

It was good to hear her laugh, to see a smile light up her face. It filled his heart with joy and a warmth that cast aside all concerns.

"There's something I need to ask you," he said and indicated Saernol seated at the wooden bench. "With all the others gone, we've run out of options and time. I need into the mists, if only for a short while."

Her mood darkened with suspicion. "Why? So you can watch over me? Keep me safe?" He took hold of her hands, refused to let her slip away, with a gentle resolve, and looked calmly into her eyes until she saw the truth. Quieter, she said, "I can take care of myself."

"I'm well aware," he said playfully. "I have the bruises as proof." His tone grew more somber. "This isn't about you or me. It's about stopping Revyn –" he squeezed her hands – "and none of us can do it alone."

Fluora nodded assent. "Alright, it is done."

When they embraced, he thought she winced, though she hugged back all the more. Her body trembled with the effort, further evidence of exhaustion. She let him go and gave a tender, lasting kiss, one that slowly yielded all her tension to welcome ease.

"You should rest," he said, glad to see her but keenly aware how weary she truly was. If only her mother would see to reason. Fluora paused at his thought, and he knew she had heard. "Is she still refusing Fezuul?"

By her demeanor, her considering gaze, it looked as if Fluora wanted to share a terrible truth. Barr guessed she already knew her mother had no intention of changing her mind.

"Obstinance runs in our family," she jested and left for bed, let her fingers trail his palm before reluctantly letting go.

Though she said nothing of him aloud, Barr knew she'd meant her father as well. Once Fluora was inside, he turned back to the once goddess.

"A few bites to break fast," he said, "then I'm off."

Saernol said, "She is far more troubled than she is telling. It is rare for any Matron to possess that much power."

"Fluora's always been strong," Barr said, "but she does seem to be finding her own of late."

"Such people," she said, in a cautionary tone, "tend to have strong emotion and poor restraint."

He balked. "That's not Fluora at all."

"No, I expect not."

Barr wasn't sure if she was offering a sort of warning or reminiscing about her past, maybe about Revyn. He felt the urge to get working, while still there was time to act.

"You'll be safer near the portalis," he said, uncertain if she planned to stay or return to Tempas. "The arachon will guard you with their lives."

"What a waste that would be." Her smile faded from wistful quip to one of solemn resolution. "Come," she said and patted the seat beside her. "Before you go, I shall teach you all I know about the language of creation." In a mindful tone, she added, "Lest knowledge of it disappear alongside me."

\*　　\*　　\*

Dhar had skimmed cloud and current halfway across Taellus, soared between the peaks and stony pillars of the northern steppes, sped through the scalding air and fiery plumes of the lava pits at Harandor, reveled past the runic walls and enchanted elements of ankaran city ruins, dove into the shadows and jagged clefts within the depths of Evergorge then climbed out the other side atop the snows of the Great Spine. He had flown without rest, pushed both body and wing to their glorious limits and set the night skies alight with the grand fires of a first child of Curoch. When at last he had succumbed to the need of returning home, to the urgency of pressing war, he bid his father farewell and turned wing toward Naerat Sanae. Though his tribute had ended, his loving memory would live on.

A traveler had brought him back to Dwendorim, and his only thought as he walked home, over cobbled roads smoothed by clay, down flowered paths of colored pebble, was a longing for Sera's touch. He hoped she fared better with her loss than he and was ready to lend comfort in any way that she needed. Just days ago, he would have considered his feelings foolish and improper, expected better of himself, of a Patron, but he had been reminded of late how precious time was – regardless of the rings in one's horns.

Sera caught him by surprise, might have even been stalking him, before she leapt out from behind a cherry tree in full bloom. Taken full on, Dhar was forced off the path and down to the heavy grass on the other side. She was atop him in an instant, wicked grin and wild laughs, as she pinned his arms and locked his thighs. Her runes and strength returned, he scarce had time to take notice or give breath to voice before her mouth was upon his in a hungry kiss.

"The geas," he said, with some difficulty at breaking free of her affection. "Does this mean –"

"No," she answered quickly, then more gently, "no, sorry, it's not Curoch. It was Barr."

Hopes raised and dashed in an instant, he felt the hollow cold take hold in his chest once more. Sera kissed him again, tender and understanding, expressed a deep desire he both admitted and would no longer restrain.

"It gladdens me to see you happy," Dhar said and let the warmth of her smile broaden his. "I thought of you as I flew."

"And now?" she asked, with an indelicate grasp.

"Sera!" Eyes wide, he looked about for others on the path or in the field, which only amused her more. "This is not a bedroom," he pointed out, to which she playfully bit his lower lip, "nor are we in private."

"I noticed," she said and continued to smile down at his modest discomfort. She pursed her lips and leaned back, folded her arms as if in thought. "What could we do to remedy this situation?"

As much as her boldness shocked him at times, he could not help but share in the joy of her zest and even admired the zeal with which she lived out each day. She was the piece of his spirit left behind so long ago, a fervor forever clumsy on his own but a work of grace and subtle peace found in the pairing.

Dhar bucked his legs free, rolled Sera to her back and held fast both arms above her head into the grass. Her strength never ceased to amaze him, incredible for a human, divine blessing or no. She would have pulled free had he been anything less than a dragon. Her tendency to calm, to completely relax every muscle, before tensing with an explosion of will without notice, was utterly and wonderfully maddening.

"We could leave the city," he offered, knew the only thing greater than her promiscuity was her passion for ending demons. Her eyes widened in impish joy at the prospect. "Is that a yes?"

She tossed him aside like he was a child.

"Race to the portalis?" She was already running as if her life depended on it, trailing shameless laughter and an as yet unmet challenge. Her taunt was barely audible as she rounded the path. "You're losing!"

Dhar growled and changed in an instant, took wing and flew past with enough force to bowl her over. She rolled forward to compensate, kept balance, and resumed her run with hardly a missed step.

"Cheater!" she yelled, words fading fast behind him.

It took quite a few moments before she caught up, where she found him lounging on a bench, head and arms splayed back as if basking in the sun. He should have known better and supposed he deserved the jab to his middle. Sera rolled her eyes, took firm hold of a hand and led him toward the travelers and merchant wagons.

"You owe me for that," she said, maneuvered through a crowd of milling arachon and alixhiran. "Ooh!" She grabbed a golden apple from one of the carts and took a bite. "These used to be my favorite."

"Hey!" The vendor fumed as they hurried passed.

Once they stepped through the portal that took them down into the portalis chamber, they found even more people coming through from Alixhir. Mostly merchants and tradesmen, the only guards in the crowd were from Dwendorim. A massive destroyer stood at either side of the portal, and two full companies of arachon kept all safe and steadily moving in an orderly fashion.

"Should we go to Alixhir?" Sera asked. They could have gone anywhere, by simply asking a traveler, but one of the largest cities in all of Taellus was just footsteps away. "It might be fun."

Sera pulled him through before he could answer, not that she would have heard him above the commingled din of banter and barter.

The other side was impressive, if but a bit burned and broken from the shapeling war. Dhar recognized it as Miller's End, once an integral and thriving part of the merchant district. Though the area had seen better days, looked rather hastily repurposed, its size and service were evidence of flourishing wealth and means, as well as a great source of pride for the Merchant's Guild.

The first and only permanently established piece of the portalis hub, the Alixhir portal was heavily guarded on both sides. Though none but the armored golems were allowed within, there were still half a dozen arachon safeguarding the portal from this end.

Sight of the city watch and hired swords, workers and tradesmen, merchants and hawkers, all manner of citizen shopping for wares, only reminded Dhar just how poorly he had been treated during his time here, when he called Alixhir home and was still apprenticed to Barr's uncle Therol. Looking back with both old and new eyes, he saw all too clearly the cruelty of men, what had become of the anaire and how ashamed they would be of their unfit descendants.

Thought of Barr, now one of his closest friends, also made him aware of their potential, that an entire race could and should not be judged by the acts of few.

Despite reason, he was struck with a feisty notion.

"I should change," Dhar said, with undertones of a growl, "right here, before them all."

Sera slipped the fingers of both hands firmly into the neck of his leathered tunic, all the permission he needed.

With a quick look about to gauge room, Dhar took his native form and rose up far above the startled crowd, with Sera in tow. A slight misjudgment of distance sent a stack of crates behind tumbling over and clattering their contents across the cobbles. Sera slid down his neck in unrestrained laughter and settled in the nook of a ridge. Lost in the excitement, she spurred him on like a horse, which drew a perturbed glance of saurian eyes.

A single snort of hot breath set her right.

"Go already!" she yelled back.

Dhar gave a roar that shook loose debris from stone buildings all around, shattered icicles along their perch under awnings and rooftops, sent snow billowing out in a ring from off the ground and put the unprepared down to their backsides. The sounds of panic ensued but fell away to muffled cries, beneath the rising winds and her enthused wail of a war call. He shook her with a chuckle and banked sharp toward the west. Something acrid had caught his nose and lingered in the air.

Smoke darkened the haze of heavy storm clouds in the distance, set the gloom in further shadow and ashen streamers. By the scent and sight, an entire village had been put to torch and left to burn.

"It's not a demon," Sera called up against the gust, "aren't any for hours out."

A mighty thrust sent them racing forward, through chill wind and a swelling flurry, with the tingle of magic augmenting their speed. He felt Sera grip her legs tighter around his neck, fingers clenched onto scales and the heat of her pressed firm against him. What would have taken the city guard hours by horse passed by in scant minutes, as icy ground and barren trees vaguely blended with fields and farmland. The devastation came into view and sharpened to a terrible clarity.

The village had been razed, with everyone still in it. Nothing remained but charred earth, the ashen wattle of homes and remains of those who burned where they fell. There were no flames left to speak of, just the crackle of dying embers and plumes of listless smoke.

"This happened before dawn," Dhar said, more than familiar with fire and its means. "Why has no one from the city come to investigate or lend aid?"

Bodies had been cruelly impaled to the cold earth, their spears jutting out, still smoked like grim candles. Some had clawed in vain at the ground to get away, a clear mark the wounded had been left alive for the fires.

"The bastards who did this," Sera said in a grave tone, tried to mask a sob, "are no better than demons."

Dhar circled once more, surveyed the surrounding woodland, fields and hillsides for any sign of a passing force. The farmland had been burned as well and salted out of spite.

"Whoever slaughtered these people," he said, "they hold a bitter grudge. There will be no reclaiming this land for some time."

Sera pointed toward the trees.

"There!" she fairly growled. "I can sense them!"

Though he trusted her abilities, Dhar saw no sign of campfires, smelled nothing of man or beast not already burned. The snow leading to her mark showed no tracks, even accounting for a fresh fall. Rather than question her insight, he gave wing and approached from on high.

Within moments, it was if they had passed through a veil of fog. Suddenly Dhar could see the heat of a hundred bodies, men adorned in the leathery scrape and metal clank of worn armor. Their scent was marred by soot and blood, with the musk of a lupine rancor. Dirtied bandits, every one, more animal than man, they were undeniably to blame for the vicious carnage.

The men sat upon fallen trees and rock around three different fires, where horse and hog had been spitted. Their raucous laughter grated in his ears, their fetid and drunken breath an assault on his senses and the lot of them reeked of death so thick it fouled the air.

Liquid fire rose up from his middle of its own accord, dripped from his maw as he plummeted to the ground. He broke earth and men apart in a billowed outburst of bloodied snow. Those unfortunate enough to survive the initial blast, the buffeted force of body against unbending bole, were left dazed amidst the resonance of shattered ears and surging terror.

"You!" one called out, a thick man in a wolf's head. He climbed shakily to his feet. "I know you!"

Sera had flipped backward through the air before he landed, came to rest in a crouch once the burst of earth and limb had passed harmlessly underneath.

Dhar recognized the voice.

"You're the traitor," the man went on, exuding *furie* and a brazen mien. "Have you come to join us?"

Khulfa's laugh was one of triumph, as if Revyn had sent a gift. Few of the others joined in, all of them once shapelings, their mirth weak and justly nervous.

Dhar spun with all his might, a few hairs above his mate, and swiped the deadly bulk of his barbed tail in a devastating circle. Through trees and armor, it shredded wood and men in yet another upheaval. Their splintered remains rained outward from the crack and cry of dying knells.

Sera snatched a large sliver to each hand, imbued them in ghostly runes and rushed forward for the living. She drove both deep into either side of a soldier's neck, pulled free his sword from its scabbard and cut free the next man's forearm, his weapon still clutched in hand as it fell. She leveled a kick to his middle, sent him reeling back into another and spun beneath a frantic strike from behind.

"No!" Khulfa shouted. "You *will* join us!"

Voices sought to enter Dhar's mind, echoes from his past in a ringing dulcet of pleading. He shook his head to clear the shroud, to shake off the nagging spell, but it clung to his weakness. It was her voice, Eoraini, just as he remembered, every lilt, every joyous play. He wanted to hear her again, to fall back into that painful bliss, and became embattled with himself within the spell.

"Lift me," she said, his first mate, his true love, once more in human form, as she was before the fall. Gladly, he did as she asked. "Bring me closer to your heart."

"Eoraini," Dhar said amidst a sob of despair. "I am so sorry. Please," he begged her, as the blade slipped ever so gently between the scales, "forgive me."

The world erupted in holy fire, engulfed her with its grasp and licked the edges of his spell. Her head jerked back by the roots, where sunfall fled to black, and the warmth of her eyes turned gray. Gone in an instant, her visage was replaced with the maddened fear of a wolf, the wide-eyed countenance of a killer. The blade in his own hand was forced across his neck, parted flesh and spell in a dark spray, a furious warmth across Dhar's palm.

His vision cleared as Sera tossed a lifeless Khulfa to the ground far below. Her eyes were stained with tearful anger.

"How badly did he hurt you?" Distraught, she ran a hand over his wound, stemmed the flow as it healed. "Oh, good. Good!" She breathed a heavy sigh of relief against his chest. "You had me worried."

Dhar brought her up to his gaze. "Not to fear," he said in a stoic show of playful charm. "I am not so easily dispatched, with the company I keep."

She leaned her elbows against him and stared up from between his nostrils with a most dubious look.

"You're a damned fool, sometimes."

"Agreed."

"But you're *my* damned fool," she said, "and I'll have words with any who speak the contrary."

Dhar had no desire to argue the point.

\*　　\*　　\*

Barr instantly noticed the changes. Wisps of fading gray still clung to his body, as a chill wind blew past and took root in his middle. There were storm clouds in the distance, marring the usual clear view of starry black. Lightning flashed out in bright, jagged strikes, lit their rolling edges in shadow purple amidst the dark. Thunder rumbled muted tremors, a low grumble on the horizon that grew to a crescendo and died away within a breath. It shook the cool waters in wheeling eddies toward his legs, lapped up against him and seemed to take warmth instead of give. A heavy scent of ozone hung about, the air charged with enough force to set arm hairs on end, and the stars overhead were more cobalt than silver.

*What's going on here?* Barr wondered, concerned the stormy visage was further proof something was amiss with Fluora, that whatever she'd been doing here was now manifest in the landscape – or it was the other way around. *Could something have altered the mists, and now it's affecting Fluora?*

*Revyn.*

Even more resolute, he conjured the mists, took hold of the rift and let the streamers fall away. A gateway to empty black, the tear between realms looked more a wound than suspended portal. Barr moved to one side and waited. It wasn't long before he heard the familiar clatter and click of umbrals, the chittering that gnawed at both memory and nerve.

One poked its eyeless head through, all inky chitin and tapered ears, tentatively felt at the rift's edges with long talons and snuffled at the air. Its mouth gaped open in a keen then snapped shut as it listened. Its behavior was vastly different from what Barr recalled of their last encounter.

*Why's it being so cautious?*

The umbral began to climb, its limbs a nightmare mix of shadow vapor and hard shell. Just as it moved within reach, the creature paused and snapped its face in Barr's direction. Its ears twitched in unison, as if it searched for a sound no other could hear. It took quick, successive sniffs, and in that moment he knew it had scented his *furie.*

Before it could act, Barr conjured a spell to shield his arm and grabbed the umbral by its neck. The creature scrabbled against him with all fours, sought to rend the flesh from his bones and *furie* from his enchantment. He let close the rift and struggled to keep its midnight claws from ripping open his stomach. The barrier flashed blue with each strike and grew weaker as the umbral fed off its magic.

Barr called a short burst of *furie* to his other hand and crushed a storage crystal. Its pieces fell away like dusted glass, scattered in the breeze and in an instant became a glyph. It was an enormous collective of silver runes and golden *furie*, intricate wards interspersed with a fine webbing of woven sunlight. The shield about his arm nearly drained, Barr forced the umbral within the glyph. Captured midair, it fought against the sunlight bonds to no avail. Unable to move, feebler every moment, all it could do was keen and soon enough had little left for even that.

He'd known the umbral would be easier to study if it couldn't resist and had spent many hours working on the glyph. The result was better than expected, though Barr detested any time lost. Each hour, Revyn drew ever closer to his purpose, and nothing and no one was ready to stand against him.

Barr looked closely at the unconscious umbral, saw its body wither and slightly burn beneath the glyph, but in the sections without sunlight, the damage was only minimal when compared to what shiardin had suffered that night in Greywood.

*Maybe this* is *a place between*, he surmised, *not fully in either realm but partly in both.*

He began searching for a Dark rune to help shift his focus, found one and followed it through. The sharp pain behind his eyes, the throbbing at his nape and overall queasiness in his middle all lessened with great practice. For his plan to succeed, he'd need to shift focus at will, as he did with the Light deific runes.

Learning their other half would have to wait.

Time went by without food or rest, as he sought the subtle nuances between realms. To shift focus required more than knowledge of the deific runes. He had to seek the different planes before him, find a way to distinguish one from another and adjust his eyes without straining. It was similar to past lives, like raugrin and celedharrin, who could see in more than a single spectrum. The move from one to the other was both a physical and mental effort, and their young spent many years becoming adept at the endeavor. Barr couldn't afford such a luxury, but neither did he need it.

Before long, he could call to mind the shades and shapes of the Dark planes, their sense and semblance of contrasts, in concept and in deed. Though it still took a bit of effort to shift his focus between, it no longer pained him to do so and he hoped in time would come with ease. He had no need of the Dark runes to spy their realm anymore, could see them rush to fore when his eyes adjusted, but he was no closer to knowing their purpose or full potential. The mere thought of it wearied him and left him longing for rest. Despite the desire for warm drink and a warmer bed, Barr pressed on with the task at hand and began to memorize each new rune.

His eyelids began to droop, heavy for lack of sleep, before he gave any wonder to how long he'd been at study. It took more time and effort than expected, to store and sort each Dark rune in his mind, and even then he doubted the umbral's glyph held every one. No creature in the Light did, at least none he'd encountered, so he assumed the same of its counter.

With an abrupt shake of his head to clear the haze of encroaching slumber, Barr started a new glyph to test interactions. Not only did he want to be sure he had each rune in proper order, of purpose and strength, he needed to determine if this half of the divine language functioned exactly like its opposite. If so, it would be a simple matter of finding correlations.

*If not...*

Barr sighed and rubbed his eyes.

He had no memory of what happened next, as the black of sleep rose up to claim him.

Chill water lapped against his ears, tingled the tips of each finger and sent a shiver from tailbone to nape. He blinked up at the clouded skies, purple tinged storm and ominous grumbles, and was puzzled by how quickly they had moved in. He conjured a chair and pulled himself into it with some difficulty. His muscles were sore, but their ache was a mere twinge compared to the knot in his stomach.

*I must have dozed off,* he thought and dried himself with a wave of warm *furie.* His clothes dried easy enough, but the rolls in his pocket were ruined. *Or collapsed from exhaustion.* He pulled an apple from the other pocket and took a bite. The umbral looked worse for wear, still alive but a bit ragged, and his practice glyph showed no sign of deterioration. *Now, where was I...*

He got to his feet and picked up where he'd left off, where one moment he was weaving a simple base into the core and the next he was on his back, confused and wet. Long hours passed by with creating basic wards in a rudimentary glyph. Luckily there was little difference in functionality between the realms. There were obviously missing runes, but he found those as well by shifting focus and studying the Dark planes. One after another, he wove wards, tested numerous variations against each other and broke them down before starting anew. He was finally ready to incorporate Light runes when a wave of dizziness blurred his vision.

Barr was exhausted, again, his body on the verge of another collapse. This time, he wisely chose to listen and took a seat. He knew a rest would do him good, but sleep was not an option. He thought the work too important and was convinced it was key to stopping Revyn.

He pulled a waterskin from his pack and drank as he watched the child's play glyph he'd forged twirl in air. After a few bites of soggy meatpie and dried fig, an idea came to mind as he pondered why Dark runes suffered damage in the Light. It didn't seem so the other way. Or perhaps he'd never been able to take notice of it before?

He went to the glyph holding fast the dying umbral and followed close a single Light rune as it passed into the Dark. It left empty from the Light astral, depleted of *furie*, and entered the Dark physical, where it was filled in an immediate burst. An empty vessel, the rune had been replenished in a surge of golden *furie*, but he saw signs of immediate decay on the outer surface as well. Just as Dark runes bubbled in the Light, this one too lost the silver edge of its sheen and began to simmer in the waves of deep violet. Once its course was run, back into the Light, the runic surface showed no corrosion nor was it marred in any way.

Barr was convinced if it'd stayed in the Dark, the rune would've eventually dispersed into nothing, just as the shiardin had.

*If Dark runes behave the same*, Barr deduced, still somewhat confused, *then why don't they fill with* furie *too?*

This time he chose one of the umbral's runes, locked sight as it hissed and bubbled through the Light astral before passing with no change back to the Dark. Barr set aside his frustration, determined to find an answer, and kept an even closer watch as it went through all three planes. First physical, then ethereal and astral at the last, he was surprised to see a shimmer of power fade with each one, like pulsing shadow flickering out to full black. It was when the rune passed from the Dark astral into the Light physical that he saw it, for the very first time, a dull flash of muted fire, black flames difficult to differentiate from the damage the Light caused.

*It's opposite*, Barr realized, with the sunken feeling of one who'd been a fool. *No wonder I couldn't see it. I was looking in the wrong place!*

Over and over, Barr watched Dark runes pass fully faded from their astral and flare with dark *furie* in the Light. It was a circulating system, carrying a disparate form of life essence. The two realms were interconnected, each a mirror image of the other. He imagined them as two halves of a whole but found the image troublesome, inaccurate. It implied they existed in separate places, like an hourglass or a sphere cut in two.

Barr was beginning to believe the Light and Dark shared the same space, at least to some degree. There were just aspects of both he was physically ill-equipped to sense.

When he shifted vision between planes, he saw them as similar to sheets of vellum pressed tightly together. Moving from one to the next was then like flipping pages in a book. All three were places he could go, yet he saw them without having moved.

That was a change in perspective, not location.

It was no different for the Dark. He could see its planes without scrying or leaving the Light. Portals and rifts were used to travel between planes and realms, like a bridge across water, but parts still occupied the same space.

Barr had a difficult time fully understanding his own notion, but it was his lacking that lay at its very center. It was akin to living in an existence limited to length and width, like a flat surface, then finding there was a whole world of height he could suddenly sense, if only in part.

*Just like discovering another set of deific runes.*

The longer he thought on it, the more it made sense. He looked down at his hands, at his body, his own glyph, and saw the spent runes pass empty into the Dark. They returned filled with the golden light of *furie*, from the source of all life in the Light, just as this realm provided sustenance for the Dark. Contrary to what he'd thought, the two realms were not at odds but were dependent on each other.

Neither could exist without the other.

He understood life, in that moment, like no other of his past incarnations. He saw everything as it truly was, the bond between realms, the divine language as a unifying force of all things, and with that insight came realization of the danger. He could manipulate the sigils within a ward, the wards within a glyph, the essence of any life, and alter its being.

Barr scrutinized the prone umbral suspended in air, watched its glyph slowly turn within the enchantment, its body gradually unravelling in a state of decay. With the ease of reaching out his hand, he touched a single rune between his fingers, at its core in the Dark, and halted the glyph. Frozen, utterly helpless, the creature was at his mercy. A single twist would undo the entire structure and crumble the umbral to ash.

He knew this could be done to any one, any living creature, anything of substance, and decided the deadly knowledge was far too dangerous to ever share.

Barr freed the unconscious umbral, opened a rift to the Dark and placed the creature gently inside. He stared into the black, what he once thought of as an empty void, and briefly wondered what might happen if he stepped through to face Revyn.

*     *     *

When he returned to Dwendorim, Barr was tired to the bone and looked forward to a much needed rest. Late morning, by the runic light, he was surprised but happy to see Fluora resting outside their home on the wooden bench. In a sea colored shawl that covered all but her hands, she appeared painfully drawn, terribly saddened and uncharacteristically defeated.

*Where have you been?* Idelle asked, her tone snippy but relieved.

*In the mists,* he replied, *studying Dark runes.*

Idelle flew in from the southern courtyard and took perch upon the fountain.

*Couldn't you do that here?*

*Not without killing the umbral.* Barr looked around and saw no sign of anyone else. It seemed all too quiet, but he admitted his senses were rather dulled by fatigue. *Where's Aren?*

*With Kaela, of course.* Done with berating, she added, *We've missed you.*

Fluora finally stirred from whatever musing had been troubling her and caught sight of him. Her eyes lit up with weary joy, smiled bright but made no move to rise. Instead, she beckoned for him to rest beside her. He took her offered hand, sat down and gave a kiss, a prolonged touch of affection that left him wanting more. When they opened their eyes again, it was clear to Barr she'd been crying.

*She's been like that all morning,* Idelle said.

"We have failed," Fluora said in answer to his worried observation. "I saw it coming, saw it happen, and was powerless to help."

Fluora seemed fragile in that moment, her hand in his weak, as if she'd lost hope and given up. He gave a squeeze of reassurance.

"You can't make yourself responsible for every dire premonition," Barr said. "There's only so much you can do." Her nod was noncommittal. "What happened?"

"They – they are all gone." Her voice caught at the memory of it. "Saernol, Tempas and his hunters. Revyn has three rifts open at this very moment, permanent footholds nothing and no one can even reach without succumbing –" she grew angry and clenched a fist, shocked Barr with the burst of *furie* he sensed well up within her "– to his ravenous blight, yet another of his diseases loosed upon the worlds."

*Worlds?* Barr thought. *Is Revyn attacking somewhere other than Taellus?*

"What happened to Saernol?" he asked. "Did shiardin enter the city?"

"No," she replied, "when you did not return, she went to aid Tempas and fell beside him. Dozens of those foul creatures poured from the rift." Her eyes looked haunted, as if she relived the memory as she spoke. "Even with your enchantment, the hunters stood no chance once Tempas was torn apart. It seems Revyn had no use for him or wanted his beloved taur to see him fall."

"The geas ended with him," Barr surmised.

"And with it all their lives."

*I was there*, Idelle said, her voice heavy with loss. *We all were. There was nothing we could do.*

"Why didn't you come for me?" Guilt overtook him, regardless of how crucial his findings in the mists were. "I might've –"

"What?" Fluora snapped. "You are not the only one with magic." She blinked back her anger with a frown, must have realized the outburst was unwarranted. "What you were doing was important," she said, more softly but adamant, "and I thought I could handle it on my own." Fluora looked away, clearly ashamed. "I was wrong."

"I didn't mean there was anything I could've done you aren't capable of," he said, equally fervent, "but I'm always here for you, to fight beside you. Together we're stronger than either of us ever could be alone. There is nothing you can say or do that will change my love for you." Barr took hold of her chin and gently forced her to look at him. "No secret, no shame, no anger or fear. I am and always will be yours, in this life or any other."

She kissed him deeply, happy with tears, and he felt the tension in her body slip away.

"You have been gone," she said, "over three days. Did you learn anything from the umbral that can put a stop to Revyn?"

Three days. Stunned, he had assumed his time there no more than a single day at most.

"I think so, yes. You saw what I was doing?"

Fluora said, "I see all in the mists, whether I want to or not."

He wondered if the children gods were still alive, if the Dark had changed them yet or if Revyn was twisting their spirits to his own design – the way the Dark had twisted his.

"Can you show me one of these footholds?"

With a nod, Fluora took them through the mists, to a barren icy field in the once lavish plains east of Garand. They stood far enough from the rift that he could barely see the violet glow of its flames. Though difficult to gauge at their distance, Barr estimated its height at thirty feet and less than a quarter as wide. There were over a dozen darkspawn around it, of varying size and shape, and they seemed unaffected by the Light.

Had Revyn found a way for them to survive in this realm? Or a means to ward against it? They appeared to be guarding the rift, made no move to engage Barr and Fluora, but it was possible they hadn't yet sensed the new arrival.

Barr looked down at the ground before him. From where he stood, all the way to the rift and around, it was blackened, broken and dead. The decay continued on, crawled toward them at a slow but steady pace. It was as if Revyn's will had seeped through and was spreading its corruption outward like a plague. He stepped a foot into the blight and felt the immediate drain on his *furie*.

"No!" Fluora yelled and pulled him back. "Have you lost all sense?"

"We have to get to that rift," he said and shook the numbness from his foot, "somehow and soon. No matter the cost."

Her anger began to rise, but she held it in check.

"That price is not yours to give."

Barr saw her resolve. "Fair enough. But one way or another, we're going to have to cross through the blight."

He knew he could survive it if he continually healed himself, just doubted he had the strength to do so for very long. Using ley lines was not an option, since the corruption spread down to them as well. What he needed was a closer look, to determine if he could close the rift from where he stood. He wanted Idelle to fly over it, but Fluora had left her behind.

Without a thought, Barr brought her through.

*You've been gone* three *days*, Idelle scolded, *and then leave at a moment's notice, again, without me? I've got a mind to drop morning meal on your shoulder!*

*Sorry*, he said and tried not to laugh, *I wasn't the one who brought us here.*

He expected Fluora to giggle, but she didn't look at all amused. In fact, she seemed –

"How did you do that?" she asked sharply, her voice accusatory. It dawned on him then, that he'd brought Idelle through the mists without going to her first. "Even I cannot do that. Not from outside the mists."

Barr felt as if he'd insulted her, as if she saw what he'd done as a show of disrespect, had in a way belittled her authority as Matron.

"I'm sorry," he said, both heartfelt and concerned. "It wasn't something I gave any thought to. I needed Idelle, saw her in my mind and brought her through. Are you sure you can't do it too? Maybe it's just never occurred to you to try." He put his hands to either side of her arms, but she pulled away from his touch as if he'd physically hurt her. "Why are you *so* angry with me?"

Fluora rubbed her forehead with a trembling hand, visibly fought for control of her emotions.

"I am not. Forgive me," she said, smiled weakly and took his hands, "please." At his nod, she kissed him, a short but sweet apology. "Being Matron is more than just a title. It is who I am, who I have become. To see you use the mists in a way I cannot... is frustrating."

"You can," Barr said firmly. "Let's put this aside for now." The encroaching blight had reached their feet. He stepped back and pulled her with him. To Idelle, he said, "I need you to fly over the rift."

Until then she'd been careful to avoid it.

*Are you sure it can't touch me up here?*

*No,* he replied honestly. *I hadn't thought of that. If it's moving outward like a sphere, it should be going upward as well.*

Fluora disagreed. "I think it is feeding, not spreading like a poison. Perhaps she could skirt the edge, to test its voracity."

*I'll give it a try.*

Idelle flew over them, where the blight ended, close enough and at a speed that momentum would see her past should she be affected. Barr breathed a sigh of relief when she circled back unharmed.

"She's fine," he told Fluora. *Could you head toward the rift? I need a closer look.*

*Alright,* she said, *but I'm not flying any lower. Those things haven't spotted me yet.*

The darkspawn were similar to shiardin, in that they had protective chitin shells over limbs and torso, but few walked upright. They looked more nightmarish animal than man and had the smoky haze of movement like an umbral.

The rift was a mass of utter dark, a pulsing shadow encircled by violet flame. Apart from the creatures, there was a uniform spacing of black rocks, like small boulders cracked asunder. Each was ringed by a purple vapor that crept along the blackened earth, and they emanated *furie* with a palpable force.

"Ley stones?" Barr seemed to be peering off into the distance but looked through Idelle's eyes. "They must be feeding the rift, keeping it open."

Left unchecked, he knew, it would continue to grow larger and its blight spread ever outward. The immediate area around the rift was darker as well, as if the soil had become one with the planar tear. There was a flickering along its surface, like lightless flames amidst the fog, that reminded him of Dark runes being replenished in the Light.

"It's dark *furie*," Barr realized. "That's been his plan all along." At Fluora's questioning look, he said, "Revyn isn't trying to break free of the Dark. He's trying to bring it here with him. He'll destroy everything, even the Dark. Neither realm can exist without the other."

*How can he even do that?* Idelle landed on a gnarled branch, in a lone and leafless dale tree. *And what's that mean for us?*

"Without some way to undo this corruption," Fluora asked, "how will we be able to fight those creatures, let alone get close enough to destroy the rift?"

"I don't know," Barr replied to them both. "The blight isn't enchantment or disease. It's another realm bleeding into ours."

*If you can't stop or undo it,* Idelle offered, *maybe you can weave a protection spell.*

"I need time," he said, "to figure something out. All I can say for certain is, whatever we do, we're going to need help. We knew this war was coming. It's one of the reasons we revived the portalis." Fluora slipped a hand into his. "It'll take more than the arachon to fight toward those rifts. We need the other kingdoms, and we have to convince them to fight, long before the blight reaches their doorstep."

"I can persuade them," Fluora promised, with steel in her voice. "I will get us to the rifts. It will then be up to you to close them."

Barr nodded agreement and conjured the mists to carry them all home.

"It's time we called in some favors."

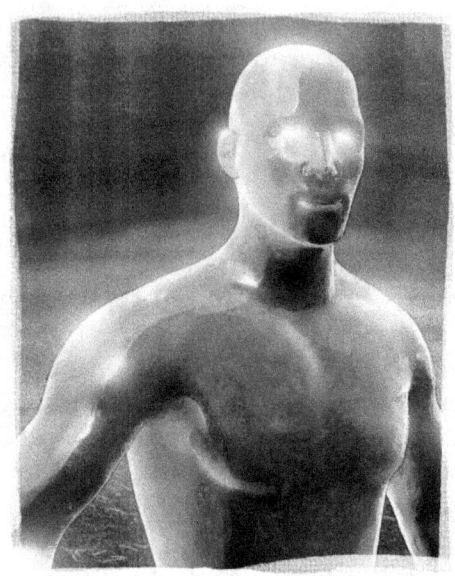

## – 8 –

luora conjured detailed images of each to mind, recalled how she had seen them last, just as she and Barr had practiced earlier at great length. She even took it a step further, had no intention of bringing them through one at a time just to risk interrupting her concentration with their inevitable protest. She had neither the time nor inclination to wait on the niceties of decorum, to offer each in turn a formal invitation and then endure the ensuing din of their racial and royal grievances. No, none would welcome the abrupt intrusion or appreciate being stolen away, but she simply had no choice. They would either cope or cry out.

Too much was at stake to care which.

She relied on premonition and past scries, for those she had never actually met. The few whose fate she had glimpsed were somewhat easier to form. Their image was not clouded by her own memories but instead enhanced by the shared emotion of having seen through their eyes. It was an impression like no other, a brief union only another oracle might have understood.

First to mind was Queen Arianaolis, her dark tresses and sky blue eyes, the sullen contours of her brow, the upturned cast of her regal nose, the pale sparkle upon her cheeks to full lips and a dimpled chin. At her arm stood Asaen Fezuul, the Arch Demon whose chiseled form looked a cooled ember blown to life. His clear black eyes rested beneath the crimson ridges of an emotionless brow, appraised all and found it lacking, gazed out at the unworthy and found solace in himself.

Next was Tuvrin, Barr's father and newest Speaker of the Sun. The stoic elf bore deep sorrow much the same as his sylvannis mantle, in careful and quiet measure, behind a veil of steely emerald. Though hardened by time and loss, his eyes retained a glimmer of hope, if not for himself then for his people. It was much the same with Teldein, Speaker of the Stars. Gray braids and pale eyes, the elder elf had guided the wyndorrin through trying times that saw an end to entire bloodlines.

Around their images went the mists, a swirl of wan tendrils that rose from will and the waters, continued on about the rest within her mind.

Adrean, shamarrin High Priestess and Speaker of the Dark, stood defiant and deadly in the face of a fallen god. At the bottom of the devaeryn, within the ocean city of Anoran-Rai, Kaeran helped fight back those Revyn had turned. Beautiful and brutal, the illysidaen Speaker of the Moon struck out with *furie* in one hand and a barbed trident in the other.

Vardikor clan chiefs swelled the line, blooded allies from the battle at Drakanon, and were joined by their distant brethren, the sankragga and krevallen. Be they king or queen, chieftain or spiritual leader, the row of powerful figures kept on until it comprised the combined might of nearly every nation upon Taellus and beyond. Once Khrona, the hotheaded red dragon Emissary, came fully to mind, Fluora finished the ranks with human kings and respective leaders from the Brotherhood and finally the Guardians. Not that they were less important than any other, she just disliked the magic hunters and had no desire to hold their faces in her thoughts for very long.

A hundred paces safely away from a spreading circle of blight, once again upon the frozen plains, Fluora put forth her will and brought them through. One by one, in quick succession, they appeared within a swirling spiral of mist, caught in the middle of whatever they had been doing.

Ruork Stonefist came through first, flagon in one meaty hand and a leg of lamb in the other. His fiery beard, ale-stained and littered with crumbs, bristled wide down over an oiled chain vest. His surprised look at Fluora and the wintry field was soon trumped by the sudden appearance of Lorrik Ironbeard crouched beside him. The red-faced chieftain hurried to pull up his leather breeches, but Ruork had already seen enough to spark a fit of laughter. He spit lamb and dark ale out over the sparse earth and leaned heavily on his cousin's shoulder as he struggled for breath.

More arrived, equally confused by the sudden change of locale as the raucous dwarven laughter.

"What is the meaning of this?" Adrean demanded, as yet others still emerged. Something must have prickled her senses, because she turned her head sharply toward the rift.

The Speaker's indignation was mirrored, in manner and word, by many others as they arrived, but Fluora's concentration did not waver. While most were startled, a few were glad to see one another and exchanged greeting in their custom. Within moments, all were present, and the combined clamor of their disapproval and discontent was enough to drown out the chill wind.

Those who had noticed the corrupted earth muttered amongst themselves or pointed to the violet fires and dark creatures in the distance.

"How dare you!" Khrona growled, caused Hunters to nervously draw their blades. His roar quieted the grand assemblage.

"Stop that this instant!" Queen Ariana snapped. Her voice echoed with power, drew narrowed eyes from the red and was met with an insolent grumble of challenge.

"Tread carefully," Fezuul warned the hatchling.

A clattering, high-pitched keen drew attention to the blight behind and a number of darkspawn at its center guarding the rift.

"What has happened here?" Tuvrin asked, just as bewildered as those who mouthed similar questions.

"Turners!" the Marshal Hunter spat.

"We don't know that," brother Dalwyn chastised. "It doesn't look of our world."

King Ferrel of Garand stepped forward. "I demand you return me at once!"

"I as well!" Hammond added, the stout King of Noria.

Knight commander Vaumont said, "We should at the least hear her out."

"Fools," Speaker Kaeran uttered none too lightly of the bickering humans, which drew a chuckle from Teldein. She crossed her thin but muscled arms in defiance when they glared her way.

"Behind you," Fluora said, her voice clear and with an air of authority, "is the reason you are here."

"Just who the cogs are you!" Farndle shot back in a gruff tone. The gnome Warden was slight of frame but not the least bit intimidated by those around him. "And why should I listen?"

"I am the one who brought you here," Fluora said, a steely edge to her voice that seemed to indicate she just as easily could have dropped them in a volcano, "and you would do well to heed my warning."

"What warning is that, lass?" Durok Ireheart asked, rather politely considering he had been stolen from his bed and still wore his night clothes. "Is this your doing?"

"No," she replied, knew they were all frightened and confused, even insulted, "it is not." She wished there was more time, that she could have done this another way. "Revyn strikes at us from the Dark. He seeks to undo life on all worlds and remake them as his own." Mention of the mad god was enough to stir not so distant memories of the shapeling war and its devastation. "Though this threat is not yet upon you, I can promise that none will be spared."

Khrona scoffed. He turned without a word and went into the blight. The scales of his foot were first to lose their luster, grayed and grew dim of life. He breathed fire down at the blackened earth, where no snow had left its mark. The molten sputum ate away soil and rock but had no effect on the corruption. As far down as the fires went, the earth was already in ruin.

To his credit, it took many more moments before he was sufficiently drained enough to fall.

Disappointed, Fluora had worried for the dragon but quietly hoped he would fare better. She pulled him to her through the mists and knelt at his maw.

"It kills all that it touches," she told him, with a gentle touch to his snout.

Weak but not defeated, Khrona lifted his head. "You have my thanks." He looked back at the spreading blight. "What is it," he asked, "and how do I destroy it?"

When Fluora stood with fists clenched in frustration, dark *furie* rose up about her hands then faded as she calmed. Queen Ariana was not the only one to take notice.

"We do not as yet know." Fluora faced the gathered men and women. "All I am truly certain of is that we cannot sit idly by." Adrean had drawn closer, seemed to scrutinize her as she spoke. "We must act and act soon, for Revyn will not wait."

The Speaker of the Dark approached and took hold of Fluora's arm. Though she did not try to remove the shawl, the sharp recoil it evinced was enough to confirm suspicion.

"You wield its power," Adrean said, so none of the others could hear. Whether in admiration or accusation, Fluora could not be sure. The High Priestess regarded her with an uncomfortable intensity but made no further attempt to touch her hidden skin. "And it is killing you."

Fluora stood firm. "Would you do any less?"

The Speaker gave a slight bow of her head in respect, a subtle indication she would not.

The Lord High Hunter grew angry. "How are we to fight creatures of the Dark if we can't even stand the same ground, let alone reach them!"

Adrean moved to stand at Fluora's side.

"We are still devising a plan," Fluora explained. "We are not yet ready to face them. What I need from all of you is to put animosities aside and give your word when the time comes you will join us on the field."

There were grumbles and glares shared among those who had warred with each other in the past, especially between the humans and elves.

Arch Demon Fezuul said, "You mean to empower your demon hunters with my presence."

"Not all of them," Fluora replied, and her eyes grew momentarily distant with premonition – *Sera bolted the door, turned and faced the others with grim resolve* – "but yes, your presence alone would be of significant use against Revyn and his forces."

Fezuul raised a brow. "Provided you can keep them from trying to kill me."

"I can make no assurances," Fluora said to them all, "not to any of you. All I can promise is I will fight and die by your side before I let Revyn destroy our homes."

Vaumont cleared his throat and asked, "How will we communicate or coordinate our armies? I assume Barr and his statue friends will want to place portals in every city."

Fluora nodded. "The arachon have designed a system of portals that all lead to a central hub in Dwendorim. With your permission, as has been done in Alixhir, they will construct a portal for your people as well. A number of you have been approached with this offer but have not yet agreed." Her eyes scanned the lot of them to gauge their willingness. "Please, now is the time."

King Tamyr agreed. "The portals are secured by forces on both sides and large enough for merchant wagons. The commerce alone has brought my people a much needed respite."

"Sorry as I am to say," Fluora said, a bit sheepish, "it would be far more difficult to send you back than it was to bring you here. I do apologize for that, but this is the perfect opportunity for you to see the portalis. Once in Dwendorim, travelers will take you anywhere you wish."

Ariana came over as the other leaders began to talk amongst themselves. She motioned Fluora a distance away and frowned at what she must have known lay hidden beneath the shawl.

"How long," the Queen asked pointedly, "do you plan to risk your life by remaining Matron?"

"Long enough to stop Revyn," Fluora replied in truth, "or until I die in the trying."

The hard set to Ariana's eyes softened to sadness, as if to say she had just lost someone dear and had no desire to see that friend's daughter die as well.

"I find it hard to believe," she said, "Barr would allow this. You have not told him."

"And neither will you. I need no one's approval," Fluora said, both of Barr and her Queen. "As much as you disagree, without me as Matron, this war is lost before it can even begin."

Ariana moved to say more, but Fluora sent her and Fezuul back through the mists to Starshrine.

"I said it would be difficult," Fluora murmured, to no one in particular. "Not impossible."

\*   \*   \*

Barr sat in a wooden chair that had hours ago grown uncomfortable, before a heavy table he'd moved outside onto the cobbles. He scrutinized a new glyph, one of over a hundred done so far. It belonged to what was once an iron ingot, stealthily borrowed through the mists from a blacksmith in Noria, but was now a melted mass of inky shavings.

Aren shifted his bulk and stretched, sprawled atop Barr's feet. They hadn't spoke of it yet, but ever since war hounds were lost in the battle at Greywood, Aren didn't like being alone. Moreover, when near Barr, he clung like an anxious pup. His dreams, while napping, had been fitful.

"I need a workshop," Barr said aloud, not for the first time, and for Kaela's benefit. He could hear her thoughts when Aren or Idelle were nearby, but as with Fluora and his companions, Kaela couldn't hear his. She put a paw on his knee and gave a questioning look. "No, not to get away from any of you." He finished changing the ward and let it go. The pile of iron shards rejoined but didn't transmute to copper, nor did they take shape as a rough edged ingot. Barr sighed down at the uneven plate, like a black sheet of vellum with the pox. "I just need more room to work with. And more materials. And a place to put it all."

The large table was littered with a number of other not-so-successful-but-not-quite-failed items he had experimented with. There was a puddle of what used to be wood, a sticky powder of cloth, a gummed residue of steel, jagged rings of dense crystal, leaves of pure jade and a stone with the supple texture of skin. In most cases, Barr simply undid the glyph to clean up, but these few he wanted to study further – if he ever had the time. Idelle had questioned whether he should toy with nature while rifts were spreading destruction across Taellus, but he asserted this was their best chance of combating the blight.

If he could change it, they could walk upon it.

*You should rest*, Kaela said, *or put your mind to a different task.*

"This is too important," he said and rubbed his eyes.

*Sometimes our thoughts get stuck*, she said, *and we think like a mallet when we should be shears or a spade.*

"I'm a mallet?"

*Sometimes*, Kaela amended, *but not all problems are nails.*

Idelle laughed. *What do you know of tools?*

*I have eyes*, Kaela said, *and I put them to good use. Do you not observe others at their tasks?*

*Not if she can help it*, Aren said and yawned.

Barr toed him in the ribs. "Be nice."

*I wasn't saying you're not observant*, Idelle said. *It just struck me as odd to hear a war hound talk of tools.*

Kaela settled in beside Aren. *Since the rebuilding, without Valar to shape the trees, I see far more of tools than I would like.*

"I could try to fix the sunlight enchantment," Barr said. "There won't be time to reweave on the field, and constant use will only break the glyph down faster."

Idelle said, *I thought you took care of that already.*

He undid the iron's glyph and wiped its ashes off the table. With a quick hand, he began to scrawl the sunlight enchantment from memory.

"Saernol helped me find a way to prolong the effect," Barr explained, "but the glyph still fails eventually. The new reduction conduits are just a temporary fix."

Unlike the entrapment glyph he'd used to hold the umbral, this enchantment needed to continue absorbing light in order to expend it. He knew the answer lay in reworking the conduits.

Aren suggested, *Why not make them so they change, depending on what needs doing?*

"Wards don't work that way," Barr replied. "They can only serve one function. I had to add a new substructure to make these change when they collapse."

*So they can change.*

"To a small degree, yes, but the ward will eventually break apart. The only way to do what you have in mind is if multiple wards had..."

Barr's words trailed off as the thought took flight in his mind through a whirlwind of supposition. His eyes scoured the runes, saw through each plane and found the room he needed in the Dark. He began to scrawl at a furious pace, tried to keep up with his racing thoughts, altered the ward at its core and linked it with another.

*You figured it out?* Idelle asked.

"We'll see in a moment," he said and finished the two new wards.

Joined at a shared center, a sphere of silver beauty, both wards moved together in perfect time, in a natural harmony, like two halves of a whole.

"There." Barr sat back to admire his handiwork. "Two separate wards, sharing the same base structures. That means they essentially act as one ward but can have two functions."

*It is magnificent,* Kaela said and followed the silver glow of runes with her eyes.

Aren yawned again. *You're welcome.*

*How does it work though?* Idelle asked. *What makes it any different from before?*

"I was trying to squeeze too much into one space," he said. "With more room to breathe, I was able to weave a second ward and link them at their base. Now when the conduit gets overwhelmed from absorbing light, the next ward is activated by the excess *furie*, transforming it into a storage node. It then stops absorbing light. Once its *furie* is depleted, the ward deactivates and reverts to the first, becoming once again a conduit." Barr chuckled at the seemingly simple approach to a complex dilemma. "Thanks to Aren, the only limit now is how many of these I can fit in a single glyph."

*See?* Kaela jested. *A rested mind leads to answers.*

Aren narrowed his eyes at her. *That had better be a compliment.*

*Of course it was.*

*So,* Idelle said, trying not to laugh at her brother, *we can destroy the shiardin. Now, how do we close the rifts?*

"I have an idea about that, actually."

Barr wiped away the glyph with a wave of his hand and started work on another. This time, rather than alter an existing material, he wanted to see if he could create something new.

"Shiardins are like umbrals," he explained as he wove. "They feed off *furie,* absorb it like my enchantment does sunlight. It evens heals them. But," he added with a sly smile, "they can also be overwhelmed by it."

*Like the demons,* Idelle pointed out, none too happy of the memory, *at the rift on Faeronthalsos.*

An odd substance formed on the table, a black ring like quicksilver or depleted mithrinum.

"Exactly!"

*You nearly died closing that rift.* Idelle was growing angry, though her tone was lost on Barr. *Or have you forgotten the burns that wouldn't heal?*

The metallic liquid pooled to a small puddle as he continued to adjust and add wards in both realms. Its surface rippled to a hard shell with a shimmer of glowing purple.

Aren sighed. *Not that I enjoy agreeing with her, but how are you going to use that much again without, oh I don't know, killing yourself?*

It resembled the chitin armor of a shiardin but with a violet metallic sheen at its edges, like the thorax of an amethyst beetle readied for war. For a brief moment, as he wiped away a base ward, the surface fluttered and looked like the flesh of an illysidaen. He tried to recreate the ward, to see what had caused the change.

*Well?* Idelle pressed

It was no use. He couldn't duplicate the result.

"I know," he said, recalled all too clearly his damaged spirit and didn't want to risk using his own *furie* like that again. "I've got something more powerful than myself in mind. Before we try that, though, I want to use what I've learned to rework my kyan."

Kaela asked, *Is there time?*

*There's already three rifts*, Idelle agreed, *and they spread with every moment. Who knows how many more he'll open before long.*

"This is especially for Revyn," Barr said and unmade the glyph. He cleared the table of ash and added, "For him, I'll make time."

*       *       *

Sera rested against the wide bole of a hornbeam, lost in the reverie of doubt and regret. She wore a bare set of borrowed combat leathers, enough to cover modesty but not impede movement. Though she had no real need of armor, it felt good against her skin, reminded of the coming battles and usually kept thoughts on the task at hand.

But these thoughts were too heavy to cast aside.

She placed a hand over her belly and wondered at the life growing inside her. It was one thing to see it in others, watch their eyes alight and manners brighten at the mere notion of bearing a child, and a very different matter to undertake it. At times she thought she could feel it within, though she knew it was far too small to cause notice. Other times she feared her choice had cost the child's life, when the emptiness of disbelief left her barren once again.

Barr had done his best to ward the unborn child against the geas but also warned it may not have been enough. There was some comfort in the measure of many lives over the one, in gauging her sacrifice in blood. At least until chilling realization fell upon her once again, no longer hidden by delusion and forced before her eyes by unshakeable introspection.

Her choice had been a selfish one, with no thought or care to anyone else. The geas had left a hole not even a child could fill, let alone the heart of a single man. Her love was but a ruse, a self-deception born of dread. It was the distraction of borrowed power, a flimsy veil for her pain, a weak bandage for her loss. Why else would she have chosen the geas over the life she had always wanted?

Sera caught her scent before she saw her, a flowery mix of mountain sage and lilac, daylily and peony. When she came into view, runic sunlight struck the pale length of curls and nearly set them aglow. Her eyes were bright as a full moon on a winter night, her bearing strong at the shoulders, and her shapely form beneath the dress had a sensual appeal. Her very presence made Sera feel all the smaller, a self-loathing wretch in the shadow of a quiet truth.

Her insecurity turned to anger and resentment.

Sera rose and walked past, without a word or second look. She wanted to brush up against her, to unsettle such perfect beauty, but didn't trust the resolve of her own desire.

"He cannot love you," the woman said, in a familiar voice that once echoed through the vast caverns of a mountain city, "not like he and I can."

"Kaolanni?"

Sera stopped and turned, gave her a shrewd look of appraisal and confusion. It should have occurred to her that other dragons could take human form. She just never expected to see one besides Dhar.

"I do not begrudge him," Kao said, tone both sad and respectful, hurt but not accusing, "this passing romance. It is easy to grow enamored of the flame that burns all the brighter for its brief span."

"Why are you here?" Sera asked.

She didn't expect a fight from the silver but neither did she discount it.

"To give you my blessing," she replied, "and a tender warning. Your pairing is inappropriate, in the eyes of my kind, and wholly unsuitable to flourish."

"I'm unsuitable?" Sera scoffed. "I don't have the time or inclination to deal with your infatuation. If he wanted to be with you, he would."

She turned and headed for the tea shop, where there were more children to be dealt with.

"You may bear his love," Kao called after, "for a time, but you will never bear his offspring."

Incensed by the audacity, Sera shot back a retort she knew one day she'd regret.

"Don't be so sure!"

She found them some time later, already well into their cups. The four reeked of bitter stout, unwashed clothes and unmasked cowardice. News of the coming war had spread through Dwendorim. An embarrassment she couldn't stomach, the others had made it known to their hosts they refused to join the fight.

Though no arachon had spoken it aloud or openly held them in contempt, Sera knew what they were all thinking but were too polite to voice. The demon hunters had grown weak, hidden safely in the city, and would rather others fight for them than risk their own blood ever again.

Sera stood in the open doorway and looked on each of them with clear disgust.

"You!" Carem shouted angrily at the sight of her. The others turned bleary eyes her way and let show their anger as well. "You're the cause of this, aren't you? It's because of *you* we're cursed again!"

Maelor slurred, "I've a mind to kill you myself."

"You're welcome to try," Sera offered. "I'll be on the field, against Revyn, where you lot should be!"

"Please!" Talburn threw his half-filled mug against the wall with dreadful aim, and it shattered to pieces in a foamy spray. "Spare us your sanctimonious drivel. I've killed demons with my bare hands, and I'll be damned if some rail of a wench is going to tell me when to fight. I'm done with it," he added, "and there's not a rutting thing you can do about it."

"I would help," Hamon said with reluctance. He took another swig and wiped his mouth on a sleeve. "Really, I would, I – I just can't anymore." He looked up to her with the frightened eyes of a child seeking solace. "I haven't slept in ages, the nightmares..." He went on, despite Carem's laughter and Maelor's foul look of derision. "I just can't. I'm sorry, I truly am."

"So am I," Sera told them all, "because no one will be allowed to sit this fight out."

"Allowed?!" Maelor roared, got up to his unsteady feet and looked as if he might fall over in a rage. "You don't control us! No one does! Not Curoch, not the geas, no one!"

Carem crossed his arms and leaned back against the wall, as if to say he wasn't moving, and smiled at her with the boastful grin of a drunken lout daring her to try.

She leveled a deadly gaze at him and let it pass over the others as she spoke.

"There will be five demon hunters on that field when Revyn and his shiardin break through to kill us all."

Sera bolted the door, turned and faced the others with grim resolve. She picked up a wooden stool, tore off two of its legs and instantly imbued them with her touch.

"One way or another."

*       *       *

*Much faster than she knew it would occur, Fluora watched from on high the bleak future of Taellus. Earth and rock fractured beneath ravenous corruption, let go their hold on root, shoot and bole. Decay led the way for darkened ruin, a browning wilt that stole all life in a deadly blossom of bitter certainty. Nothing withstood its grasp, not creature or plant, naught of any substance. Worse still than the inexorable blight radiating outward were the hundreds of darkspawn left free to roam the tainted land unharmed by the light.*

*Dozens more rifts had already opened and started to spread, with new ones tearing through the realm barrier every moment. Revyn's children scrabbled through in all manner of nightmare forms. Shiardin were his scouts, clawed across the blackened landscape with a terrible speed. Once valkstrun secured the rift, waves of kourai stepped past and took their place upon the field. Heavy soldiers, naturally armored, bladed limbs made each one a living weapon. When the rift grew large enough, they moved outward in packs to make room for the garaenu, lumbering monstrosities like walking siege. Deiken swept in after, winged horrors that flung dagger-like barbs from their long tails and regrew the projectiles in an instant.*

*There were others of varied task and ability, but each shared the same purpose. They were meant to transform the whole of Taellus, turn the land and all its life, or tear apart its stubborn remains.*

*She looked down upon the frenzy of corruption, the wide circles of blight spread across lush and barren land alike, over emptied settlements and the poor souls caught unaware, and saw purpose in the chaos, sound reason in the sum of seeming madness. There was a pattern to the rift placement, with a goal that could only be seen from the vantage of an oracle.*

*At the center of it all she saw the Mirror Pool.*

Fluora forced away the premonition. She still refused to wear a mask or blindfold, had chosen to grow strength and restraint instead, but began to doubt her conviction. Control was everything to her of late, both with the mists and her seer sight. If the length of the unbidden vision was any indication of resolve fading, the stabbing pain in her arms and legs were a desperate cry.

The wounds kept getting worse, had opened further and bled freely but were not yet marked by infection. Her plan to save Barr from his fate, all the pain and suffering she had endured, would be for naught if her body failed before the deciding moment had come to pass.

She carefully pulled back the shawl where it stuck to the reddened bandage and bit her lip to stifle an outcry. She needed to redress the almond-shaped sores, for the second time this day, and weave the ruined shawl anew once again. It was a tedium she had no choice but to bear, but when she unraveled the sticky cloth, she was overcome with a dread fear her time had run out.

The outline of the wounds, where the skin had been eaten away, had gone to black. There was no festering scent or discharge, no new discoloration but the dry and hardened edges. It reminded her of the wasting black, when an umbral strike had nearly killed her. This pain, however, had grown deeper than the flesh. It sapped her spirit at times, in fits of dizziness and nausea.

Fluora inwardly admitted, with a reluctance akin to defeat, that she needed help from a practiced healer. Her own magic, the mists, was not enough to counter the old lesions, let alone their darkening edges or those newly formed across her middle. Desperate and more than a bit frightened, she sought out Qilahd, the jade eldarath who had accompanied her to Alixhir.

She found him at the Academy, on the second floor of the great study. He was reading from a heavy tome, a thick work bound in leather and rich wood, its pages painstakingly inked and adorned with sketching done in silver.

"My apologies," he said and looked up from writing notes on a separate parchment. "I did not hear you come in."

"I did not wish to disturb you," she said and pulled up a cushioned chair to sit beside him, "until you had finished. Am I interrupting?"

"Not at all. I was just following up on an herbal cure for a fevered cough." He leaned in and spoke quietly, though only a handful of other arachon were present in the massive chamber. "Our new friends from Alixhir take a dim view of magic, healing or otherwise. I thought to find another way to aid their sick."

"That is most thoughtful."

"Is everything alright?" he asked, mild concern upon his emerald brow. "Have you taken ill?"

"No," she replied, with a second thought to her visit, "no, nothing like that." What if she could not persuade him to remain silent? She looked down at her forearms, every moment a struggle not to cry out from the pain, then back to the doorway she had come in. "Are you sure this is a good time? I could return later –"

"Is there ever a good time to need a healer?" He was trying to be genial, perhaps even make her smile, but when he gingerly touched a hand to her arm, the sharp recoil startled him to a deeper worry. "What happened here? Show me."

He held out his hand and patiently waited.

Fluora eased her anguish with a deep breath. "You cannot tell anyone of this," she said in a firm tone, "not even Barr. If that is a problem, I can leave –"

"You have my promise," Qilahd said and still waited. "I care more for your well-being than the talking of it."

With a glance toward the other arachon, she asked, "Is there someplace more secluded we could go?"

Qilahd gave a nod and stood. "Follow me. We can use one of the private studies." He led her past the open rows of tables, beyond the bookshelves and curio stands, to one of a dozen side chambers with a wooden door. "Take a seat," he said, indicated a chair and sat opposite her with anxious curiosity. "Alright then, let us see."

She carefully removed the shawl. Despite the fresh dressings, blood had already begun to speckle through. He helped unravel the bandages with a slow and steady hand, noted her distress and did his best to lessen the pain. Fully exposed, the array of wounds across her body looked more grievous than she expected but on par with the stinging burn that seemed to torture her from within.

"How did this happen?" Qilahd asked, in a tone that seemed both astounded by the extent of damage and afraid to hear their cause. "More importantly, why must it remain secret?"

He already held both her wrists and had begun to send healing warmth up their length. It tingled the skin with a brisk flare, like stepping through a portal from the runic sunlight of Dwendorim to the bitter winds and icy snows of Greywood.

"It has to do with my becoming Matron," Fluora tried to explain. "My bond with the mists grants power unlike any other, power we will need to win the fight against Revyn." She winced when the chilling warmth reached her middle. "Unfortunately, it comes at a cost."

Qilahd jerked his hands back. By the wide glow of his eyes, something had gone amiss.

"There is more at work here," he said, looked down at the grayed tips of his jade fingers, "than the physical. I can try to mend the wounds, but I fear they will occur again in short time." He looked relieved when the color returned to his fingers. "It felt as if your injuries sought to –" Qilahd shook his head and gave a reassuring smile. "I am sure it is nothing."

He took hold once more and began to heal with a greater fervor. The warmth felt more like fire than the soothing balm of midday sun, slowly raked up her arms beneath the skin and touched upon each lesion as if hot sand coursed through her veins. Though the sores began to close, the fiery torment grew too much when it had reached its way down to her belly.

"Stop!" Fluora cried, tore free of his grasp, and dark *furie* engulfed her wrists of its own volition. It took long moments for her to calm, but when she finally settled, the black fires died away. "My apologies," she said, voice wan from the ordeal, "it may be too much to bear in one sitting."

Qilahd was distraught but focused on his own arms. From fingertips to either elbow, the once vibrant jade had gone to gray and his silver runes had lost their luster. Fine cracks had appeared along the surface, as if the stone might fracture and crumble at any instant. Fluora began to fear he would not recover.

"I am so sorry," she said, uncertain what to do. "I will fetch the others. Just wait here –"

He motioned for her to wait a moment. The weak shades of stony life worked their way back to his arms, but neither one looked as if they would be fully restored for quite some time.

"That is a relief," Qilahd said and fairly sighed with nervous joy. "I have never seen an affliction like this. Are you sure there is no telling Barr? His skill at healing is surpassed by none. He would be far better suited –"

"Please," Fluora said, "he cannot know. Too much is at stake now for me to break my bond with the mists."

"Alright." He considered the sores on her forearms, where many had closed but not mended. "If we are to deal with this in sessions, perhaps there is a way I might ward you against further damage – or at least mitigate it somewhat."

"That would be much appreciated."

He placed a tender hand above her heart and began to weave with the other. Barely a rune had filled the air when he stopped with a puzzled look. He continued to feel her heartbeat for a long moment, regarded her with a mix of happiness and concern, then pulled away and sat back.

"There is a problem, I am afraid." He seemed to be searching for the right words. "You are carrying twins. I would say congratulations are in order, but…"

Fluora could only blink in return.

Pregnant? That changed everything. She could not keep such news from Barr. Not for very long. What would he say, once he knew? Would he dissuade her joining the coming fight? There would be no hiding her condition. He would see what she had become, what she had kept in secret all this time.

As if loath to say it, Qilahd continued, "One has already been affected by the bond you spoke of. I can try to ward the children as well, but only the other will likely be born unharmed."

She snapped free of her stunned silence. "What of the other?" she asked, shaken by sudden fear.

"There is no way of knowing," he replied honestly, "not so long as the bond persists. Only time may tell."

Was she to weigh the lives of her unborn children against Barr's? Against the countless others who would die if she stood the field against Revyn as anything less than Matron? She knew her powers stemmed, in part or whole, from the Dark. What if this was the god's doing?

"Is it possible," she asked, "that Revyn is responsible for what is happening to me? Could he be manipulating my connection with the Dark?"

Qilahd shook his head. "I truly have no idea, but he no doubt knows more of that realm than any other yet living." He must have seen her deep thought as a sign of desperation. "Would you turn to him for aid?"

Her manner hardened in an instant.

"I would sooner die," she said with grim assurance, "and take my children with me than suffer his touch on either one."

"If this is in any way a result of his doing," Qilahd sagely offered, "that may very well have been his intent."

*     *     *

Barr scried one of the new rifts Fluora had shown him. It stood within the frozen sands of a ravine just south of Salianne, a mere two-hour ride by horse from the jade city. Over twenty thousand naga made a home in Valsimar, their grand capital at the heart of the rallan nation. The first three rifts had been spreading at an increasing rate, but by that measure this new one would reach the city by next morn.

Valkstrun had only recently secured the rift, so its radius was barely a hundred paces. Four shiardin stood guard, waited patiently for the blight to spread. It was the perfect opportunity for Barr to test his theory.

He carried Aren and Idelle through the mists to the blight's edge. When the hound had learned of Barr's plan, he insisted on coming along. That they had left while Kaela was in Geilon-Rai was something Aren would have to deal when they got back.

*If we get back,* Aren said.

Idelle swooped past him. *You should be so lucky.*

Four sets of beryl eyes were trained upon Barr. The shiardin made no move to attack but looked as if they might come loping after at any moment.

*She could've come,* Barr said. *I didn't plan to put us in any danger.*

*No.*

Barr could feel the anxiety course through him, the guilt of having survived while other hounds fell within sight. Aren was determined not to lose another friend, especially not Kaela, and would say nothing more on the matter.

The pull of dark *furie* sent a flutter through Barr's stomach. A violet mist had formed and clung about the darkstones. It wouldn't be long before the Dark broke through and began to spread.

He knew he couldn't enter the blight, not without expending a huge amount of *furie* to keep himself healed. He would've had to use his own, since the ley lines under the blight were corrupted. At best, it was a losing battle. Luckily, he had something else in mind.

Barr knelt at the blight's edge and studied its runes, looked for any sign of Dark encroaching on their realm. What he saw, the spent and damaged sigils, was a bit of a disappointment but not wholly unexpected. The breach was closer to the rift. What he examined was the result of its touch.

He began to alter runic structures, the corroded and blackened wards, their depleted glyphs on the verge of collapse, in the hope of changing the damaged earth to something that could withstand the Dark. It meant not only shifting and reworking runes, as he had done in his experiments, but including the new deific runes as well. If he could weave a new substance, one that suffered no damage from either realm and wouldn't drain those who walked upon it, he'd be able to approach the rift without harm and disable its glyph – given enough time.

The depleted wards weren't behaving as he'd hoped. Once reworked, they remained dormant. Even filling the runes with his own *furie* only sparked a temporary flare of life. The blight's drain was constant and shut the ward down before its material could change.

*Barr*, Idelle said in a tone of warning.

The amount of *furie* it would take to counter the drain was more than he was willing to spare. He thought of drawing from a ley line further away, where it had yet to be corrupted. It would then be a matter of whether he could maintain his concentration as a living conduit and still have the presence of mind to reweave a glyph.

Aren gave a low growl. *Barr!*

*What?* He looked up and saw three shiardin had joined the others, with more stepping through one at a time as he watched. *Seems someone's taken notice of my tinkering.*

*Do we fight?* Idelle asked, circling above.

He could undo their glyphs, turn each shiardin to ash, but it would take at least a moment to look for one of the right runes. Even if he managed to undo a few, there were still too many for them to handle.

*Not against that,* Barr replied and looked down to the ley lines far below. He had to take a step back to avoid the growing blight. *I may have a better idea.*

The rivers of golden *furie*, the lifeblood of Taellus and every other world in the Light, seemed to struggle with the corruption, forced it back in a violent thrash. Its fight was to no avail, though, because the darkstones tapped and turned a ley line's *furie* against itself. The only way to stop the spread was to sever the connection – or the ley line itself. A glance further ahead showed the rift had been opened over four intersecting ley lines, so it could draw as much as possible in this area and in doing so spread faster.

*I don't know if this will work,* Barr said in way of caution. To be honest he wasn't sure it could be done at all. *You may want to stay back from the rift, Idelle.*

He reached down through the earth with his will and touched upon a line. The echo of a hollow knock far off in the distance signaled connection with his spirit. Its *furie* bubbled up to his middle, filled his body with renewed energy and sent a tingle from head to toe.

*Alright,* he said and readied his mind to strike, saw the exact wards to break asunder. *Here we go.*

By force of will, Barr severed the ley line.

The violet glow about the darkstones fluttered and began to fade. A narrowed gaze from one shiardin had them all scrabbling across the blight in an instant, claws tearing at the earthen ruin as they ran with all speed. While the half still connected to the darkstones calmed to a black morass, the other end of the ley line spewed its *furie* up through Barr.

No longer merely tapped into its power, Barr stood as capstone to a raging torrent he had no hope to control. The best he could manage was direct its flow, to focus its intensity through his body and will. Already he could feel it singe the edge of his consciousness, as it blurred his vision in a haze of golden luminescence.

Barr held a hand outward, tried to channel the rising *furie* overwhelming his senses, and sent a ray of light coruscating toward a shiardin. It took the creature full on, as a spray of molten sun, and ate away its every rune in a single breath. Chitin armor flared one brief moment, cracks spread wide like lava flows, then burned through and away in a flurry of dying ashes.

*Barr!* Aren cried out beside him. *Your arms!*

The other shiardin suffered similar fates, reduced to remnants of sparked shadow and a sputter of ash within the light. As the darkspawn disintegrated, the abundant flow of power built within to a worrying devastation. It scraped along his veins, raked hot claws beneath the flesh. Barr knew with a sinking certainty, it would burn his spirit before long.

He destroyed the darkstones next, scorched each in turn to cratered stains upon the blight. The violet fires about the rift began to flicker. Barr ignored the searing pain within him and sent the flow into the Dark. The keens of untold dying echoed back. The rift began to wither, shrank in upon itself, and the agonized shrieks seemed to fade into the distance.

When the rift closed, it left behind a decimated land, but all trace of the Dark was gone – and with it went the blight.

*Let it go!* Idelle yelled in his mind, over the din of splashing *furie* tearing through and broken free.

*Not yet!* he called back. *I need to mend the line!*

Barr reached down for the other end, as corruption bled out into the blackened earth. He took hold of it in his mind, saw it collapse like a severed artery as the last bits of darkness seeped away. Without any release, the flow burned all the stronger, made it difficult to focus. He had hoped bringing the two ends together would allow them to reattach and heal on their own. When that didn't occur, to his dismay, he tried repairing the wards but was too distracted by the power bearing down on his senses. With reluctance, he ended the connection and set free the roiling flow.

He immediately regretted the decision.

The ground beneath him swelled, sent him reeling and to his back, as earth cracked with a release of golden steam. Soil and rock exploded upward in a deadly spray, narrowly missed Idelle and rained back down in hissing smoke. The earth shook with violent tremors, as the heat began to rise in visible waves. Barr struggled to unsteady feet with Aren's help and watched in abject horror as the broken ley line did more damage than had the blight.

*Get out of there!* Idelle swooped low and would have carried him off had he not stumbled. *Damn it!*

On his knees, arm around Aren to hold him steady, Barr reached back down with his mind to either end of the sundered ley line. Try as he might, there was too much turmoil to maintain a fixed view of its glyph on the flow's side. Forcing them together had no effect, he had no way of healing it on his own and the land beneath him was melting with no end in sight.

*I can't fix it!* he told them, terrified and confused, frantic for a solution.

Where the blight had left earth a still and lifeless black, its counter was weaving a savage storm of molten storm and heated air strong enough to set the soil to swirling embers.

*We have to leave!* Aren cried against the tumult.

In an attempt of desperation, Barr opened a portal to Faeronthalsos and touched a shaky hand to the ground on either side.

"We need your help," he said to the land.

It was his hope the verdant world would use his body to heal Taellus. Already damaged from within, he knew what it would cost.

"Please."

Barr screamed against the surge of an all-consuming power, his senses drowned out within the channeling of Faeron's will. It pulsed through him, end to end, with the force of a tremor, scorched clothes to smoking ruin and set his flesh to smolder beneath the golden light. The air came alive within its tide, sent splashes to the ground that erupted in green life. He was vaguely aware of the two ends moving closer to one another, as his body gave way a little more with every breath.

Aren, too stubborn to leave his side, suffered beneath the embers in an endless whimper. Idelle's feathers had flared orange at the tips and would have engulfed her in flames had she stayed in air any longer. She tumbled to the ground within the once blight. Skin blistered, Aren nuzzled Barr's cheek, forced him to pay attention. In the only way he knew to save Barr, Aren offered himself to lessen the burden.

*I can't do that to you.*

Aren gave a pleading look. *You don't have a choice.*

*We always have a choice*, Barr said, his smile wan and cheeks flecking away into cinders within the storm. *I love you both.*

Barr sent them into the mists.

The ley line was mending, but his body would fail before it finished. There was little enough left for him to draw upon, his *furie* pushed to the limit of endurance in just keeping him alive for this long. Eyes closed, skin shedding flakes of ashen embers, he called upon the only force within him he knew of that was greater than this life.

He appealed to his soul for aid.

*I know you can hear me,* he said to his higher self. *If I die here, I'm at peace with my decisions. But all you've strived for will be lost. There will be no more lessons, no more chances to ascend. Revyn will see to that. I know I'm just a small part of you* – Barr grinned against the end – *but I'm the only life you have left.* He chuckled and braced for death. *Besides, it's not like you have anything better to do!*

Barr was enveloped in the soothing cool of a silver light. A crowd of luminous bodies stepped outward from his own, encased in an equal glow, and placed a hand upon his shoulders. Elf and dwarf, human and orc, faeron and dryad, plus a number of other races, men and women of all shapes and size, even a child efreet, each lent him their strength in a show of love. Ghostly figures stepped further out from those around him, all warmth and argent glow, and touched upon the shoulders before them. On and on it went, until Barr was surrounded by thousands. He and all his past lives became as one.

The ley line mended, his body whole, Barr took in a deep breath. He let it loose and looked down at his hands with a great calm and understanding.

"Thank you," he said to Faeronthalsos, removed his hand from its touch and closed the portal.

The earth around him began to heal. Upward and out, life sprang anew. Blackness faded from the soil, left behind a rich brown. Roots renewed and grew their reach toward the sun, where across the surface a lush blanket of grass paved the way for budding trees.

Barr sat back on his heels, put both hands upon his lap and looked out at his other aspects with a warm smile.

*My thanks to you, as well,* he said, *to all of you.*

They returned a knowing smile.

From the outskirts of the circle, each one stepped forward and into those ahead, rejoining their separate parts once again. Within moments the ring of varied lives had collapsed inward, until those immediately around Barr took their step and were gone.

*     *     *

Dhar flew high above Taellus, through chill wind and winter flurry, but kept below the storm-laden clouds. Six more rifts had been opened during the night, according to Fluora, and in the madness of their making, she had seen a greater purpose. From his vantage, the spheres of blight were no more than blackened stains within a vast blanket of snowy white. He had followed a wide circuit over every major city on this continent in the few hours since they had spoken. The rifts were too sparse, spread too far apart to discern a true pattern, from any height or perspective. Her premonition had simply not yet come to pass, and for the sake of a dear friend, he hoped it never would.

He turned and headed for the Mirror Pool.

Revyn must have had a reason. The god was a fool but had always been clever – terribly cruel and twisted, mad beyond a doubt, but clever. Perhaps corrupting the pool was the only way he could enter Taellus. Why then were his shiardin able to pass through the rifts? Maybe Dhar's old friend was somehow key to the god's survival in this realm. Either that or a means of conquest.

Regardless of the god's intentions, Dhar had to warn his friend of the coming danger.

Minutes later he landed upon the frosted sands of its shore, opposite the cobbled road to Garand. Cold wind blew through leafless boughs in the trees all around, a pale whisper of sadness in its song. The pool was as it had always been, from the first moment they had met during his exploration of this new world. Its waters were clear but more silver than blue. They showed nothing of its bottom and chose what images to reflect. Its center churned with argent bubbles, where the stream of life fed in, and the whole of it felt alive with a hushed presence of the divine.

Water rose before him in the form of a man from the waist up. He appeared as hardened quicksilver, solid from within but fluid on the surface. A living mirror, he reflected bits of his surroundings, but not all were recast in the image. Bald and well-muscled, a handsome man of middle age, he greeted Dhar with a broad smile and a happy tone.

"It is good to see you," he said, craned his neck to look up, "and doing so well I might add."

Dhar changed and greeted him eye to eye.

"It has not been quite that long." Dhar gripped the offered hand at the wrist in a firm shake. "Not including the short span before our last."

"What are a few centuries between friends?"

Dhar returned the wry grin with a wistful laugh. Just hearing his voice again, his passion for the moment and the slight echo of its timbre, brought back memory of their countless days spent in lively conversation. Few he had ever met during his travels had a clearer insight or intuition. Which only served to make this moment all the more harder.

His friend noticed the somber turn.

"What troubles you?" he asked. "Something from the past or more recent?"

Dhar replied, "It is the future, I am afraid, yours in particular. I was told a premonition, one where Revyn plans to corrupt your waters with his rifts from the Dark."

247

"I had guessed as much."

"Have you seen them?" Dhar was curious if the pool might have sensed or intuited something others may have missed. "His rifts and the tainted creatures he has woven from nightmare?"

"Somewhat," the pool vaguely admitted. Despite their millennia as friends, he had always been guarded about his visions. "I can feel their touch, even now."

"What do you mean?" Dhar asked. "You can sense their effect on the land, or has the corruption already reached you?"

The Mirror Pool considered, as if he weighed the result of sharing a hidden knowledge against the damage ignorance of it might cause.

"I was formed with the creation of Taellus," he said at last, "used as a conduit between this plane and the astral. It was through me the children gods worked their magic, exerted their will upon the lands – and oftentimes their children." His gaze trailed off to distant memory. "There is a stream there, in the astral, that feeds directly into me. Its source is a waterfall I have tried many times to follow up its course but to no avail. It goes far higher than I the strength to traverse it." His tone grew thoughtful. "I have heard it said, by more than one of the children gods, that the fall existed before them. It may well be the source of all *furie* for this realm."

Revyn's crazed scheme became clear.

"That must be why he wants you," Dhar said.

The pool gave a worried nod. "Every ley line, on every world, passes through me. It could be Revyn needs that power to break free from the Dark."

"No." Dhar believed it went further. "I suspect he is already free, was never trapped to begin with. He can step through at any time, anywhere he wishes. I think his plan is to corrupt the entire realm at once, use you to spread the Dark through the ley lines to each world."

"If that is true," the pool said, eyes downcast, "then there is little I can do to stop him. I will fight, of course, but we both know I cannot hold out for very long against it."

Dhar gritted his teeth, refused to lose a good friend without a fight. He looked out across the water and saw the battle yet to come.

"If it is true," he said, "Revyn will enter here. This is where it will happen, the final battle for all life." He met his friend's gaze with firm assurance. "My kind and I will do all we can to help. Entire armies are being formed as we speak."

"Perhaps you can assist me in another way," the pool said in a considering tone, "if you are willing." At Dhar's prompting, he continued, "Until now, I saw no need, but... If we bound our spirits, together we might be strong enough to resist." The pool regarded Dhar with a measured look. "It would also grant you access to the very heart of my power, the waters."

"Anything you need," Dhar said in assent.

Silver water rose up around him in tendrils that formed a swirling column. *Furie* thrummed in his ears and caused a twinge in his middle. When the pale water receded, Dhar was somewhere else. He stood before a beautiful waterfall of argent light that splashed down into a stream. It was surrounded by rich soil, lush grass with wide blades, exquisite trees in full bloom and a multitude of colored flowers. For as far as his eyes could see, the world appeared in the midst of spring at its most luxurious height, like an endless sunny day of clear blue skies and gentle warmth.

Clinging to the fertile ground was a thin layer of cool mist. It stretched off to the horizon, like a lazy blanket of calm. The Mirror Pool stood before him, risen up from the stream.

"I had no idea you could do that," Dhar said, "or that this place even existed."

The pool said, "I am a consequence of creation, a force that will always strive for balance."

Dhar pushed fog about with his foot.

"Though this place looks nothing like it," he mused, "the way you brought me here reminds me of the mists. Yet another place Revyn has sought to corrupt. Luckily, he failed in the attempt."

"Ah, yes," the pool said with a growing sadness, "my sister. She was always one for theatrics."

His demeanor became grave, and he looked away. When he turned back to Dhar, there was a hint of shame and even fear in his eyes.

"As for Revyn failing," he said, "I am not so sure."

# – 9 –

 t had all been a ruse. Barr hadn't thought to question why they opened in fairly isolated areas, days away from all but the remotest of villages. Only recently had blight from one spread far enough to reach a sizeable town and caused people to flee in fear for their lives. Revyn had known all along what they would do, had waited for the right moment to strike a decisive blow, not to take or turn one kingdom at a time but remove all resistance in a single move.

The panicked screams had alerted Barr to it first, before he felt the chill charge of dark *furie* across his skin. He rushed with all speed and sinking dread toward the chaos, the frightened merchants and tradesmen all scrambling to get away while arachon struggled to usher them past. He pushed through the throng to meet it head on, to face the worst possible scenario, the only hole in his plan to defend Taellus.

Barr raced toward the new rift in the portalis.

Every ally they could muster was connected to that chamber. If blight spread through their portals, untold lives would be lost and the joined armies laid to waste before ever seeing a single battle.

Idelle asked, *Is this why Revyn hasn't just opened a rift to the Mirror Pool?* She flew above him, as he ran, with Aren not far behind. *To cripple our armies first?*

*Maybe.* Barr fought against the tide of terrified men and women, dodged between or shouldered aside those in his way. *One might not have been enough to corrupt it.* He saw two travelers beside the portal leading out from the portalis, both glad and angry they hadn't yet closed it. *But a dozen or more, converging from all directions?*

*Visions aren't perfect*, Aren said, forced humans from his path with sharp barks or sheer bulk. *Fluora could be wrong.*

It didn't matter anymore. They had bigger problems at the moment, and Barr wasn't sure what he'd do if –

Blight seeped through the portal like withering flesh, blackened cobbles beneath its touch and startled the travelers into stepping back. Violet fires rose up either side of the portal and engulfed it, darkened its center to empty black until it resembled a rift. Both arachon tried in vain to close it but were forced out of reach by the growing ring of corruption.

*Damn*, Barr said and stopped short just steps away. *I'm going to have to go in.*

*What can we do?* Idelle asked.

Shiardin began to come through, one after another, and immediately attacked nearby arachon. Barr drew both kyan and strode forward. No longer ironwood, their blades were now a mix of gemlike onyx and black crystal, their pommels of smoothed chitin shot through with veins of glowing purple. He sliced a shiardin across its chest, was already past to stab another, as its glyph unraveled to crumbling ash.

Arachon champions were already prepared to face off against darkspawn, their enchanted blue steel blades all the more deadly for Barr's sunlight spell, but there was still no way for them to walk upon the blight. The further it spread into Dwendorim, the more lives would be lost. Barr had no choice but to leave them behind, to enter the portalis and hope he could deactivate the rift.

*Stay and fight*, Barr told them. *I'll see what I can do from the other side.*

He called up a protective barrier, a shield of blue light that encompassed him head to toe, and stepped into the blight. Its magic flared upon contact but fought the constant drain. The link to his spirit had stayed open, and he hoped it would remain so. It was like having access to another ley line, one from within and far more powerful. He used it now to keep at bay the Dark's touch but knew it would falter before long. Two more fell to his blades before he entered, where dozens of shiardin pressed forward to reach the fray and valkstrun secured the foothold with their bodies.

The chamber was dark, its stone and sigils given way to blight, but for the glow of purple mist along the floor and over portals on either side. The grayed and crumbled remains of Destroyers littered the blackened rail paths, and the dying screams of men and women echoed back throughout the room.

Barr recalled the rift near Salianne fading after he'd sent the overwhelming flow of *furie* through. Destroying the darkstones had helped to weaken its hold upon the land, but he believed the rift only closed when something on the other side succumbed as well. Whatever it might have been, he was certain it was how Revyn spread the Dark into their realm. Unfortunately, the only way to be sure was to go there for a look.

His binding glyph came to mind of its own accord. He sent it out by will alone and caught three shiardin in its grasp. They hung helplessly in air on his left, as he dispatched two others on the right with precision strikes. It took moments to see into their core, to find the right runes. With a mental twist, he undid a single ward and collapsed their glyphs. Their embers floated down into ashes and joined their brethren's upon the blight.

With a deep breath, he stepped through.

The barrier flickered as he entered, a wan shade of ocean blue beneath the onslaught of violet. Its light faded with each heartbeat, as will and ward began to waver. The drain intensified, tugged at Barr's middle like hungry hands upon the cord that linked him to his spirit.

Darkspawn leapt from swirling dark, like shadows within lamplight. Those entrapped remained in air. The few who dodged his glyphs, who moved within reach, met their end by blade or *furie*.

The land itself seemed alive, a roiling mass of mutable soil that clung in tendrils and flailing wisps. Black crystal trees reached ever outward toward the sun, a dim orb of violet fire and chilly rays, then stabbed down into the earth with jagged fingers. Vapor bubbled up from their tops in pale smoke and lilted across limbs overgrown with stippled moss. Thin blades of pale grass swayed within the wintry pull, as flowers turned his way with eager petals all aflutter.

What buildings could be seen had rounded edges and sharp protrusions. They looked more like the husks of fallen monstrosities than anything shaped by hand. Only the obelisk before him seemed tooled to a design, its sides smoothed to a glossy sheen and base embedded in the ground. It thrummed with enough force to shake the soil and surrounding mist, in radiating waves that could be seen as much as felt.

Darkspawn fliers filled the cloudless skies, a swarm of black stars that spiraled wide and sped toward him. Shiardin stepped out from the hollowed dead in answer to their cries, snuffled the air and turned his way. Other creatures appeared, clawed up from below the surface or dislodged from the trees. They were blades given life with deadly purpose and moved with horrific speed.

Barr did his best to quickly study the obelisk, to scour its runic structure and ascertain its every function. The intimate bond he now shared with his spirit allowed him to call to mind and execute complex glyphs, without need of a storage crystal, but it still took some time and effort. He knew with alarming certainty he could not act fast enough to deal with all the darkspawn and decrypt the obelisk in time. His barrier was nearly gone. Soon he would be forced to heal against the Dark's touch or flee back through the rift.

He just needed to figure out how it worked. Once he knew that, how it forced the Dark through to their realm, he could hopefully find a way to stop it from the other side or ward against it to safeguard the portalis. He was forced to unmake some caught in his binding glyph, as the number he could maintain was limited by lack of concentration. He'd glanced and understood most of the obelisk's wards but not enough yet to grasp what it was doing.

Ashes swirled from the commotion, stung his eyes and caught in his throat. The more that attacked, the more adept he became at their unmaking. There were too many of them though, and the swarm was on the verge of overwhelming his attention. Claws raked against his back, the barrier gone with a sunken fear in the cold pit of his stomach.

Barr called healing warmth up to embrace him, to fight off the corruption, undo damage from the Dark and mend the inevitable wounds that would come. Shiardin died by the dozen, frozen in place and unraveled like the strewn pieces of a winding puzzle. Barr had memorized the obelisk's glyph, studied it in thought as darkspawn rushed to their demise.

Some of their attacks made it through, by sheer force of numbers. Though able to heal himself free of their disease, as he had Fluora's infection from an umbral, the toll it all took was more than he could bear. He edged back toward the rift as he fought without relent, unmade darkspawn by thought alone and wracked his mind for an answer.

*There!*

He caught sight of the connection, the wards working in tandem, and was confused enough by what it meant that he only narrowly avoided being skewered. The glyph, its entire structure, was designed as both a portal and a rift that channeled *furie* inward. So instead of bringing two places together, like folding a sheet of vellum, or tearing through to another plane, the obelisk tried and failed to do both. The resulting damage, however, caused a wrinkle. Given time and *furie*, it would continue to grow, like crumpling parchment, and force together all planes of existence.

A resounding boom echoed from off in the distance, followed by the keen of an immense throng closing in. It looked as if the world had come alive in a writhing mass of dark bodies, with all eyes and scrabbling claws intent upon him. They sought to end him with an increased urgency, as if Revyn knew what he'd found.

Barr grinned at the thought.

He rolled forward and struck through the obelisk in a single swing, cut in half and unwound its glyph. *Furie* nearly gone, he hurried back through the rift as it began to close. He then destroyed the surrounding darkstones with a plunged kyan through each of their middles. Once the rift fully closed, the Dark receded back. The blight's touch still stained the stonework, but it no longer spread into the city. All the portals returned to normal, though he was afraid to imagine what damage had been done.

With the portalis secured, at least until he could ward it against another rift, Barr began to imagine taking the fight to Revyn. He could seek the god out, face and unmake him, put an end to this war. His only obstacle was the Dark itself. If he found the means to survive its touch, without expending precious *furie*, he could walk the other realm as if born to it.

As if he too were a darkspawn.

\* \* \*

Sera looked down at her hands. The cuts had healed with no trace, not within or between runes, as if nothing of her deed remained. She left their stain in the wash basin, though part of her wished to keep it, to carry their sticky remnants as a warning – both for herself and the newly awakened hunters. Theirs was a life not meant for complacence. It was violent, necessary and would only end in blood.

An arachon had heard their scuffle but was too late to intervene. He'd escorted her home, stood watch at her doorway, had no doubt alerted others and was awaiting a decision. Would they throw her in a prison cell? She wondered if one even existed. This city was like an idyllic dream on the verge of waking, a child's fantasy in stained glass just begging for a hammer. They might see it that way or perhaps as she did, as a service to all, a needed sacrifice for the greater good. Banishment was another option. Remove her from the city, never to return again. Not much of a punishment, really. Secluding her on a mountaintop or a desolate island would be worse. They could simply demand an apology and forgive her, even thank her for getting rid of such louts.

Sera laughed. "Now who's dreaming?"

The obsidian looked in through the window at the sound of her voice and turned away once he was sure she was still alone.

It didn't matter what they thought or decided for her fate. They'd need her in the coming fight, would *have* to let her fight. No one was better suited to face Revyn and his creations. They could quibble over niceties and her breach of etiquette if she survived.

Screams sounded in the distance.

Sera was out the door and down the road before her guard could voice complaint. The cries were those of men and women, though no race could be discerned. Since the portalis had been completed, the market streets were all aflutter with varied bodies and their noise. Dwarves may have tended toward a deeper timbre, elves a bit more nasal and measured with their words, gnomes pitched higher than she cared for, with humans hurried in pace and so varied in manner they were distinguished by locale, but the commotion she heard now was a frantic mix of them all.

She moved fast enough to dislodge cobbles, leapt up to a roof and slid along its shingles. A quick glance to the north showed people running for their lives from shadow figures with beryl eyes.

*Shiardin!* Ceramic shattered beneath her feet as she ran toward the fray. *There's a rift in the city!*

A forward spin through the air took her steadily to the ground, where she stood as a lone pylon parting the sea of rushing terror. Atop a helpless man, screaming on his belly, a shiardin bit deep into a shoulder and didn't let go its hold until the victim changed completely. His skin blackened and turned hard, like the shell of an iron beetle. His fingers and toes grew to hooked claws, and when he turned toward Sera, his eyes had gone a glowing green.

She recalled everything Fluora had said of the dark creatures. Avoid their teeth and claws, or be turned and become one of them. They feed on *furie*, either magic or life essence, and are weakened by the sun.

"Sure," Sera said and looked about for anything she could convert into a weapon, "there's lots of sunlight to be had in an underground city."

Champions attacked the two shiardin as they rose to face her, arachon in full suits of enchanted blue plate and wielding blades of vibrant yellow, like slivers of the sun. Others bore them as well, cut through the mass of black devils, causing shrieks and hissing wounds.

"Now *that* looks like fun," she said and ran after another pair. They were headed toward a command being overrun and forced to fall back. Shiardin swarmed over those brought to the ground, bit into stone and drained them to a dull gray that split and crumbled. "At least we don't have to worry about them turning."

Sera ran straight for the shiardin and shouldered the first into the rest. She snatched up a sunlight blade, a short sword with nice heft, and faced them with a look of feigned surprise.

"Apologies," she said. "Did I interrupt?"

She grinned wide and charged forward, sliced clean through an arm outstretched to claw her from the side, grabbed hold of another to her left and flung its foolish owner through the air like a rag doll. She cut off a leg at the knee, claws at the wrist, stuck her blade through a shoulder and on up. It quickly became clear that wounds were not enough. The best way to end one, she imagined, was to take its head.

Just as she had in the tea shop.

The first to lose its top spewed dark blood with a violet sheen across the grass, dropped to its knees and toppled over before disintegrating into ash. She avoided claws and took another, dodged a barbed elbow and took its head with reflex born of the divine. One lunged at her with teeth to fore and caught a blade between its jaws. An arachon cried out at her left, had needlessly allowed its arm to intercede a bite on her behalf. Sera chopped through its neck and into the graying bloodstone, pulled free her blade and gave a wordless nod of thanks.

The arachon champions were not faring as well, had lost dozens to debris and would have been forced to fall back even further into the city had Sera stayed hidden in her home. Everyone else was all but useless. Worse, they bolstered enemy ranks when they fell. It wasn't her duty to save them, or anyone for that matter. She was a killer by nature, a hunter by design. The only reason she put herself between a large group of them and the shiardin was to save her the trouble of having to kill them when they turned.

"Thank you!" a human merchant said to her once the immediate area was clear.

Shiardin had stopped coming through the portal, but there were plenty enough left that giving thanks seemed nothing short of foolish. He'd meant well, was sincere, but his frailty only sickened her.

"Don't thank me!" Sera shot back, was already on the move toward another pack. "Take up a weapon and fight! Defend yourself!"

She ran toward the heavy pieces of a broken pillar. Its bloodstone remains littered the field, and two full commands had chosen to take a stand there. She cut a swath of shiardin between the blocks, fought to the west side and screamed a challenge to their front. Shiardin rushed her, to no avail, and died at her feet. It was only when a jade golem was pushed back into her with great force that she fell. She landed hard on the slick grass and narrowly avoided bring brained by a sharp rock to the back of her skull. When she moved to rise, however, her left arm held her back.

From elbow to palm, her forearm had become lodged between a boulder and fallen golem. Two shiardin were already upon her. She struggled to keep them at bay with precise kicks and her free sword arm, but there was no time to wriggle free or force the arachon's body aside. She kicked one away, sliced free the other's head, and in the brief moment of respite slammed the pommel of her sword down into her caught forearm.

Sera bit her lip and drew blood, as the bones broke and set her lose. She got up and finished with the other shiardin, took out her pain upon it by cleaving its head in two from top to bottom. Wrist held firmly in place between both knees, she pulled the broken arm until its bones aligned. She snatched up another sword, felt the healing tingle burn its way through and rejoined the fray with a renewed vigor born of anger.

\* \* \*

*Fluora thumbed the edge of the leather sack, felt its supple roughness in her hand, caught scent of its musky oil with a faint mixture of ozone and enchantment. It was lighter than expected, not for its size but for what she knew he had hidden away inside. Far larger within than without, there was no limit to what it could hold, or none she was aware of.*

*All twelve Emblems were inside, the living swords they had used to weaken Revyn and defeat his army of shapelings. Forged by the children gods, magic artifacts come to life, each one was a force of nature and granted power beyond measure. Alone, they could tear the land asunder with chaos and destruction, or they could coax it to flourish with love and guiding care. But together...*

*Together they could undo the gods.*

She realized what it meant. The moment was growing near when her vision would coalesce into a reality she had dreaded since first they met. That still, after all her time spent in futile preparation, she was too weak to stop it, rankled only slightly less than his damn complacence.

*I understand*, he told her, over and again in vision, as if happy, at peace, accepting of his fate. Each time she saw it play out in seer sight, it drove her further into madness and despair. She wanted to shake him until he truly understood, until he realized giving in is what hurt her most.

Fluora sighed, forced down the pain and resentment, and called up the mists to carry her through to the pale statue of Saernol. It was said this is where Aislin was first found, cradled in her arms, a gift for the faeron to aid their bond with the mists. The mithrinum blade had helped to keep umbrals at bay for generations. Though Fluora had no need of it, she could not help but wonder if its touch would mend her wounds.

She motioned her hand through a swirl in the air, trailed mist in its passing. When the rings of wisp grew solid and spun of their own accord, she reached through their middle and pulled free a leather sack from out of time. A single breath of intent dispersed the rings into a haze and collapsed the hidden pocket.

As in premonition, she ran a thumb across its edge. It was her right as Matron to bear Aislin, as it had been Daesidaoli's and all those who came before her. It had aided her people in maintaining the balance, kept the Dark in check and its creatures from breaking through. Was she strong enough without its power, or did she owe it to all of Faeron to take back what was theirs?

Barr would want all twelve, she knew. But did he *need* all of them? Her premonition had not changed or faltered in any way. Nothing she had done thus far made a difference. Perhaps this was how she took his fate into her own hands, by forcibly altering his choice.

*It should be mine!*

Fluora dropped the sack in alarm. Her hands shook and mind raced. The thought was not her own.

It had sounded from within, spoke in her voice, bore with it her emotion but felt alien in purpose, as if its desire was not her own until the words rang out in her mind.

*Barr will need all twelve Emblems*, she asserted in thought. *I have seen it.*

*What if?* The words echoed through premonition that should not have come to pass. *What if I did have Aislin? I could have saved my mother. I can still save Barr, save our twins from growing up without a father.*

She shut her eyes tight, but the visions had no need, showed behind the lids, in pressing thoughts that would not abate.

*What if I took them all for myself? I could do it right now. There is no one to stop me, no one else who even knows where they are. I could use their power to end the war before it begins, close the rifts, heal the blight...*

*Destroy Revyn.*

*I could, once and for all, put an end to his madness. How many lives would I save? How much suffering and* loss could be avoided if I but acted on my own, with no need of aid from Barr or any other? In one fell swoop, I could destroy Revyn and his children, unite the known worlds as the gods had intended.

*I would be their savior.*

*They would love me, all people and races, respect me as an equal, respect my power and ability. They would admire my courage and strength, for doing what was right, what was needed, when no one else would. When no one else could! The Emblems should be mine, need to be mine. No one else is strong enough to wield them all.*

*I would be foolish not to take them!*

"Stop!" Fluora yelled, and the power in her voice sent ripples outward through the mists. "I know what you are doing," she said to Revyn, whether it was the god, fatigue or madness affecting her thoughts, "but it will not work. I will not be manipulated nor plied as your puppet. You may hold sway over the Dark, but my bond is as great."

*What if...*

She cast aside the useless notion, steeled her nerves and mind then took up the leather sack. She fastened it to the sash at her waist, was ready to carry it to Barr when a premonition took hold.

It was of the battle at the Mirror Pool, a time now fast approaching. She gasped as she saw it, their means to overcome the blight and fight upon it. Revyn knew of it as well and had chosen to quickly strike. With his attack on the portalis, there was no other way to mobilize their armies but the mists.

Fluora stepped through to Sera in an instant, at the aftermath of the attack in Dwendorim. No shiardin came through the portal, but the ring of blight continued to spread. The hunter's eyes widened in surprise at her arrival but soon narrowed to cold purpose.

"What's happened?" Sera asked. She gripped her sunlit swords as if ready to leave that very moment.

"Revyn opened a rift," Fluora explained, "inside the portalis. Blight has spread through every portal and into the connected cities."

"That explains all this," Sera said and indicated the destruction all around, "but not why you're here, in front of me."

"We can counter the blight." Fluora surveyed the area with a keen eye as she spoke, counted their losses and adjusted her plan accordingly. "It is time to gather at the Mirror Pool and ready to face Revyn." She regarded Sera with intent. "Are you ready to fulfill your destiny?"

The hunter cocked an eye, her dim view of fate made all too clear.

"You don't care that I killed them?"

Fluora replied, "They needed to die, to make way for new hunters, ones willing to fight. We shall carry them to the field as well, when we gather all the others."

"What about the portalis?"

"Barr is doing his best." Fluora straightened the sack at her waist and squared her shoulders. "For now, I will bring as many as I can, as quickly as I can."

Sera nodded. "Alright. What's in the bag?"

"A few things Barr will ask me to fetch," Fluora replied, "when he returns from the Dark."

Disbelief and then shock crossed the hunter's face. At last she laughed with a shake of her head.

"You oracles are a strange lot," she said, "talking of the future as if it already happened."

Fluora winked. "I have been waiting for you to say that since I arrived."

With a chuckle of her own, she called up the mists and carried them through.

\*    \*    \*

Back outside his home, Barr worked a glyph with all speed and artful precision. From nothing but knowledge of the divine language and the will to wield it, he wove a new material capable of existing in both realms, one alive yet not living, born of Light and Dark but dependent on neither to survive. It drew *furie* from both systems of ley lines, acted as a dual conduit, intensified the gathered magic until its power grew tenfold and plied them in unison to replenish spent runes.

It looked an amalgam of shadow and light, violet chitin and brilliant sunstone, with black vapor and pale mist shot through in tendrils. As a shaper, he had given Protectors form by firm thumb and skilled hand, but as a weaver of life, he shaped the new dawnstone by force of will, into a golem like no other.

*Why weren't you trapped*, Idelle asked, *like Revyn?*

Glowing blue runes began to form across its surface, a deep hue like vibrant moonlight through a sapphire.

*He isn't trapped*, Barr replied. *He never was.*

Idelle seemed dubious. *But how did he survive? Did the Dark change him?*

He worked the outer runes to safeguard the golem against tampering and prevent connection with any other consciousness or spirit. Revyn knew the divine language as well, might try to undo the creature, but of equal risk was the god attempting to supplant the bond.

*He changed himself,* Barr said. *He wouldn't have been able to continually heal for very long. The only other choice was to adapt. As for why he stayed, –* Barr took a step back and eyed the glyph, checked for the slightest of mistakes and to be sure he'd left nothing out, *– I can only guess. He took advantage of his surroundings and time away from the other gods, created life as he saw fit and*

266

*schemed an end to all else. What troubles me most,* he said and activated the glyph with a spark of *furie,* smiled when the golem's eyes opened a bright and vivid blue, *is that he's unaware his plan will destroy everything in both realms, or he* is *aware and intends to follow through out of spite.*

*So, he's like a child with a toy and would rather break it than share.*

*Essentially,* Barr agreed.

He took a seat on the ground against the fountain and began to clear his mind of all worry, anything that might weigh his thoughts.

*Do you really think this will work?*

Idelle eyed the golem with apprehension. Its body looked male, without the obvious attributes, but its face was plainly made, as if no thought or effort had gone into it – because it wasn't coming back.

*There's only one way to find out.*

Barr sent his consciousness out toward the golem, like searching for a ley line, and connected to its glyph with a faint knock.

It was strange at first, looking down at his own body but feeling both. He was, for all intents, in two places at once. Thought of it made his head swim, so he pushed it aside and focused solely on the golem.

Its vision was somewhat clouded by the pale azure of mixed *furie* but clearer for the bolstered sense of magic. He saw the runic structures of life as a dim extension of silver, in a sphere extended outward like a second body. The designs were plain to see and moved in time a stately course, wove through one another, a seamless harmony of dance.

*Can you still hear me?* Idelle asked, her voice off in the distance of a body left behind.

"Yes," he said, the spoken sound far different from the one in his mind. "This may take some getting used to."

He waved a hand through the air, caused a circle of runes to shimmer like water.

*What happens if it dies with you in there?*

Revyn's glyph appeared in scry within the circle, not as it had been in Geilon-Rai but close enough that it was not too difficult to find. The god thought himself secure, hidden in the Dark, and hadn't bothered to ward against it.

"The connection will sever," Barr replied, "and I'll snap back to my body." He regarded Revyn's new form with revulsion. "Hopefully, it won't hurt."

Another wave ended the scry, as it drew the god's notice. Barr called up the mists and stepped through to the Dark.

The chamber was immense, as required by Revyn's bulk. His physical body had become an immutable mass of bulbous pitch and barbed tendrils. Languished upon a throne of smoky black crystal and violet haze, two legs and arms could be discerned but all other trace of his once self was no more. Even his eyes, deepset beneath the twist of a thorny brow, had become as beryl flames, two lambent emerald suns upon the face of unyielding madness.

Dark *furie* emanated off him in waves, a shadow fire that warped the air until his visage seemed illusion. The sheer force of it unsettled Barr, gripped his middle with cold sickness and refused to let go. Its pull tugged at his senses, gauged his every facet with a curious touch of will.

"I have been expecting you," Revyn said, his voice a low rumble from the depths of a frozen cavern. "How fitting you should come to me as a puppet."

Barr knew the god's game, how he taunted with one hand and probed with the other. There was nothing left to say between them, so he remained quiet and studied Revyn's glyph from afar.

"I understand your reticence," the god went on and shifted his great weight. He looked down upon Barr with nothing more than mild interest, as if he posed no real threat. "After all, you have much to lose. Too much to face me in person, it would seem." His smile was a wide and gaping maw of jagged night. "Tell me, how fares your faeron wench? Has she told you yet she is with child?"

The cold grip tightened at his surprise, worked up his spine with a chilly touch.

Revyn added, "Twins, actually. I already have one in my clutch." The chill tingled Barr's neck like a wintry noose. "How long do you suppose before I have the other as well?"

"You spew lies and deceit," Barr said, "like they were weapons." He had found the runes he was looking for, took hold of each with his mind. "I will hear no more of them, nor will anyone else."

Barr exerted his will in a twist to each rune. His surprise grew to uncertain fear when it met with firm resistance. He realized Revyn fought against him, kept in check his touch upon the god's runes.

Revyn's laughter boomed throughout the chamber in a raucous echo. When at last it faded, Barr could hear the innumerable clicking of chitin legs against stone, as thousands of darkspawn drew near from all around.

"Why lie when the truth hurts all the more?"

The cold grip turned upon his own runes, tried to unmake the golem, but Barr found he could resist as well.

"Seems we're at a draw," Barr said, wove blades to either hand and readied to attack.

269

"No," Revyn replied evenly, "we are not."

All manner of darkspawn rose up over the broken crystals and fallen pillars that circled the chamber. At their head were ten figures, no bigger than a shiardin. Covered in oily pitch, each bore the jet resemblance of a child god.

*Oh no*, Barr thought as he caught sight of Saernol. A stab of sadness struck through his heart. *What has he done?*

They resisted as well, would not be as easily undone as the foolish shiardin that rushed in and fell to ashes. No matter how many he unmade, more hurried to fill their places. In the end he was overwhelmed, swarmed over and held down as the once children gods closed in around him.

Together they tore the golem apart.

*   *   *

Barr untied both leather laces and pulled loose the opening. Fluora stood beside him at the wooden table in their courtyard, had brought the sack to him not long after his connection to the golem had been severed. The base of his skull still thrummed with the vivid memory of being torn to pieces by twisted remnants of the children gods.

Revyn's words ran the edge of his thoughts, haunted each moment with whispers that dared, even pleaded in sadistic laughter. Barr could have looked. A quick glance of focus, and her glyph would reveal the truth. More than a petty desire to resist the deranged god, he refused to betray Fluora's trust.

He reached into the sack, past the physical limits of its material to the glyphed astral pocket linked inside. He willed Aislin to hand, pulled her from the sack and set the mithrinum blade upon the table. An image of Roena as a child, twin sister from his life as Alloric, flashed in his mind.

"I almost missed you," she said and elbowed him in the ribs, sparking a fit of laughter in them both.

*I hate those things*, Aren grumbled from beneath the table. Both he and Idelle disliked the emptiness they felt when an Emblem spoke with Barr. They could no longer sense him, as if he'd somehow disappeared.

It was a brief vision but the only way Aislin knew to greet Barr. He smiled at the joy thought of his once sister brought with it. The happy moment soon faded when his mind settled upon the fact Roena had been his twin. He began to wonder if Aislin knew what was troubling him, despite her time hidden away.

Idelle looked down at the blade in disdain. *Hopefully this will be the last time we need them.*

Barr was careful to hide his thoughts. He wanted to simply ask, but even the small twinge of doubt that had led to the question felt an insult to her integrity. What if it was true? Did it matter she kept it from him? This was hardly the time to risk thought on the future.

"She is beautiful," Fluora said and ran her fingers along the blade. Her dress and shawl put aside, she wore a set of sylvannis leathers and her ironwood mask in preparation of the attack. "Would it not be wiser for us to distribute the swords amongst our ranks?" Her hand slid down to the pommel. "She and I would do well together."

Image of an older woman came and went, her arms crossed and brow furrowed. Her displeasure had no need of words.

Khaela came next, a sphere of sunlit wave and silver glow upon her pommel. Her voice called to mind the chill spray and rolling waves of the ocean.

*You look well*, she said in a happy tone.

271

*As do you,* Barr replied and chuckled. To Fluora, he said, "I mistook my premonition." His past life as seer Kheran had given insight to a future that'd led him to hide the Emblems. He had believed no one should ever wield that much power. "I thought the man sheathed in light had been Markus. When he died, I didn't know or really care who it was. Until I saw Revyn and what he'd done to the other gods."

One blade after another, he pulled the Emblems free and set them on the table. Uinbro stood by, a ghostly figure with an amused demeanor.

"You now believe it was you," Fluora said and then amended, "will be you."

*Of course it is,* Uinbro said, admiring his own blade. He looked up with an eyebrow cocked. *Who else could it be? Certainly not her.*

Barr cleared his throat for attention, as the last was pulled free. His head had gotten crowded.

"It is me," he said. "I can't affect Revyn's glyph. This is the only way I can see to defeat him."

"There is Sera."

Without him needing to ask, each Emblem began to change. Their blades rippled and flowed like quicksilver, spread and hardened to separate pieces of plate armor. Barr took up Aislin, now a bracer, and fastened her to his wrist.

"If I'm wrong," Barr said, "we'll at least have tried."

Fluora helped him secure Khaela, now a gleaming cuirass of silvery gold.

She said, "If you are wrong, you will have delivered all twelve Emblems to Revyn's hands."

*What if she's right?* Idelle asked. *Twelve wielders on the field, fighting back shiardin, might be better than a single person with them all.*

Barr sighed as he fit Drakha into place.

*No,* Aren said. *This fight isn't about how many of those things we can kill or keep back. It's about Revyn. It's always been about Revyn.* He slipped out from under the table and shook out his thick coat, stood before Barr as the last piece of armor went on. *This is our best hope to kill him, and I'm going to be there when he falls.*

The voices had gone quiet, as each piece was put in place. Their power tingled every inch of him, prickled his senses with brimming *furie.* He'd at long last become his premonition, the man in silvery gold armor, the man sheathed in light...

The slayer of gods.

To his shock and dismay, the Emblems slowly began to brighten and shimmer. They rippled once again, as if taking new shape, but rather than their metal spread or recede, each sank into his flesh. Their glow set his skin alight, as all twelve fused together and became one within his body. Like puddles of water drying in the sun, each dissipated deep inside and left no trace but growing light.

He still felt their presence in his mind, but that too was beginning to fade, to seep down into his thoughts as a single pool. Their memories came flooding in, washed over his own and commingled in a swirl of confusion. It was a barrage of visions, many lifetimes all at once. He'd strained against the assault, held his breath and tensed without knowing. When finally he was forced to let it out and take new air, realization swept in alongside.

There were far more than a dozen lifetimes in the mix of visions, incarnations of the same twelve spirits but memories beyond their time as Emblems. Stunned by the implication, Barr stood speechless in speculation. He'd thought lives were exclusive to a soul, like fingers to a hand. A soul was the highest form of existence. It sent out aspects of itself to experience the wonders of life and learn all it can, until that one moment of ultimate clarity, enlightenment, when the soul had reached the end of its journey and ascended.

To what, he didn't know.

But if life from one soul could join a second, that meant souls were not the higher beings he had thought. They were also aspects of something greater, not leaves to a branch but untold branches to a tree. The children gods had created the worlds and all life within the Light, but this realm had already existed before them. They had knowledge of the Dark but only guessed its real purpose. None of them had been able to pierce true understanding of the realm, because they too were merely aspects.

"No," Fluora said, her voice choked in disbelief. She shook her head against the tears. "Please." She grasped at his front, as if it to hold him firmly where he stood. Motes of golden light rose up from his dissipating form. "I did not see it before. I thought I could –" but her voice had drifted off into the distance, lost beneath the weight of a culminating awareness, "somehow fight it."

She'd been stricken with a realization of her own, with a look of horror and overwhelming sadness. It was as if a great fear had stood before her, a premonition she had seen a thousand times before finally come to pass, right before her eyes, despite all effort and sacrifice, all love and loss.

*Barr?* Idelle asked, her voice frantic. *Where are you going?*

Fluora pulled him closer, held him back by love and will, an anchor of desperation. The light of her essence paled beneath the growing glow.

"You can choose to stay," she insisted, pleaded. She kissed him deeply, a clamoring attempt to sway him that ended in a burst of tears.

*What's happening to you?* Aren asked. He nuzzled at Barr's hand. *Why does it feel like you're leaving?*

Barr tried to relay the depth of his love for her in a smile, with a tender hand upon her cheek. He saw the summer glow of ascension reflected back in her eyes and in the tears streaming down.

"I understand," he told her, wanted to explain it all, to sweep her up in his joy, shake her free of the needless sorrow and hollow rage, as his body continued to become one with his spirit and rise.

Fluora held even tighter, refused to let him go.

"For me," she implored. "Stay."

Barr tried to put aside the influx of awareness, the joy at what awaited. It was difficult to focus. The physical world seemed so hazy, but Fluora remained clear. His love for her held him back. The time left for him to decide was short.

He saw all too clearly the sacrifice before him, the true choice he was dread to make. He saw the spreading dark in her as well, what she was willing to give up for him. He saw their children and what each would become without him. While part of him argued such thoughts served no purpose, not anymore, the rest put forth they were all that truly mattered. He loved Fluora with all his heart, more so than any other that had come before. He loved Idelle and Aren, all the people in this life, but what he was faced with losing...

"You don't know what you're asking."

"Yes," she said, "I do. You can hold off ascension for another life." She kissed him once more, so fervent in her decision. "Let this one be mine."

If only it were that easy.

"Alright," Barr said, his glow all but faded. It was then he realized his choice had been made long ago, at

Starshrine when first they met. He'd forego all for love, for Aren, for Idelle, for their children and...

"For you."

\*   \*   \*

Dhar knelt before the stream and watched the scry within its waters. Over a dozen armies had gathered in the now treeless fields around the Mirror Pool. Arachon had made short work of the task. Though the way had been cleared for thousands to arrive, the field was still littered with fresh trunks and thick roots. As with every blade, axe and hammer, every arrow, bolt and stone, those too had been enchanted with sunlight glyphs. The whole looked a webwork of sunny veins upon the land, as if life coursed through it and stood ready to face the Dark.

Dwarves drank and sang out to the coming nightfall, each clan and royal bloodline joined against a common foe for this first time in generations. All differences aside, at least for a short while, distant kin shared a pint and told stories of old.

The elves were less raucous, more composed in their preparation. Though they too had agreed to temporarily set aside the disparities that long ago had driven them apart, some distance still remained between each race, rank and calling.

The respective minotaur clans had no qualms with one another, but the kheos and daumon stood opposite ends of the field. It was the same for the faeron and their once allies, the dryads. Numerous races were between those, all armed and armored, faced the pool and waited with an equal trepidation. Sadly, none of them stood idle for very long.

As night fell, the rifts appeared.

Two and three at a time, all around the Mirror Pool, they opened in the midst of milling soldiers. Chaos and death ensued, as shiardin poured through and over the poor souls they first encountered. Shouted orders rang out to rein in the turmoil. Armies turned inward to face the invaders, while the pool itself went untouched. The varied darkspawn only showed interest in their prey and tried to turn all they faced.

It was when the darkstones took root that Revyn's plan was made clear, when the corruption broke through and began to spread its blight. With dozens of rifts open, encircling the frozen sands, their touch would shortly reach the pool.

Forced back from the blight, the defending armies would soon be hard pressed for footing. The time had come for Dhar to act. He roared down into the waters, a bellow from the center of his very being that rippled out across its surface and every ley line the worlds over.

Dragons descended from the storm clouds, each and every last, as Dhar called up the waters. Carried through to the field, he arrived in air to the swirl of silver tendrils. He let loose another roar, one of such force that even the darkspawn took pause to turn and look. No longer was he merely the last Patron of all dragons, scales aglow in the golden hold of the Light.

Dhar was Patron of the Winding Waters.

He landed hard upon snowy ground and caused an uproar of life. Where his bulk touched, the land bloomed and blossomed to verdant growth. It rushed out from him like a halo of emerald mist, turned all to a vibrant lush of green grass and myriad flowers. With it came a summer glow, a radiance emanating from within that pushed back against the blight.

His breath rained down over the land and shiardin alike, no longer a stream of molten fire but a burst of liquid *furie* like the golden rivers of a ley line. Darkspawn keened in untold pain, as its touch burned through each and left behind nothing but flared cinders and further bloom.

A massive rift appeared at the foot of the Mirror Pool, one nearly as large as the pool itself. Through it came a lumbering monstrosity of oily darkness and jagged chitin shell. Taller than Dhar ten times over, it trudged forward on two legs and shook the earth with each step. The beryl eyes and hateful mien told him what it was, as its bellow sent out a shockwave of dissonance and murky sputum.

"Revyn," Dhar said and growled *furie* from his maw. Whatever darkness had twisted the foul god to such a state, its ministrations paled in comparison to what Dhar had in store for him.

A familiar, wild cry cut through the din. Sera, caught in the throes of bloodlust and holy fire, ran toward the dark god with four new demon hunters in tow. Not only did Fezuul join their defense, as he had promised, he brought with him the other three Arch Demons as well. Their combined presence gave the hunters incredible power, enough to scorch the earth as each passed, but he knew with it came the gnawing pain of refusing the compulsion.

"It certainly does not seem to be slowing her," Dhar said and nearly laughed, as Sera charged through the dark intruders and left a wake of smoldering embers.

A crack pealed through the air with a bright flash of silver blue, as if the skies had opened up and loosed a bolt amidst the battle. When the sphere died away, two figures stood the field. Resonance of their mingled *furie* was enough to set his ears to ringing and stomach all aflutter.

Barr and Fluora had finally arrived.

*   *   *

He handed her both kyan. She didn't need them to accomplish the task she'd set herself, but it made him feel better all the same. He had no need of weapons, not anymore.

Barr held in place by will alone the tens of shiardin all around him. Fluora gave him a nod and smiled, then disappeared through the mists. He almost felt sorry for Revyn.

Almost.

Dwarves slashed through the frozen darkspawn with sunlight axes and hearty laughs.

It was up to Barr, they'd agreed, to deal with closing the rifts. Fluora had wanted Revyn for herself.

*Ha!* Aren skewered another shiardin, had used his considerable bulk to force the creature back onto a sunlit spike within a bulwark. A second shiardin lay pierced beside it. Both still wriggled and keened, as their bodies wasted from within.

*You're enjoying this too much.* Idelle dropped one into a pitfall full of similar spikes. *It's unsettling, really.*

*Oh, please!* Aren frowned up at his sister. *You're ahead by three, so don't tell me you're not having fun.*

Barr unmade eight darkstones and the obelisk on the other side. He could see through the rifts now, saw far more than he would've liked.

*It's a bit satisfying,* Idelle admitted, *and nice to know you're keeping track. I am too, by the way, and even Kaela has you beat.*

Aren grumbled as she took hold of another.

Dwarves and taur made short work of the shiardin Barr froze, as he moved from rift to rift. Revyn bellowed out in laughter, loud enough to give Barr pause. So large was the god, Barr could see his glyph from across the distance. He could've unmade Revyn by force, tore the glyph apart rune by rune, but no longer thought it his place to do so. It all seemed so futile now, the senseless slaughter and vies for power. But neither could he leave unanswered the grievous acts the god had done. Barr considered and made a choice. He reached out across the battle with his mind and masked the immense glyph to match the other children.

Revyn was now mortal.

Barr saw the shock and dismay, as Revyn looked down at his hands in a growing, helpless rage. His next outcry brought with it ten shadows in a surge of smoke. The once gods surrounded Barr, their bodies twisted by Dark and deadly intent. Weapons in hand, they rushed toward him as one.

He conjured blades of pure light to either hand, short like kyan but far more fatal to the darkspawn. Ghostly knights clawed up from the ground beside him, as spikes of molten metal flashed out and pierced the attackers. They stopped to reassess, as realization quickly dawned that Barr somehow wielded the power of their Emblems. Already committed, each tentatively approached.

Balsina and Unther were held in place by the metal spikes through their middle and a growth of ironwood bladed vines around feet and hands. Illusory knights cut them in twain with sunlight broadswords.

Celene fell by fire, blinding tendrils that snaked up and around her frame before burning utterly through, while Veralnon succumbed to ice. Jagged frost spread up his legs, encased them with its touch. When he forced a step forward, his right leg broke free without its foot. The frost continued on up, until at last he toppled over and shattered upon the snow.

Herne stopped and clutched his head with a terrible scream. His nightmares, given life, tore him to pieces from within. Wynter slipped into the earth, up to his waist, as if the ground had partly swallowed him. Thorny vines rose up and overtook him, pierced his chest and came out his mouth.

Kraug and Kierna made it close, he a double-bladed axe of obsidian and she a trident of blackened steel. Barr pushed aside their attacks but would not put them to an end. He destroyed their weapons with his own and let the Emblems do the rest.

Only Saernol got truly close, so saddened was he to see her, what had become of the light inside her. All of them had been remade by Revyn's cruel design, but hers stung the most for their short time spent together.

"I'm so sorry," he told her, heartbroken at such a loss. "If only I'd known sooner –"

Curoch's blade pierced him from behind, a longsword of midnight hue. Barr looked down more in surprise than any pain, saw his blood along the blade drip from the edges. His heart began to beat faster, as he looked up to see her once more. He may have dropped his blades. His fingers had gone numb at the tips. He thought she might speak, as she stepped in close enough to feel the cold of her breath upon his lips. She too drove a blade in, a dagger of starry black. It went up under the ribs and felt as if winter had taken root in his chest. He felt the blight within him before he saw it in the wounds.

Its darkness began to spread at an alarming rate.

\* \* \*

Fluora appeared upon the snowy sands, where blight had yet to reach. Revyn was ahead, the once god now a nightmare parody of his former self. He was an enormous mass of hardened pitch, half again taller than any trees that remained, and walked upon two legs like pillars of ebon stone. The ground shook with each slow, deliberate step, minor quakes that threatened to falter balance.

Shiardin came rushing toward her, with hundreds of kourai not far behind. Their bladed limbs clacked and made violet sparks as they ran. Garaenu lumbered out from the giant rift behind Revyn. Some crashed thick arms against the earth to propel themselves forward, while others plodded ahead on muscled legs, their heads jutting out with blunted chitin like battering rams. The piercing keen of a thousand deiken followed after, winged horrors so close-packed their swarm nearly blotted out the skies.

She felt a numbing tingle at her feet and looked down to see the blight. Her chest sunk into a pit of cold and sudden fear. It had reached her much faster than she expected. A frantic cry in the back of her mind warned to jump away, but she knew it was too late. The blight had moved past with enough speed that it already touched upon the water behind.

There was nowhere to run.

To her surprise, the blight did not affect her as it had the land or any other living creature she had observed in its grasp. There was a spreading numbness, a cold that crawled up her flesh with a shiver of dread, but it did not blacken her flesh or drain her of all *furie*. Her connection with the Dark must have granted some protection. Either that or she had given in too much for too long, and her body had become attuned with the corruption.

Its touch still stained her skin, riddled her body with growing lesions that pained her every movement. She had thought the dark *furie* was damaging her spirit, her body from within. What if it was far worse, for her and both her children?

What if it was changing her?

The rattling cries of a demon horde rang out to her right, where Fezuul led hardened elders against kourai. A roar startled her from reverie, shook her in the waves of its intensity. It was Dhar, a towering figure of light that cast aside blight with his touch. The ground beneath her bloomed to life, as Revyn strode past in a single step and entered the Mirror Pool.

Fluora steeled her nerves and called up the mists. In an instant she was in the air before Revyn, kyan gripped tightly in each hand. She felt herself start to fall, drove the blades deep into midnight flesh and pulled down with all the strength she could summon.

The once god's anguished outcry caused hundreds of his nearby children to stop mid-attack. As one, they all turned and scrabbled back to his defense. A tall figure appeared amidst them, sent darkspawn through the air with the onslaught of his arrival.

"I will idly watch no longer," the man said in a voice that boomed across the battlefield. "I will not forsake my oath, but neither will I allow you, brother, to destroy all we have created."

It was Laeryk, the Watcher. He conjured a gleaming scythe to one hand, as others joined his side. Fluora knew who they were, had seen each in premonition. All the lesser gods had come together, a final fight for their survival.

Fluora disappeared through the mists again, struck between chitin plates at Revyn's chest, then once more at his neck. He tried to swat her with meaty hands but was too slow to come close. She flitted from one spot to another in the span of a breath, cut away at his dark flesh with a single-minded ferocity. Darkspawn climbed up his body in droves, determined to put an end to her assault.

She growled in frustration. Why was there no blood! The wounds clearly pained him, but her attacks seemed little more than an annoyance.

A large barb struck against chitin by her head. Other deiken joined in, swooped past and tried to claw her as she vanished into mist. Darkspawn were everywhere, across Revyn's tattered flesh and in the air all around. A wing flapped through her hair, caused her to lose grip and begin to fall. Though the onset of fear took hold, she kept composure and called up the mists. She appeared atop a chest plate as a deiken crashed into her at full speed.

Fluora struck her head against the chitin, split her ironwood mask and together they tumbled toward the ground.

\*   \*   \*

Sera watched her fall, saw the limp body turn in air and smash against Revyn. More dark fliers darted by and were struck as she passed. In one heart-wrenching moment, Fluora bounced against a leg and hit the water. Shiardin screeched in a frenzied attempt to reach her, but their bodies hissed with white smoke upon touching the silver pool.

Though the presence of Arch Demons pained her to the core, Sera had steadily grown used to the inferno in her middle. The other hunters hadn't fared as well. They had either succumbed to the geas, fell against the horde, or perished within the double-edge of enveloping pale fire. Either way, she felt secure in her decision.

Water bubbled at the touch of those same holy white flames, but Sera was first to reach Fluora.

"Dhar!" she yelled, her voice amplified by urgency.

He'd been trying to get to Revyn, but the enemy was intent on bringing the dragon down. He heard Sera's call and left off the fight to join her. One moment he was breathing *furie* upon the darkspawn, incinerating them in a blast of liquid magic, and the next he was beside her, in swirling tendrils of water that collapsed down to the pool in a shower.

"Get her out of here!" Sera said and took up the seer's blades, imbued them with her touch.

"What will you do?" Dhar pulled Fluora to his arms, and water began to rise about the two of them.

Sera narrowed her gaze toward Revyn.

"I'm going to end this. Now."

She moved with divine speed, leapt over two bladed darkspawn and took their heads as she passed. When she reached a massive leg, she dug in with one sword and started to climb with the other, used both to pull herself up the flesh of the dark god.

Revyn screamed with enough force to shake her grip on one blade. She quickly recovered, kicked a shiardin in the face and resumed her ascent. Others tried to stop her, to send her back down toward the water. Her holy fire kept most at bay, as well as burned a chalky trail up Revyn's leg. Only the fliers gave her trouble, though she managed to slice more than one's wing when they flew too close.

Sera looked up at her goal. With a fierce grin, she bunched up her legs against Revyn and leapt up toward the other leg. She drove both swords in and had doubled her distance up. Again she jumped, climbed the towering god one mighty leap after another. Bit by fleshy bit, killing darkspawn in her path, she reached between the thorax plates and sliced an opening.

She secured both swords to her belt, gripped the new wound at either end and pulled it further apart. Shell cracked and split, hissed beneath her touch. With a final throaty pull, she managed to widen the gash enough to burrow inside, just as a massive fist came crashing down from behind.

Sera heard it then, the racing *thumpity thump* of his heart. She flared her aura of holy fire, to the muted echo of an agonized cry. Swords in hand again, she burned and cleaved a path through dark sinew and hardened muscle. Veins appeared within the breach. It was the first time she saw his blood, a viscous black fluid with a touch of violet fire. The closer she came to his heart, the more blood she spilled.

Its foul touch tried to change her, burned away at her flesh, but her body had already been claimed. The geas healed her as fast new wounds formed.

She heard the clack of darkspawn clamoring through from behind, desperate to reach her before she put an end to their maker. Inky tendrils lashed out, as the heart came into sight. Its violent rhythm shook the chamber, caused surrounding flesh to pulse. She sliced free of one ropy appendage at her wrist and two at her ankles. The others burned away to piercing cries that shook his body.

The head of a shiardin appeared, as she took a firm footing. Sera brought up both blades, and with a roar of pent-up pain and frustration, of all the sorrow and loss suffered at Revyn's hands, she embedded each deep into the throbbing muscle. Another shout brought them down in a smooth motion. A black morass flushed out upon her, tainted the air with its foul stench and beryl steam.

More darkspawn clawed their way in, tried to reach her but were too late. She stabbed at the heart with a relentless ferocity. Any shiardin that got within her reach swiftly died between strikes. The world began to tilt, as the dark heart slowed and beat its last.

Sera dropped the blades, wrapped her arms within the tendrils and braced. She felt more than saw Revyn plummet into the Mirror Pool. When next she opened her eyes, all around began to harden and ignite with the glow of spreading embers. The darkness collapsed about her, into crumbling ash and smoking ruin. Breath heavy, still surprised to be alive, she looked out at the god's remains diminishing within the light.

Her holy fires subsided, immediately eased the pain in her middle to a dull and empty ache. The demons had wasted no time in their departure.

Covered in dark blood, sticky with its touch, she climbed out, fell to her knees and laughed. Not because Revyn was finally dead, good and truly gone, but for her sudden desire of a bath. She glanced over the edge of the dead god's fading carcass, down at the silver waters of the Mirror Pool and longed for a dip.

An impish look crossed her face, but her reflection disapproved.

Sera only laughed all the more.

## – 10 –

arr appeared through the mists, outside a tailor shop on Clothier's Way. Garand, like all the other major cities still connected to the portalis, had flourished through healthy trade and arachon good will. The cobbled street was busy with people of varied race, but none had taken notice or seemed to care at his arrival.

A bell above the door rang out as he stepped in. Barr walked up to the worn counter and put down a bundle of finely made tunics that had seen better days. A fairly young man, at least for a master tailor, came out from the back room. He had chestnut hair, a slight build and a ready smile for his customers. His hand was rough, when they shook in greeting, from long years plying his trade.

"Good to see you again," Nedryn said and gave the bundle of his handiwork a critical eye, "though I didn't expect to see these quite so soon."

"Sword practice," Barr said in way of explanation. "Even the teacher takes a cut now and then."

"Mmm hmm." Nedryn probed the tears in each tunic. "They're clean, I suppose. If I didn't know any better, I'd think you'd cut these with shears."

Barr returned a look that seemed to say only a fool would do such a thing.

"Are my others ready?" he asked.

Nedryn nodded and reached under the counter for two clean tunics bundled neatly in twine. Barr slid two silvers across but paid no mind to what he supposedly had come to retrieve.

"I'd tell you to take better care," his natural father said and grinned.

There was no need to finish the jest. Despite the quality of his needlework, most people preferred a visit to the grandeur of Dwendorim's marketplace.

"Why have you stayed all this time?" Barr asked. It was a question he'd wondered at many times before but feared he already knew the answer. "Because of all the others?"

"No," Nedryn replied, waved off the notion, "nothing like that. I've dealt with all manner of folk since the portal opened. They're mostly like everyone else. Some are just fine, others I could do without." He scratched at his chin and said, "Truth be told, I waited too long. Now there's a list long as my leg just to ask."

"I could probably help with that," Barr offered, "put in a good word at the right place."

Nedryn looked dubious.

"And what might that cost me?"

"Not a thing," Barr said. "It would save me a trip through the portal. Think you could do it, though?" He studied his father closely, hoped the years free of Daesi's curse had brought with them a change of heart. "Live among so many strange and different people? Elves and dwarves, gnomes and minotaurs, nymphs and sylphs? *Dragons*? Not to mention the arachon."

"The talking statues?" Nedryn hesitated and gave a chuckle. "They can make a man uneasy. Rather lovely, though. Artful, you might say. Don't think they've much use for clothing."

"Not so much," Barr agreed, "but plenty others do."

Nedryn considered, a faraway look to his eyes. When he returned his attention to Barr, he seemed reluctant to ask.

"Spent much time there, have you?" At Barr's nod, he continued. "Ever come across any fairies?"

"Faeron," Barr said. "They prefer to be called faeron. And yes, I have. I've actually been to Aranadir." Nedryn looked in askance. "Their largest city, on Faeronthalsos."

"Oh, I see. I used to know one," he said, "a long time back. Most charming and beautiful woman I'd ever met. Could brighten a rainy day with her smile. Her name was Daisy," he added, with what sounded like regret, "like the flower. I wronged her, you see. I do still love her, though. Think about her every day."

Barr nodded in understanding. "I've met many faeron in my travels, but none were named Daisy. Perhaps you meant Daesi?"

"That's what she called herself." Nedryn gave a short laugh, as if he found some relief in sharing his story. "No matter how many times she made me say it that way, to me, she'll always be Daisy."

"Hundreds of faeron live there," Barr said, "but I only know of one Daesi who visits from time to time. I could pass along a message, if you like."

Embarrassed, Nedryn said, "No, I couldn't impose on you like that. As for moving? I'd have to think about it. I've built a decent life here for myself. Not sure I should go looking for the past."

Barr placed a scrystone on the counter.

"If you decide you're interested," he said, "hold this in your hand and picture me in your mind. We'll be able to talk."

"Magic?" Nedryn was shocked. "You expect me to use magic?"

"People use magic every day. The portalis wouldn't exist without it." Barr added in reassurance, "The days of Guardians hunting turners is long gone. If it makes you feel any better, it's not *your* magic."

Barr gave his father a sly grin.

"It's mine."

\* \* \*

Barr returned to his office at the Academy. It was quiet for the moment, almost peaceful. Years had passed since the Darkening, when worlds came together to fight for the lives of all. Yet little had changed in his day to day. He was busy with different matters but always busy just the same.

Moments like these had become all too rare.

He smiled at the thought of his mother upon her throne and imagined she must have felt the same way.

With the turn of a single rune, one only an adept of the divine language could see, he opened the astral door hidden within a mural on the wall. Once through the starry black, he entered a large chamber of wide couches and cushioned chairs, stone floor and a warm fire. Its walls and ceiling were the same star-strewn midnight.

He closed the door with a thought, poured himself a cup of water from an enchanted clay pitcher atop a table at the room's center and left through a corridor lit by oil sconces on either side. He went past numerous doors of polished wood and two adjoining hallways before coming to the library.

The largest collection in existence, it held tomes from every culture, the histories of all known races, librams from countless weavers and untold scrolls that had yet to be deciphered. It even contained all the lore left behind by Laeryk and what remained of his devoted children. A heady scent filled the room, vellum and dried ink, tooled leather and... boiled potato with honey butter?

Barr chuckled.

He knew he'd find Ashear there, lost in the pages of one book or another. Much like Protectors had been the peak of arachon craftsmanship, Ash was the culmination of all Barr had learned throughout his lives, his greatest creation – aside from the twins, of course. Ash sat at a long wooden table, stacks of books spread out before him. The massive chamber was lit by runic light from the ceiling. They had always been careful to avoid fire of any kind within the library.

"Just a moment," Ash said from across the distance, without looking up. One last page, and he stood, ran to Barr with a wide smile. He nearly knocked Barr over with the enthusiasm of his embrace. "I'm so glad you're here! I've much to show you. Has it been long?"

Ash was a construct, like the dawnstone golem Barr had made to kill Revyn in the Dark, and only in part like what the arachon Protectors had become. He was far more complex, not necessarily better but greatly refined. Ash was flesh and blood, appeared human in almost all respects, and had the full range of emotions one would expect. He was alive but also warded against a soul. Ash could live, grow and learn, just like anyone else, but would never take part in the cycle of lessons that led toward ascension.

"Not very." It was difficult to tell the passage of time within the astral. "What have you been up to?"

He looked roughly Barr's years but had only drawn his first breath just months before. He didn't age in the same way and would live the span of many lifetimes. His core glyph was inscribed within his body, across every bone and organ, every muscle and vein. There were two others as well, linked with and woven into the first. The one across his skin, in tight rows of fine sigils, could only be seen in direct sunlight and even then was only visible to strong weavers with a keen eye.

Ash led him to a far table, where plates of sugared fruit slices chilled above bowls filled with ice, and honeycakes steamed as if freshly baked.

His other glyph floated just above the flesh, a thumb length away. It existed in all three planes, within both realms, and would expand as he gained new knowledge. Whether that came from study or experience, it allowed him to learn from his mistakes. None of its runes could yet be seen, but given time the glyph would grow to an encompassing sphere of pale silver – again, hidden to all but the strongest of weavers.

Barr loved him as a son, wanted to protect him from any injury, physical or otherwise. He thought it best to keep secret Ash's origin, to let Ash decide for himself when or to whom he would reveal it – if ever.

"I know they're your favorite," Ash said and offered him a cake. "I tried to make them just like the ones you brought last time." Barr took one and bit off half. It had a fluffy texture and sweet grit, with a taste of vanilla that immediately brought him back to his time with Tuvrin and the sylvannis. "Except without all the fire and messy bowls."

Barr was caught by surprise.

"You *conjured* these?"

Ash finished one in a single bite and licked the honey from his fingers.

"Not bad, right?"

"You have no idea." Barr laughed and took another. "Aren lives for these. He'd love you to no end if you made him some. Though, he'd pester you to no end for more."

"I think I'd like that," Ash said and put the plate back down. "Someday."

They had agreed he could leave when both felt he was ready. Ash was bound by a basic set of instruction runes, three imperfect rules at best, meant to guide him through life and his interaction with others. While Barr was confident he was ready, Ash was not so sure.

"I trust your judgment," Barr said and clapped him on the shoulder. "Whenever you're ready."

Ash only nodded in reply. His mood then brightened as a thought struck.

"Can you stay awhile?" he asked. "I've been reading about Danarriden. I've got some questions, if you have time."

"Of course." Barr walked over to a cushioned seat at a nearby table and indicated for Ash to come join him. "We can discuss anything you like."

"Anything?"

Barr couldn't help but feel guilty each time he saw Ash. If he'd bound himself to the same rules, Barr never would have made him.

*Do no harm, if it can be avoided.*

*Seek out and preserve knowledge worth sharing.*

*Leave the worlds in a better state than you found them.*

He'd purposely left room for interpretation, to let Ash best decide how he wanted to contribute to the lives of others. No more than a moral grounding, they surpassed what Barr had nearly done.

"Whatever you want."

Ash didn't even need to consider.

"Tell me what it's like to have a soul," he said, then shortly after added, "and why it is you don't want me to have one."

His original intent had been to pass on all he knew, all he had learned from every life, especially this one, regardless of the inherent danger. Keenly aware such knowledge posed a dire threat, he'd also thought it too precious to just discard. His plan had been to create the perfect vessel, a living container in which to store what he knew, but one capable of deciding whether those who sought it were deserving of being taught.

He thought differently now, was afraid the knowledge would change any deemed worthy into one who was not. Worse, they could make a catastrophic mistake, affecting countless lives. Revyn remained a perfect example of a single being who had wrought havoc upon the rest.

Despite the change of heart, Barr saw no reason to unmake Ashear. He hadn't taken a life since before his near ascension, nor would he ever do so again.

"It's like being many people at once," Barr replied, "except you usually can't talk with the others or see who they are or know what they're doing. I make decisions, or so it seems to me when I do, but ultimately I'm not really in charge. There's an unseen force directing my path. I can choose what to do along the way, turn left or right, even stop walking altogether, but I have nothing to say about the road itself. I've been put on it for a reason, one

I'm not privy to." Barr shook his head at how poorly he'd described it. "Think of my soul as a puppeteer, and I am its puppet. I'd much rather you weren't hampered by any strings."

"Hmm." Ash smiled at the imagery. "I'm glad for that, though somehow it still seems appealing, to be a part of something so much larger than myself."

"That's really just a matter of perspective. You're a part of this time, a span that includes millions of lives. Within you is the power to affect them all," Barr said with insistence, then added with some mirth, "hopefully for the better."

Ash laughed and rolled his eyes.

"You have such grand expectations. What if I fail? What if I choose to do nothing but sit here and read until my body gives out?"

"So long as you're happy," Barr replied and went back for another honeycake. "That's all I really care about." He took a bite and asked, "So, have you been practicing at all? Besides these, I mean."

"Magic?" Ash grinned with excitement. Barr knew how much he loved their challenges. "I've got some tricks I think you'll like."

"If they're anything like your pastries," Barr said and finished his cake, "I'm sure I will."

\*     \*     \*

Barr arrived at his home in Dwendorim hours later. Sounds of laughter and the occasional joyous squeals of the very young filled the air. He realized, with a sinking feeling, he'd returned late for the harvest festival. One occurred every other week, but Fluora had made a habit of gathering all their friends and children at the park.

*They must already be there.*

*Food's all gone*, Aren warned, lethargy in his voice.

*Yes*, Idelle said, *you made sure of that.*

*Not my fault he's late.*

*It's alright*, Barr said and headed out toward the park. *I've already eaten.*

He saw them all not far away, seated in the grass upon blankets and pillows. Aren sharply raised his head and sniffed at the air.

*You had honeycakes!*

Kaela and Idelle laughed, as Fluora turned Barr's way. He thought she might be upset, but she only smiled and shook her head.

*I might have*, Barr said.

"Why do you tease him so?" Fluora asked, as Barr sat beside her on the blanket. "Just give them to him already."

"What's the fun in that?" He would have laughed but for the elbow in his side. "Oh, fine. Here."

Barr reached into a pocket and brought out a cloth napkin wrapped around three cakes. He placed them in front of Aren to let the hound decide their fate. Idelle swooped in and snatched one before Aren could say a word.

*Hey!* Aren growled at his sister. Kaela raised a brow. *I would've offered her one*, he complained, *but that's just rude!*

"Better hurry," Barr warned. "I think Sasha's caught their scent."

Aren quickly ate his in a single bite. Kaela sighed, as one long used to such behavior, and offered her piece to Sasha, the only daughter from their first litter. While the pup rarely left Ana's side, she made exception for a honeycake – something she'd clearly inherited from her father.

Barr leaned over and kissed Anaraelis on the head. She giggled in return but remained focused on a handful of flowers she'd picked. Long, sable hair and rounded ears, chestnut eyes and thick limbs, she was every bit her father's daughter, a breathing half of Barr's heart. The other half, her twin brother, shared Fluora's crimson curls, freckled skin and blue eyes, but like his sister each orb was ringed with white. Neither child appeared faeron but for the faintest rainbow glint upon their skin when the light caught them just so.

While Ana had been bonded with Sasha when the pup arrived, Idelle insisted her firstborn go to Balaodrin. Koren hovered in air, dangled a blue ribbon from one talon and led Bal on a merry chase. The boy tripped and fell more than once but always pulled himself right back up to renew the chase, laughing all the while.

Dhar sat across the way, Sera's head in his lap, and watched with a broad smile their daughter dance about in the grass, playing hand in hand with Fluora's brother. Renaerrin looked a faeron boy of twelve, but in truth was little more than a year older. The rate at which he'd aged was surprising but less so than his demon blood having no effect upon the geas. And while Reina had somehow inherited her mother's curse, as if it had become part of her in the womb, she wasn't burdened by its compulsion or considered one of the five demon hunters. She had all of their markings but no holy fire as of yet. Reina was as much a marvel as her cambion friend.

Dhar's other son, by Kaolanni, spent most days with his mother at Naerat Sanae. The only other gold dragon, he'd been prized and fawned over since hatching but was occasionally allowed to visit Dwendorim. Unable to take a human form yet, he romped about as a child nearly as large as a mature red. He and Fanarin made a mess of things, tore up grass in wide swaths with a small tree here and there, but the two had been fast friends from the time they'd met.

Barr looked on them all with a sense of wonder, of pride and contentment at what they'd become. Fluora slipped a hand into his and gave a squeeze. Of course she knew what he was thinking, might have even known it before he did. She'd given up her role as Matron but was still an oracle after all.

He kissed her hand and turned her way, saw the crimson curls shot through with silver, felt the frailty in her touch. She'd sacrificed so much of herself, and he loved her all the more for it. He considered briefly what he'd given up as well, though he tried to keep such thoughts at bay. If Fluora ever discovered the truth, that he'd done far more than merely postpone his ascension, she would be wracked by guilt, unable to enjoy their life together. It was better she didn't know his next life was a clean slate, the start of a new and different path.

It was better no one would ever know.

## About the Author

Joe has been writing for most of his adult life, in between bouts of serious online gaming. He continues to write fantasy novels, in both adult and young adult genres, in his selfish need to create worlds that amuse him. That others enjoy the work is a happy coincidence but one that he fully appreciates.

With a Bachelor of Arts in English from the Arizona State University, he is both an avid reader and addicted gamer. He writes novels full-time and longs for the day when those efforts pay some bills – seriously, even just one bill would be nice. For those of you who purchased copies of any of his books, he is eternally in your debt. Note: this is not a legally binding contract.

He lives with his wife, Lori – who is not only a doctor of both internal medicine and psychiatry, she's *also* an avid gamer! His daughter, Ada Rose, is eleven at the time of this writing. She has yet to read a single one of his books, but at least she reads others. They all live happily ever after in the perpetual summer that is central

Arizona (technically there is a winter, for about three weeks in January).

Joe attributes much of his success in life to good looks, incredible talent, luck, modesty, air conditioning, friends & family and his DVR – though not necessarily all in that order. Oh, and his computer.

He hopes you enjoyed this book immensely and will share it with a friend.

And as evidenced by the picture, he's both a fan of Adventure Time and a silly, silly man...

If you simply must, you can visit him online at jagiunta.com.